FIELD OF

SCREAMS

book four of the matchmaker mysteries series

elise sax

Field of Screams (Matchmaker Mysteries – Book 4) is a work of fiction. Names, characters, places, and incidents are the products of the author's imagination or are used fictitiously. Any resemblance to actual events, locales, or persons, living or dead, is entirely coincidental.

Cover design: Sprinkles On Top Studios
Edited by: Novel Needs and Lynn Mullan
Formatted by: Jesse Kimmel-Freeman

Printed in the United States of America
elisesax.com
elisesax@gmail.com
http://elisesax.com/mailing-list.php
https://www.facebook.com/ei.sax.9

For Susan Cambra, super reader and super woman
And also for Joan Varner, thank you for reading and for your support.

ALSO BY ELISE SAX

Matchmaker Mysteries Series

Matchmaker Marriage Mysteries

Goodnight Mysteries Series

Agatha Bright Mysteries

Operation Billionaire Trilogy

Partners in Crime
Partners in Crime
Conspiracy in Crime
Divided in Crime
Surrender in Crime

Five Wishes Series
Going Down
Man Candy
Hot Wired
Just Sacked
Wicked Ride

Five Wishes Series
Three More Wishes Series
Blown Away
Inn & Out
Quick Bang
Three More Wishes Series

Standalone Books
Forever Now
Bounty
Switched

CHAPTER I

Blood is thicker than water, bubeleh. You hear what I'm telling you? Family is important. Only your Aunt Tilly is going to hold your hand during your hemorrhoid surgery. Your girlfriend from high school isn't going to want any of that. I speak from experience. So, don't poo-poo family. But on the other hand…family isn't necessarily always right or helpful or kind. That's why we're in business, dolly. Aunt Tilly may be great for hemorrhoids, but she has no place sticking her nose in her family's love life. So, tell your matches to ignore their mother's/sister's/cousin's advice. It's all drek. Tell them to smile and nod and make a beeline for our house. We'll set them straight.

Lesson 69, Matchmaking Advice from your
Grandma Zelda

Grandma handed me a platter of cut vegetables, and I tried to make a place for it over one of the three sweet potato casseroles in the filled to bursting refrigerator. The casserole topped with pecans instead of marshmallows.

Who eats pecans when they can eat marshmallows?

And who eats sliced cucumbers for Thanksgiving? It sounded unpatriotic to me.

Grandma handed me a bowl of Cool Whip and canned fruit. "Meryl calls it, ambrosia," Grandma said. "I don't know why they ruined a perfectly good tub of Cool Whip with fruit. I think you can wedge it between the cranberry sauce and Sister Cyril's potato salad."

I had my doubts that there was room for Meryl's ambrosia, but I had piss poor spatial skills, and Grandma was usually right about those kinds of things. I gave it a shove, managing to get the ambrosia in by knocking Sister Cyril's potato salad against the refrigerator's light bulb and breaking it to smithereens. Light bulb shards flew everywhere, covering every plastic-wrapped dish that Grandma's guests had brought in advance of Thanksgiving.

We stared at the destruction in the now-dark refrigerator. There was a good chance that someone was going to chomp down on the stuffing tonight and wind up with internal bleeding.

"See? You did it," Grandma said. "Everything's in nice and tidy. Let's have a snack."

I closed the fridge and ordered a pizza. Grandma adjusted her breasts in her Ann Klein knockoff power suit and took a seat at the kitchen table. I poured us both some cola and sat down across from her.

"Is it gross to order a pizza four hours before Thanksgiving dinner?" I asked her.

"No, I think that's fine. It's bad to let your blood sugar dip."

Our pizza arrived a few minutes later. Ever since Grandma fixed up Angelo Pitoro, the owner of the pizza shop, with a pretty, double-jointed gymnast, we never had to wait more than fifteen minutes for a pie.

I chomped down on my second slice. "Is it possible to have too much of a good thing, Grandma?"

I was afraid of her answer, but I was definitely having a lot of a good thing lately, and I was worried about it.

"How could there ever be too much of a good thing?" she said, taking another slice of pizza.

She had a point. Good was pretty good.

"Unless the good thing isn't really a good thing. That's a common mistake. Are you sure about your good thing?" she asked.

"Well…"

"Sometimes, we can confuse good and bad, especially when it makes our toes curl," she added, wiping the pizza grease off her lips with a napkin.

I had a lot of toe curling going on recently. I thought I was keeping my sort of relationship with Detective Remington Cumberbatch on the down low, but Grandma had a way of knowing things that couldn't be known. It was feasible for her to be perfectly aware that I had been doing the dirty mambo with a muscle-bound hottie.

I had lived with her for the past six months after she asked me to help her in her matchmaking business. Since then, I made a handful of matches and got myself into more than my share of trouble, and now I was stuck between three men. One was angry with me, one wanted more than I could give him, and one…well, I kept falling on his penis.

"I might be confusing good and bad," I said, taking a third slice of pizza. I was eating a lot these days, even more than I had been eating since moving to Cannes, California to live with my junk food-eating Grandma. Sex and carbs…good or bad? "What should I do?"

"Go with your heart. Always go with your heart. We're in the heart business, and that's always my advice."

I tossed my pizza onto my plate, my appetite suddenly gone. "I'm confused about my heart," I said.

"Who isn't, dolly? Congratulations, you're human."

I didn't want to be human. Being human was confusing, too.

Grandma patted my hand. "Ovaries are demanding. Little bitches. Thank goodness mine stopped demanding years ago. It's going to be fine. Eventually. But right now Meryl and Bird are walking up the drive, fighting about mashed potatoes. This is going to be a hell of a Thanksgiving. Why don't you get some fresh air and come back at three? Save yourself."

"Are you sure?" I was dying to get out of there, but I

felt guilty leaving Grandma by herself. Not that I could help her. She was an expert at handling large groups of crazy people, which was pretty much the entire population of our town.

"Yes. Go quickly, or you're going to run into them on your way out. And don't spend too much time curling your toes. Thanksgiving is at four o'clock."

I hopped up from my seat and skipped out of the kitchen. I was wearing jeans and a turtleneck, but it was freezing outside, and there was no way I could go out without a coat. I bolted for the hall closet and grabbed it just as the front door opened.

Meryl walked in first. She was the town's blue-haired librarian and came to Grandma's house every Monday to give her a selection of books, since Grandma never left her property line. I was more of a sitcom rerun type than a bestseller hardback type, so we didn't have a lot to talk about with each other.

She walked in with Bird Gonzalez, who owned the most popular hair salon in Cannes. Bird believed in the power of a good rinse and set, and there was no way she would ever let her hair go blue. It must've taken a lot of self-control for her to not attack Meryl's head with a bottle of auburn hair dye.

"Are you going somewhere?" Meryl asked me as I put on my coat. "You're not staying for Thanksgiving? You got someplace better to go? Did someone die again?"

Since I moved to Cannes, I got a reputation for

stumbling over dead people. I was like a bloodhound for corpses. A one-woman dowsing rod of death.

"Nobody died, Meryl," I said, affronted. "I don't know what you're talking about."

"You are kind of like a murder magnet, Gladie," Bird said. She held two large paper grocery bags, and she handed me one of the bags after I put my coat and hat on. "You could at least help with the groceries. Besides, I have something to talk to you about."

I couldn't imagine what she had to speak to me about. Bird was a business owner with toned arms and a knack for cutting hair. I was a struggling matchmaker, living with my grandmother, who just ate three slices of pizza and couldn't button her jeans. I hadn't gotten my hair done in a month. Perhaps she wanted to chide me on my split ends. But I was saving my money for other things, like tampons and soap.

Last month I made the most money I've ever made as a matchmaker, and I was trying to make it last. Still, I didn't have any more clients on the horizon. Most people went to my grandmother to get matched, and why wouldn't they? She had the gift, whereas I just had a gift for murder and mayhem.

"Don't look at me like that, Gladie," Bird said. "I wasn't going to chastise you about the state of your hair, which is terrible, considering you're not one hundred years old like the rest of the people in this town. You should keep up your appearance. Don't you want to attract a man?"

Meryl snickered. "Don't you know anything, Bird? I thought you were up on all the gossip. Gladie is swimming in men."

"Is that true?" Bird asked me. "I thought that was done."

It was totally true. I was swimming in so many men, that I was taking on water and drowning fast. I was going down for the second time, waving my arms in distress, but there wasn't a lifeguard to be had.

"No, that's not true," I lied, wagging my finger at Meryl. "I'm not swimming. I don't even have a toe in the water."

Meryl and Bird stared at me for a moment. "You're a terrible liar, Gladie," Bird said.

I followed them into the kitchen with the groceries. Grandma was still sitting at the table. She was totally relaxed, even though it was Thanksgiving and her house was about to be invaded by hordes of hungry people.

"I warned you to be quick," Grandma said to me.

I put the bag down and helped Meryl and Bird organize the groceries. I didn't take off my coat, because I was still determined to get out as soon as I could, and I didn't want to get roped into cooking. Food preparation and I don't get along.

"Well, bye," I sang.

"Wait. Take this," Bird said. She rummaged in her purse and handed me a large jar of peanut butter.

"Uh," I said.

7

"It's your new diet. I've noticed that you put on a few pounds to go along with your split ends," Bird explained. I sucked in my stomach, but it was no use. Swimming in men packed on the pounds. "Did you know that the average Thanksgiving dinner is five thousand calories?" she asked.

"That sounds like a lot," I said, but I was probably eating the equivalent of a couple of Thanksgiving dinners every day for the past month. I had grown especially fond of brownies.

"Starting after dinner, you're going to do just what I've been doing. It's great. Every time you want something sweet, just shove a spoonful of peanut butter in your mouth. Oh!" Bird spun around and dug a spoon out of one of the drawers and handed it to me. "You'll need this, too. Take the peanut butter and the spoon wherever you go. Trust me. It works."

"Bird, you have more diets than socks," Grandma said.

"Zelda, I'm forty-two years old, and you can bounce a quarter off my ass," Bird said, proudly.

I didn't know what it meant to be able to bounce a quarter off your ass, but I was pretty sure nothing would bounce off mine. It would probably sink in and disappear. Eww. Maybe Bird was right. Maybe peanut butter was the answer to buttoning my jeans and having a firm butt. I was nowhere close to forty-two, but Bird was beating me in the in fit race.

"Thanks, Bird. I'll give it a try."

"Now that that's done," Meryl said. "Can you talk some sense into this woman about mashed potatoes, Zelda? She's going on about olive oil. Olive oil! In mashed potatoes! Can you imagine?"

I tucked the peanut butter and spoon into my coat pocket and left before they inducted me into peeling potatoes or worse. I'm not a slacker, but I'm not a cook, either. Not since my tragic two days as a sous chef for a fine eatery in New York.

I walked outside and closed the door behind me. I shivered and turned up my collar. It was a colder than usual winter, and it usually got pretty cold in Cannes. The town was settled in the 1800s after a gold rush, but the gold dried up pretty quickly. Located high in the mountains east of San Diego, Cannes was now known for its apples, pears, and a glut of antique shops in its historic district.

Grandma's house was right in the center of the historic district, one of the oldest houses in town. It was a large Victorian, beautiful and perfectly preserved. It was also the center of activity for most of the townspeople, not only for matchmaking but for every committee, group, event, and holiday.

I turned the corner and walked down the street toward Tea Time, my favorite place to get coffee, despite its name. Tea Time was located in a converted western saloon, but was now devoted to exotic teas and scones. It still had the original bar, but hand-knitted tea cozies sold for ludicrous prices next to it. The shop was run by Ruth Fletcher, an eighty-five-year-old crotchety woman, who despised coffee drinkers.

I tried to open the door, but it was locked. Through the window, I could see Ruth standing at the bar, wiping it down. I knocked on the window. "Ruth! Ruth! It's me, Gladie. Open up. I need a latte."

There was a good chance I was risking my life, asking Ruth to open her store on Thanksgiving to give me a coffee. I would probably get a better response if I was asking for lapsang souchong or at the very least, Earl Grey.

"I know damn well who it is," she yelled from inside the store. "I can see you. You think because I'm old, that I can't see or I've lost my mind? I'll have you know that I see better than you, and for sure I have a better mind than you. Go away! I'm not opening up on Thanksgiving. This isn't Walmart. I'm a Democrat, for Christ's sake."

I didn't know how to argue with that. Ruth was pretty vocal about labor rights. I cupped my hands on the window and peeked inside. "Come on, Ruth. Please! I need coffee. You don't know what it's like. I'm swimming. They're fighting about mashed potatoes."

She waved her towel at me. "Get your hands off my window. I just had it replaced. Wasn't it enough that you demolished my shop?"

"I wasn't the one driving!"

Last month, two cars in two separate incidents crashed into Tea Time. Ruth paid contractors double to get her shop up and running in record time. I figured there was some kind of connection between her long life and the shop. Like it was her beating heart…if she actually had a heart.

Or maybe there was something to the health benefits of tea.

Ruth marched toward me and unlocked the door. I skipped over, but she blocked me from entering.

"What's wrong with you Burger women? You all have a screw loose. Go away. It's Thanksgiving. I'm busy. I'm not opening to you."

She tried to pull the door closed, but I stuck my foot in the doorway and I pulled on the door for all I was worth. We did a tug of war, but Ruth was stronger than I was and was closing it on my foot.

What was it with everyone? Even though they were all older than me, they were in better shape than I was.

"Geez, Ruth. Do you eat peanut butter?" I grunted.

"What?"

She stumbled, and I ripped the door open and hopped inside.

"Please, Ruth. Just one latte. What could it hurt?"

She pursed her lips. "Don't get me started. I'm sick and tired of you latte, mocha, caramel macchiato people. Where's the culture in this town? Shakespeare is dead, I tell you. Dead!"

I wasn't a reader and I had dropped out of school, but I was reasonably sure that Ruth was right. Shakespeare was dead. Despite her protests, she walked toward the bar, intent, I guessed on giving me what I wanted. She probably figured it was better to do it and get rid of me, than have me continue to bother her.

"Zelda's house is filled with wackos, I guess," she said, turning on the espresso machine. "Same thing every year. That woman opens her house and lets all the Looney Tunes inside."

She had a point. There were a lot of loonies coming to Grandma's today. "They're not loonies, Ruth. Just people trying to get together for a holiday. I guess you don't go in for holidays."

"Of course I do. What do you think I am? You're the Philistine, not me."

I didn't know what a Philistine was, but it probably wasn't good.

"I have the turkey cooking upstairs, and I have a few guests coming over," she explained.

"Julie?" Julie was Ruth's niece and some-time employee at Tea Time.

"Are you kidding? That girl would burn down my place or worse. I haven't let her around here since I renovated. I got her a job at the ice cream shop. Let them deal with her. Anyway, isn't she going to Zelda's with Fred?"

I had matched Fred and Julie up a couple of months ago and they were still sweethearts. I gulped. "Julie's coming to the house?" It was a terrifying prospect. She was known for wreaking havoc, even more than me. Well maybe not more than me.

"How's that latte coming?" I asked Ruth.

"If you wanted instant coffee, why didn't you just stay home? Everybody wants immediate gratification. You wouldn't know finely crafted, good quality if it bit you on the ass."

As if on cue, the door opened and Detective Remington Cumberbatch walked in. He was tall and massive, a lot like The Rock but even better looking. I knew that under his clothes his body was painted with tattoos. Seven of them. My pulse quickened, and my mouth watered. I almost forgot about my coffee.

"We're not open," Ruth snapped. "See what you started, Gladie? Now the whole world is coming in here. What do you want?"

Remington gave me a pointed look, which said so much… Sex. Raunchy roll in the hay. Even Ruth caught on.

"Oh," she said, raising an eyebrow. "Well, bless those who still have hormones."

She handed me the latte and I gave her a few dollars. Without saying another word, I left Tea Time with Remington. He held the door open for me and I stepped outside. Ruth was right. I still had hormones. In fact, I was following Remington in a cloud of hormones, unaware of most of my surroundings except for the muscular backside of my hot lover and a stream of thirsty people walking into Tea Time, now that it was open. I thought I heard Ruth yell at them, but I was too distracted by Remington's massive body and the nakedness I knew was underneath his jeans and pea coat.

"We really should stop doing this."

Remington stopped and turned toward me. "You want to call it off? You're in charge. I'll follow your lead."

I bit my lower lip. Giving up on casual sex was like stopping heroine or even worse, chocolate. "Did I say that?"

CHAPTER 2

There's all kinds of love, bubeleh. Remember, I'm a very open-minded old lady. There's also all kinds of ways that love blooms. Usually, love needs one on one time. Bonding. But some of your matches get nervous when they're one on one. They prefer social gatherings. These are the social butterflies...people who need to flit and fly around to be happy. So let them flit. Let them fly. What does it hurt? If they like to kibitz around at a party, give them a party. But while they're at the party, go ahead and slip them a surprise while they're flitting and flying. They got to land sometime, so make them land on their love match. Turn that butterfly into a happy caterpillar.

Lesson 88, Matchmaking Advice from your
Grandma Zelda

Remington Cumberbatch was all about the easy. He

was kind and gentle and a terrific lover. But I wasn't in love with him, and he wasn't in love with me. We just seemed to fit together nicely and he was a great distraction.

And orgasms are nothing to sneeze at.

We laid in his bed side by side. I rested my head on my arm, staring over at his *Fast and the Furious* poster, which hung next to a poster of Princess Leia in a metal bikini. Remington was a geek in a sexy tattoo, muscly kind of way.

"I like when you're on top," I said.

"I like when I'm on top or you're on top or we're side by side or I'm behind you or we're standing up…"

"Okay. I got the picture. Bless the people with hormones."

That was the extent of our usual conversations. I didn't talk about my home life, and he didn't talk much about himself, either. It was all about the easy, and real life is nothing about the easy.

He turned toward me and gathered me close, kissing down my body. His lips left burning hot trails and made me want more. Just like M&Ms…I could never get enough.

"You haven't had enough?" I asked, and he maneuvered his body over mine, pushing my legs apart with his knees.

"I can go another round," he said, pulling my legs up over his shoulders. Sex had been really good for my flexibility. Much better than yoga.

Remington entered me with a delicious slowness, dragging out the ecstasy as he touched every inch of my core.

Then he found a just right rhythm that he knew I appreciated. I pulled his head closer and kissed him, letting our tongues play together in an echo of the rest of our bodies.

"Another round," I moaned, breaking from the kiss, as my eyes rolled back in my head, and my G-spot was caressed until I shuddered against him with a gentle climax. He followed my lead and climaxed, his back arching and then falling against me, careful to hold most of his weight with his forearms.

"I better get back," I said, after lying in the afterglow too long. "It's probably a madhouse, and I should set the table or something."

Remington sat up, and I ogled his chiseled abs and his massive shoulders. I had a strong desire to lick him, but that would start things all over again, and I really had to get going. This quickie was taking longer than it should. Maybe I should eat some peanut butter instead, I thought.

"Okay babe. I'll see you for dinner," he said, his voice low and rough.

"What? What did you say?"

He stood and stretched, making me gasp. I turned away so that I wouldn't jump him. He walked toward his bathroom. "Your grandmother invited me to dinner. Four o'clock, right?"

I broke out into a sweat. "There's going to be a lot of

people there," I said. A lot of people I didn't want to know that I was doing the nasty with Remington. My life had gotten very complicated. The easy ended at Remington's door.

He made a gun with his fingers and shot me. "Don't worry, babe. I'm as cool as the other side of the pillow."

I peeked up and down the street before I exited Remington's building. Thankfully, the coast was clear. It had been a dicey month of hiding, espionage, and secrets. I hadn't intended on having an affair with Remington, but it just happened. Guilty by reason of sluttiness.

I walked down the street with my head turned down against the cold and the shame. I sipped the last drops of my latte just as I reached Ruth's shop. The door was wide open and people were coming and going.

I tried to sneak past, but Ruth spotted me and called me in. A strong survival instinct made me pretend that I didn't hear her, but Ruth wasn't fooled. "If you don't come in here, you'll never drink another latte in your miserable, traitorous life."

"It's not my fault," I whined. Tea Time was a hive of activity. It was wall to wall folks, drinking hot beverages. Ruth was making tea and coffee at a breakneck pace. Her face dripped sweat, and she looked like she was going to murder me.

Where did all the people come from? It was Thanksgiving. They should have been home, cooking. I figured that nothing made people want to hide more than big family get-togethers.

"Well, who the hell's fault is it? Get these people out of my shop."

Even though she wanted to kick them out, Ruth didn't stop serving. Tea Time was her life. It was in her blood. Nothing gets in the way of retail.

"Gladie Burger. Is that you?" I felt a sharp fingernail poking my back, and I turned around. She was familiar, but I couldn't place a name to the face. Grandma was the one who knew everybody. I just watched as the people came and went from her house.

The woman with the pointy finger was in her fifties and perfectly preserved, probably with her share of fillers. She didn't have a hair out of place, and she was dressed just like my grandmother but with real designer clothes instead of knockoffs. And her clothes fit, whereas Grandma's always looked like they had been put on with a shrink wrap machine. She pointed at me with her beautifully manicured finger.

"Do you think it's appropriate to get a Thanksgiving invitation on the Monday before the holiday?" she asked, accusingly. I didn't know how to answer. I never got an invitation to Thanksgiving. I shrugged.

"What does that mean?" she demanded. "I'm asking you a question. Your grandmother invited me on Monday. Monday. Like an afterthought. Like she didn't want me to come. Me!"

Frankly, I was surprised that Grandma had invited anybody. I thought they just showed up, like ants to a picnic. Her house was open, and whoever wandered by at the right time got a good dose of turkey and cranberry sauce. That is, if they brought it, because my grandmother didn't cook. Remington's invitation was the first I had ever heard of and now this woman was the second.

"I'm sorry?"

"Is that a statement or question?" she asked. "I'm a very busy woman. You know who I am?"

I didn't know who she was, but I didn't think that was the right answer.

"Shut the hell up, Mary," Ruth said, placing herself between us. "Of course she knows who you are. Everyone in this town knows who you are. Mary Trench. You're the one-percent. You're the evil capitalistic, imperialistic overlord of our sleepy little town. You're the reason we've had the same mayor for twenty years, even though he's a moron."

"Slander," Mary breathed. "Slanderous bitch. I'll have your shop for this. You won't have a pot to piss in after I get through with you."

Ruth's face turned red, and I got my phone out to call 911 in case she had a stroke. "I'll cut off the hand that gets near my pissing pot," she yelled.

It was obvious that Mary wasn't used to being spoken to like that, but who was? You walked into Tea Time at your own risk, as far as I was concerned. Ruth had her own philosophies about customer service.

"Slander! Threats!" Mary screeched.

"Truth hurts," Ruth said.

Mary shook with anger. I held tight to my cellphone. Someone was going to need medical aid. It was just a matter of time. She turned toward me, her fury directed at me.

"Tell your grandmother that George and I will be there at four, despite the insult," she said. "We have enough class to rise above it."

"Is that what they call it these days, Mary? Class?" Ruth said.

I thought Mary was going to blow. Her face was beet red, noticeable even from under her thick makeup. I put my hands over my head in case I would get some of the fallout. What did they say to do in case of nuclear attack? Oh yes. Duck and roll. I was sure I could duck, but I wasn't sure I could roll. Luckily, Mary turned on her high heel and walked out of the store before I had to take evasive maneuvers.

"You're going to have a swell dinner, Gladie," Ruth said.

Cars lined Grandma's driveway and up and down the street. There was a steady stream of people filing into her house, even though it wasn't four o'clock yet. Since Grandma didn't cook, they were all cooks as well as guests.

Inside, Grandma stood in the parlor, answering

logistical questions from her guests, such as where the good china was or how they were going to fit five long tables into a space that could only hold three. I looked at the staircase, longingly. I loved pumpkin pie, but I wanted to hide in my bedroom upstairs even more than I wanted pie. It was doubtful I could get by the hordes of guests without them noticing, though. Besides, they only made me claustrophobic. Upstairs there was someone in particular who made me feel a lot worse than merely shut in without air to breathe. She was asleep, and I wanted her to stay that way.

I took off my coat and stuffed it into the hall closet, which was now packed with coats. I closed the door to see my best friend Bridget Donovan standing next to me. She pushed her big owl glasses up on her nose.

"Oh good. You're home. It's chaos around here. Same as every year, but your grandmother always gets it done," she said.

"It smells good."

"I know. Normally I don't celebrate Thanksgiving on principle. I mean, this is a de facto celebration of genocide and thievery, but I can never pass up sweet potato casserole." Bridget was Grandma's bookkeeper and a militant anti-everything. She got a lot of joy out of being incredulous.

"There's marshmallow topped and pecan topped. Your choice."

"Why would I eat pecans if there are marshmallows?"

Bridget was right. It was chaos. But there was some kind of organization behind it that I couldn't see. Within half an hour, the tables were set up with lit candles and beautiful centerpieces. I did as I was told, helping out with the setting of the tables, bringing food platters, filling pitchers, and opening wine bottles.

The kitchen was packed to the rafters with townsfolk. It was like a war zone, with each cook fighting for their recipe to come out on top.

"Bird," Meryl said. "If you don't put down the olive oil, I'm going to throw out your peanut butter."

Bird held up the bottle of olive oil. "You wouldn't dare."

"Oh, wouldn't I?"

"You probably don't need me here," I said, trying to step out of the kitchen.

"Baste the turkeys!" Meryl and Bird shouted at me in unison.

I had no idea what "baste the turkey" meant, but it didn't sound good. "When you say baste, what does that mean exactly?" I asked.

A warm, strong arm came around me and wrapped itself around my belly, pulling me against an even warmer and stronger body. Even though I hadn't exactly been intimate with that body, I would know it anywhere. Tall with eight percent body fat and legs that had climbed every major mountain in the world, Arthur Holden, now known as William Burton, was hugging me and kissing my neck. It was enough to make a strong woman weak, and I wasn't a strong woman.

Whore. Whore. I was such a whore.

The air shifted, as the atoms rearranged themselves. I held my breath. Women-- young and old-- stopped what they were doing. Their mixing spoons hung in the air, dripping cream, stuffing, and whatever else they were preparing.

There had been a lot of speculation about Holden in the past. Some thought he had shot Osama bin Laden, where others thought he was a butt model. Nobody had guessed the truth, that he was in witness protection and was really a famous explorer. Why would they guess that? Butt model was a lot more realistic.

Forgetting that she had a spoonful of mashed potatoes in her hand, Bird ran the spoon over her hair, as if she was brushing it, leaving a trail of potato in her hair. Meryl giggled like a schoolgirl and stepped back, knocking into a container of cream and sending it spilling to the floor.

Holden had a way of making women crazy. I couldn't figure out why he was interested in me, but he was. He had come back into town to pack up his house and leave again, but I thought he was waiting around for me to go with him. I wasn't entirely sure that's why it was taking him so long to pack, because I was being careful not to be alone with him too much. Remington was all about the easy, but Holden was all about the hard.

I turned around in his arms and looked up. His attention was fixed on me, which was difficult since it was bedlam around us. Grandma's friends had spilled the entire dinner on themselves in the aftermath of Holden's tidal wave of sexiness. He studied my face, as if he was trying to read an answer there. I averted my eyes, like I was distracted by the ceiling.

I'm such a coward.

"I. Well. So," I sputtered. I couldn't seem to make out a sentence. My tongue had swollen, and my brain had swelled, pushing against my skull. Holden had that kind of effect on me.

"You look beautiful," he said.

"I do?"

My tongue swelled even more. I worried that I was going to die like that, in the arms of a man who loved me while I had another man's sexy all over my body.

Whore.

My grandmother walked into the kitchen. "You better get him out of here, bubeleh. Otherwise, I'm going to have to lick my dinner off Meryl's body, and I'm just not into that."

I took Holden's hand and walked him out. Bridget was standing just outside, clutching her belly. "Are you all right?" I asked.

"I think it's gas. I snuck some raw sweet potato casserole. Can that kill me?"

I had also snuck some sweet potato casserole, and now I was worried about dying, too. I looked at Holden. "No, I think you'll be all right," he said, smiling.

"I haven't been feeling like myself for a while now," Bridget said. "I haven't even been in the mood to protest the new box store in town. Maybe the election got me all out of sorts."

Normally, Mayor Robinson ran unopposed. Voters didn't actually like him as mayor, but nobody else wanted the job. Besides, our town was so small that there wasn't a lot for mayor to do or get wrong. But this year everything went to hell, and the election had become an extended mess.

"Mayor Robinson is bad enough," Bridget said. "But what if the other guy wins? Can you imagine Mayor Darth Vader?"

Holden snorted. "Mayor Darth Vader. You've got to love this town," he said.

"I think we're ready to take our seats," Grandma announced. The house was busier than I'd ever seen it. Twice as busy as grandma's Second Chances singles meeting. I took a seat near the middle of the room between Holden and Bridget.

Guests took their seats, and there was a slight scuffle at the head of the table when Mayor Robinson pushed another man out of his way. "The head of the table for the head of the town," he chortled. He was a big chortler. Everything he said he thought was riotously funny.

I noticed the woman from Tea Time, Mary, sat at his right hand and next to her was a man that definitely went with her. He was in his fifties, wearing a custom suit, with an irritated expression on his face like he was either constipated, had just lost a big bet, or was forced to go to Thanksgiving dinner at my grandmother's house. Across the table at a respectable distance away, Remington sat, surrounded by half of Cannes's single female population and two of its male single population. He had garnered a lot of attention.

Bridget grabbed a couple of rolls and took a big bite. "Ha, that's funny. I feel totally fine now. Hungry, though," she said with her mouth full.

Holden took my hand and gave it a gentle squeeze. My body got warm, and I sort of melted against his side. "I'm so glad to be sharing this evening with you," he said.

I couldn't look him in the eye. I was wracked with guilt. He was perfect…rich, sexy, kind, successful, and he wanted me bad. But instead of jumping into his arms and allowing him to love me and give me a life I'd only dreamed of, I was grinding hips with Detective Remington Cumberbatch on the sly just because it felt good. Really good.

Had I lost my mind? I had a headache a few days ago. Could that have really been an aneurysm? Maybe I had multiple personality disorder, but instead of personalities, I had too many men. Would that make me crazy?

"Can a woman have too many men?" I whispered to Bridget.

"Are you asking *me*?" she asked with her mouth full of bread. Bridget was a militant feminist. Militant everything. "I think one man is too many men. Like bedbugs or lice. They're parasites who suck the life and soul out of women. Not that I believe in souls. That's just Judeo-Christian hogwash." Bridget clutched at her chest. "Wow, I've got wicked heartburn. I'd give my right arm for sausage stuffing."

Yum. Sausage stuffing. With my mind on the men in

my life, I'd almost forgotten about the food. I was surprised that I was hungry after what I had packed in already during the day, but I was ravenous. My pants had been tight since I moved in with Grandma and adopted her junk food habits, but recently I couldn't stop eating. If I continued like I was, I wouldn't be able to fit through the door, and probably I wouldn't have to worry about having too many men.

I refused to step on a scale, but I couldn't button my jeans. It was almost like I was pregnant.

Pregnant.

I gasped. My body convulsed, and I knocked into my cutlery, sending a soup spoon and a salad fork flying across the table. The salad fork hit Julie's boyfriend Fred in the forehead and dropped down on his plate, making a loud noise, but not louder than Fred's scream.

He rubbed his forehead, but he seemed all right. "It's a good thing it wasn't the dinner fork," my grandmother noted. "He would have been a goner."

Sister Cyril crossed herself and mumbled a prayer.

"Are you okay?" Holden asked me. I felt him studying me, and for a moment I worried that I had a big sign on my face with "pregnant" flashing in neon.

I snuck a glance at Remington. Two old ladies and a middle-aged man were leaning toward him, like they were trying to breathe him in, and maybe they were. He was smiling politely back at them. I wondered if he could have super sperm, capable of swimming through a condom to make a woman pregnant. I watched his biceps bulge against his shirtsleeves, as he popped an olive into his mouth.

Yep. He could probably impregnate a woman, condom or no.

"I need a drink," I said. Holden quickly poured me a glass of wine and handed it to me. My hero. Totally responsible, like a good father should be. But he wasn't the father.

"Uh," I said, looking at the wine. I put the glass down on the table without drinking from it.

No wine? Pregnancy sucked.

With everyone seated, the Mayor stood and waved his arms around, like he was swatting at flies. "I am just so happy to be here at Zelda's beautiful home for this beautiful meal on this beautiful day in this beautiful town," he said and then guffawed loudly.

"Oh God," Sister Cyril moaned.

"I'd like to thank you all for your support," he continued, slapping Mary's back loudly and making her lunge forward against the table. "We had a fun election. We could call it a trial run. And now we can just prepare ourselves for an even more fun election coming up during Christmas time. A holy election, as it were. Maybe I'll dress up like baby Jesus for it. Oh, that would be fun. A Christmas election! How can life get any better than that?"

Bridget grabbed a third roll and took a bite. "Life could get better if we ate," she whispered to me.

I agreed. Even though I had eaten three slices of pizza and drunk a large latte, I was definitely down for a big helping of mashed potatoes, even if it was made with olive oil.

"I promise you I won't let the Dark Lord be your leader," he continued.

"The Dark Lord was Voldemort in Harry Potter," Meryl interrupted. "Darth Vader was just Lord Vader or My Lord."

I had no idea what they were talking about, but it wasn't the first time. I wasn't a science fiction fan or into politics, not since I worked two days for the PTA in Idaho.

"Well, whatever he's called, I have a plan to beat him," the mayor said, jovially.

"Good luck," Bridget whispered to me. "I hear Darth Vader is ahead twenty-five points in the polls."

"It must be because of The Force," Holden whispered.

"I have some plans that are sure winners," the mayor announced. "I wasn't going to talk about them here…"

"Thank goodness for that," someone muttered.

"But it's Thanksgiving, so why not give you one more thing to be thankful for?" the mayor continued.

"Yes, but you dropping dead would be too much to hope for," someone else muttered.

"So, first thing Monday morning, I'm initiating the first of several new initiatives. As of Monday, the 'Fresh Air for Cannes' law goes into effect. Simply said, it will no longer be legal to break wind in the town's limits. Shall we eat?"

The mayor sat down and flicked his napkin over his lap.

"Did he say what I think he said?" Bird asked.

"Breaking wind means farts, right?" Fred asked.

"Legend. Epic legend," said Remington.

There was a lull. No one said a word, and I imagined they were all concentrating on not farting. I jumped when Grandma cleared her throat.

"I think we could start, Mayor, by going around the table and whoever wants to, can say what they're thankful for," she said. "I'll start. I'm thankful that there's love in the world, that people find their soulmates and have a lifetime of love."

Holden squeezed my hand, and I swallowed.

The declarations of gratitude went around the table until it got to Remington. "I'm thankful for it all," he said and smiled. I held my breath, but he was true to his word. He didn't look my way and never let on that he and I had gone for a tumble in his sheets every day for the past two weeks.

Whore.

Plus one.

Ruth's niece, Julie was just about to say what she was grateful for – – probably for having all of her fingers and toes, despite her accident with a food processor last week– – when there was a loud stomping down the stairs. I closed my eyes, knowing full well who was making the noise and dreading what came next.

I wished for a time machine or a teleportation device, or just to be invisible or to not exist. But none of my wishes came true. No matter how hard I wished, my mother was there, her hair a rat's nest on her head, her lipstick smeared past her lips and over her cheek, and her clothes wrinkled, like she had slept in them, and of course she had. She was in that sweet spot before she had finished sleeping off her drunk, right before her hangover started and she had to contend with being sober. She was meanest during her sweet spots.

"What the hell?" she screeched. "You started without me? I live here, you know. What am I thankful for? It sure isn't my daughter or my mother-in-law."

I closed my eyes and prayed that someone would fart.

"Who's that?" Mary Trench asked.

"Luann, we've saved a seat for you over there," my grandmother told my mother. "You're just in time. We haven't started yet."

My mother stared at the table and seemed to think about the prospect of eating. She used to be a beautiful woman, but time, booze, and cigarettes had taken their toll on her. She used to have long, thick dark blond hair like mine, but now it was short, thin, and washed out. Her skin was sallow and she was rail thin. She liked to drink her calories.

I hadn't seen her for years and only a few times since I had left home when I was in high school. And now she was back, living in her former mother-in-law's house for the past few weeks, spending her time drinking, sleeping, and screeching. I didn't know why she was there or how long she was staying, but Grandma told me to be patient, and I normally did what my grandmother told me to do.

"And there's wine," Grandma added. That clinched it. My mother dragged a chair over the floor, making a hell of a racket and threw her body down on it with a huff. She crossed her legs, wrapping one around the other like a snake and grabbed a bottle off of the table.

Ladies and gentlemen, meet my charming mother.

"I'm thankful for Gloria Steinem and the First Amendment," Bridget said quickly and spooned stuffing onto her plate.

I was thankful for Bridget. It was unusual for her to eat when she was given a platform to decry a whole list of social injustices. But she wolfed down the stuffing and served herself more, and it cued the other guests to dig in.

It was a free for all. Platters of food were tossed like footballs, mounds of food scooped onto plates and eaten like it was everyone's first and last meal. I was no different. Yams, stuffing, cranberry sauce, and turkey. It was all delicious, and I figured if I was pregnant or going to kill myself, I might as well carbo load.

With the diners' mouths full, there was a welcome quiet, but it didn't last long. There was a brief tussle over which mashed potatoes were the best, and Mary Trench and her husband were going at each other about funding the mayor's campaign.

"You don't seriously want Mayor Darth Vader in this town?" she asked him, her voice rising over the other conversations around the table and the sounds of chewing and clanking of cutlery on plates.

"I don't give a good goddamn who's mayor. It's not like we even need a mayor. And if I want to let rip, I'll let rip. Nobody's going to tell me what I can or cannot do with my rectum."

"This is a lot like a dinner I had in Libya," Holden said to me.

"Starting the campaign off with a bang tonight," the mayor said. "We're heading off to the Black Friday sale at Walley's, which is starting a day early. I'm going to be a greeter. That way they'll associate me with the joy they get out of electronics at greatly reduced prices."

The mayor smiled from ear to ear, delighted about his campaign strategy to get voters at the new boxed store just outside of town.

"I hear they have slow cookers for five dollars," Meryl said.

"And peanut butter for fifty-cents a jar," Bird added.

There was a lot of excitement at the table about Black Friday a day early at Walley's, and most of the guests made plans to go over there after dinner.

"Walley's is one more sign that the fascists are winning," Bridget said, shoveling cranberry sauce into her mouth. "I may go, too, and protest. Convince sale hunters that they're part of the problem instead of the solution."

"I'm going to get a portable heater for fifteen dollars," Julie, said, excitedly.

"Don't let her near the portable heater, Fred," Grandma said. "It will end badly." You didn't need a third eye to know that.

"I would buy antacids, if I were you," the mayor said, happily.

"I can't believe you wrote a check to this guy," Mr. Trench said.

"Mind your own business!" Mary shrieked in my direction. I looked behind me to see who she was yelling at, but there was no one there.

"You! Busybody girl! Mind your own business."

"She's not Busybody Girl," Fred said. "She's Underwear Girl."

I had accidentally showed the entire police force and fire department my underwear once. I mean, while I was wearing them.

"She's not Underwear Girl," Meryl said. "She's Death Girl. She's stumbled on enough dead people to fill a cemetery."

There was murmuring around the table, agreeing that I was Death Girl, and they reminisced about my run-ins with murder victims. They were right. I was Death Girl. Even though I usually passed out at the sight of blood or any kind of violence, I had recently been involved in one death or another.

"I'm not Death Girl!" I yelled.

"You're so Death Girl," Bridget said to me, as she took a bite off a turkey leg.

I turned toward Holden. "I'm not Death Girl."

He patted my hand. "You couldn't fill a whole

cemetery. Maybe just a small section of a cemetery," he said.

I pulled my hand away. I didn't like being the center of attention, the main topic of conversation. Death Girls weren't extroverts.

"She's a Death Girl because she's a busybody. Busybody!" Mary Trench shouted, wagging her finger at me. "She's always sticking her nose in where it doesn't belong."

"What's wrong with being a busybody?" Grandma asked. "In my experience, busybodies are some of the most productive members of society." Grandma was the number one busybody. She was Wendy Williams on acid.

"She has the gift," Grandma continued. "If you have the gift, you have to be a busybody."

"I don't have the gift," I said to Holden. My grandmother had the gift, not me. She paired people like magic. She knew who should be with who just by looking at them.

"I'm sick and tired of hearing about 'the gift,'" my mother sneered. Her plate was clean because she hadn't put any food on it, but her glass was seeing a lot of action. "What did the gift do for my husband? He's six feet under. Gladie is just using this matchmaking crap as an excuse to sponge off her grandmother."

I gnawed at the inside of my cheek and picked at the cuticle on my thumb. Her words struck home. I wasn't a good matchmaker, and I was sure I didn't have the gift. My grandmother had been extremely generous letting me stay with her. Was I a sponge?

"You're not a sponge," Grandma said. "You have the gift."

"How long have you been here, Gladie?" my mother shrieked. "Months. And what have you done? Nothing. Just like your whole wasted life. You're a failure. A quitter. Just like high school. Just like everything. Who do you think you're fooling? You're not fooling me. I know who you are and what you are."

She grabbed a bottle off the table and stormed up the stairs. Nobody said a word. They were either in a collective state of shock or they agreed with my mother's assessment. But the quiet didn't last long. Before my mother got to the second stair on the staircase, the front door burst open and Darth Vader stormed in.

I heard his real name was Irving Schwartz, but he had it changed to Darth Vader a couple years ago when he either had a psychotic break or just wanted to make a point. He dressed in head to toes Star Wars, his long black cape dragging behind him wherever he walked, way too long for his five-foot-two frame.

Even though I wasn't interested in politics, it was hard not to be aware that a man named Darth Vader was running for mayor with his stormtroopers by his side and Darth Vader theme music blaring at his events. The election ladies didn't take him seriously and left his name off of the ballot, and that's what sparked the lawsuit and the second election planned for December.

I doubted Grandma invited Darth Vader to Thanksgiving dinner. In any case, we hadn't set a place for him or his storm trooper friends he brought along.

He threw open the door and let it bang against the wall. His theme music blared, and he made a loud breathing sound.

"I will be mayor," he announced, his voice high-pitched and muffled in his black helmet. "I will create an inter-galactic empire with Cannes as its capitol!"

"Would you pass the stuffing?" Bridget asked me. "When are the pies coming out?"

I was having a hard time keeping up with her. My stomach was ready to explode. Was that the baby growing? My head spun at the thought.

The mayor and Mary Trench stood. "How dare you come here?" The mayor shouted at Darth Vader. "This is my constituency!"

"I'm not feeling well," Bridget moaned and clutched onto her stomach.

"These are good people, not like your constituency," the mayor continued.

I couldn't believe that Darth Vader had a constituency, and I wondered if the mayor was using the word wrong.

"I'll go where The Force tells me to go!" Darth Vader breathed.

"This food isn't for you!" Mary shouted.

To prove it, the mayor took a forkful of stuffing and

slammed it into his mouth. "You shouldn't do that," Grandma said, but it was too late. Mayor Robinson bit down and yelped in pain. Blood spurted out of his mouth, like someone had turned on a faucet in his mouth.

"I told you not to," Grandma mumbled. "Gladie, take Bridget to the bathroom. She's about to blow."

I turned to Bridget. She was green, and she had one hand on her belly and one hand over her mouth. I jumped up, grabbed her hand, and ran for the bathroom. We just made it when she blew.

After, Bridget rinsed her mouth at the bathroom sink. "Wow. I have no idea where that came from."

"I do. If it crawled, flew, or sprouted from the earth, you ate it."

Bridget pushed her large glasses up on her nose. "I was starving. I couldn't get enough. I was feeling fine and then all of a sudden, pow."

"Pow."

"And now I'm hungry, again. I could go for a slice of pecan pie. How about we eat in the kitchen. I think it's safer in there."

"I'll watch you eat. I don't think I could take another bite," I said, but watching her eat gave me an appetite again, and I ate two slices of pie before my grandmother walked in.

"Mr. Holden took the mayor to the hospital. They're going to put five stitches in his tongue and send him on his way. He's going to sound even dumber. Anyway, the Trenches stormed off in a huff, but the rest are here, waiting for dessert."

I looked down, guiltily at our decimated pie. "Sorry."

"We have enough, but take out a bag of trash to the curb and take your policeman with you. There's something you need to talk about."

I belched. "He's not my policeman," I lied. "I'm not sure I want to talk to him."

She handed me a bag of trash. "You can make bank on that."

"What?"

She shrugged. "I don't know. I just got it with my radar. I don't know what it means."

I took the bag and walked out. With the mayor, my mother, the Trenches, and Darth Vader gone, the dinner guests had calmed down. I caught Remington's eye, and he extricated himself from his admirers and followed me outside.

It was freezing. "It smells like snow," I said. Remington slipped his warm arm around me and pulled me against his side. He was a man of very few words, but we didn't need a lot of words in our relationship. I wondered if that was going to change, now that I might be pregnant.

We walked down the driveway and stopped at the curb where the trashcan was waiting to be picked up for trash day. I was thankful for the dark night, because I was having a hard time looking at Remington in the eye. There was a big secret I wasn't telling him, and I wasn't planning on telling him. At least for now.

"Give it to me gently," he said.

"I think we need to take a break. A temporary break."

He touched the side of my face and trailed his finger down my cheek and cupped my chin. "I always figured we wouldn't be forever. Not with the other guy around."

I wondered which guy he was talking about. "It's not that," I said.

"Give the guy a break. Don't be afraid."

I still didn't know which guy he was talking about. I was afraid of two of them. Petrified. "I'm not afraid," I said.

"Well, you know where to find me. You feel me?"

"I feel you."

"I'll always be there for you, Gladie. You can make bank on that."

"Okay," I breathed. It was hard not to jump on him and wrap my legs around his waist. He was the only easy part of my life, and I was rejecting him. "I might be knocking on your door soon."

And giving birth to his baby.

Without kissing me goodbye, he turned on his heel and walked away. I watched the shape of his large body walk down the street. He moved like an athlete...strong and lithe. I stood, holding the trash bag until he was gone, having turned down the next street. I was either very brave or very stupid to let him go. But I had a lot to figure out in my life, and his easy would just make it harder.

I opened the trash can and dropped the bag inside, but the can was overflowing, and I had to push on the bag to get it to fit. I moved around the contents to get it down further because we would have more garbage bags before the night was done.

I stuck my hand in the can. There was something long and heavy sticking out. Somebody had obviously stuck their trash in our can. It was long like a baseball bat, but it was covered in cloth. I pulled it out and tried to see it in the dark.

I gasped, sucking in a lot of air.

CHAPTER 3

Have you ever had an old shmata that you couldn't bring yourself to throw away? I had a sweater like that. It was stretched out with coffee stains on the front and holes in the elbows, but I couldn't bring myself to throw it out. Sometimes a shmata worms its way into our heart, and we can't part with it. This is often true with our matches...they have shmatas in his or her heart. Love shmatas. Do you understand what I'm talking about, dolly? These love shmatas are past loves that maybe shouldn't be past loves. Maybe they should be current loves. Maybe it's not time for them to move on to a new match. It's our job to investigate these shmatas and make sure they need to be thrown away. You see, sometimes they're not shmatas at all but beautiful silk shirts that should be kept forever. Don't let them throw away a silk shirt, bubeleh. Silk shirts are precious and hard to replace.

Lesson 59, Matchmaking Advice from your

elise sax

Grandma Zelda

I felt myself drift off into a black cloud, only dimly aware that I was still holding it in my hand and walking back up the driveway to the house. Inside, the guests were eating pie and drinking coffee, discussing normal topics like sports and cable prices. Then, they noticed me.

"Why is Gladie holding a severed leg?" Meryl asked.

"Oh my God, she really is Death Girl," Fred said.

"Help," I moaned. "Leg. Foot. Help."

Somebody from somewhere helped me to a seat. I was still in a half-dream state. It wasn't like me to remain conscious when I was holding a severed limb in my hand. I mean, I passed out when I worked as a receptionist at Fresno General Hospital for an hour and a half.

But no matter how much I wanted to slip into a gentle, relaxing coma, my eyes wouldn't close, and I couldn't let go of the bloody leg, which I was firmly grasping in my right hand, as if I was holding the torch at the Olympics.

Time passed. I wasn't sure how much, but people came and went, commenting about the leg or snapping their fingers in front of my face. It was hard to focus on the here and now. My mind was drifting off to a place where it didn't matter that there was a lifeless body part in my hand.

"Hello, Chief Bolton," I heard someone say in the distance. It was Grandma. But normally she called him Spencer like I did. Had he changed from Spencer to Chief Bolton in the past month since he got his feelings hurt? He had worked up a seething anger at me and when I had seen him a couple times in town since then, he gave me the evil eye, as if I had committed war crimes or spit on the flag.

I smelled his expensive cologne and then noticed his designer shoes. Spencer was a vain metrosexual that made my toes curl without even touching me. He was a womanizer who almost committed to me, but our timing was off. At the moment when he finally let his guard down, I got down and dirty with Remington.

"Are you kidding me?" he said.

"Leg. Foot. Leg," I heard myself say, and I was relieved and somewhat surprised that I could still speak.

"Let go of the leg," he ordered in his best cop voice.

"Leg," I said.

"That's right. Let go of the leg. Give it to me."

"Leg. Foot. Leg."

"Give me the leg, Gladie. Right now." At the sound of my name, I blinked. Spencer usually called me Pinky, in honor of my underpants. Calling me Gladie meant that he was really angry or the situation was really serious. The here and now came back into focus. I could see Spencer clear as day and a room full of horrified people staring at me and the bloody, severed leg that I clutched in my hand.

My fingers loosened on the leg, and Spencer took it with a gloved hand.

"Gross," I said.

He handed it to another cop, a young one I didn't recognize. He must have been new because I was pretty familiar with the police force.

"Gross," Spencer agreed. "Why did you have it?"

"I don't know. I'm lucky that way. Do you have anti-bacterial gel or a wipe?" I held up my hand, as if I was hailing a cab. I doubted there was enough antiseptic in the world to clean my hand. I might have to cut it off. "Or a saw?"

"Where did you get the leg, Gladie?" Spencer asked me, seriously.

"Is that how we're going to play it?" I said, affronted that he was calling me Gladie. I understood he was angry at me, but he didn't have to be cruel.

"What do you mean?"

"You know what I mean." I wiped my leg hand on his perfectly pressed suit. I was pissed.

"Nice," he said. "Very nice."

I touched his beautifully groomed hair with my leg hand. He pursed his lips and scowled, like he was going to kill me.

"Where did you get the leg?"

"In the trash can. I was taking out the trash."

Spencer nodded and ordered his men to search Grandma's trash and all the trashcans on the street. "What the hell are you doing?" he asked me.

"Who are you talking to?"

"You."

"Who's that?"

Spencer's face turned a light shade of purple. "Listen Pinky, stop sticking your nose where you don't belong."

I stood up and leaned into him. "I was taking out the trash!" I yelled.

"Only you take the trash out and find body parts."

"It wasn't my fault! It was there!"

He pushed against me until our bodies were touching and he was looking down at me, our noses an inch apart. "Don't find anything else. Nothing more. Do you hear me? Not a leg. Not an arm. Not a fingernail. Nothing. Don't ask a question about the leg. Don't wonder about it. Don't dream about it. Don't show up at the station. Don't pester my men. Don't pester me."

"That's a lot of don'ts."

"Don't."

A tall, thin man tapped Spencer on his shoulder. "Hey, Chief, are you ready to go, now? I'm going to be late for dinner."

Spencer hung his head down and ran his fingers through his hair. "Mr. Sullivan, you live down the street. Wouldn't you rather go home?'

"No way," Mr. Sullivan said. "I stole a pack of gum. Fair's fair. You must take me to jail."

Spencer sighed. "I have a murder to solve. Can't you just ride it out with your family?"

"I'm not spending one more holiday with my family," Mr. Sullivan explained to me. "Jail is quieter with better food."

"There's a double feature at the Cannes Landmark," I suggested.

"The jail has a killer pecan pie," he countered. I couldn't argue with that. Besides, if I had thought of jail instead of Thanksgiving with my family, I would have stolen a pack of gum, too. Mr. Sullivan had the right idea, as far as I was concerned. I was done with it all.

With the cops gone and the pies finished, Grandma's guests started to file out. "I have to take him to jail and write up reports," Spencer said. "Remember, no more dead stuff. Nothing."

"Do you think I wanted to find that leg?" I asked.

Spencer held up his hand with his thumb and forefinger an inch apart, like he was pinching something invisible. "A little bit."

"No. I'm done with death. I'm done with busybodies and love and everything."

"Music to my ears."

"Bridget went to get her sandwich board," Grandma told me. "Take your coat with you. Be careful of the free, dolly."

"What? Where am I going?"

"You're taking Bridget to Walley's for the Black Friday one day early sale. She's going to protest, and you're going…well, you'll see."

"I'm tired, Grandma. I need to bleach my hand," I said.

Bridget had changed the message on her sandwich board from "Gerrymandering is Stalin's Love Child" to a simple "Walley's Management are Labor Criminals" for our trip to the Black Friday a day early sale.

I drove her to the store, just outside of town, in my ancient Oldsmobile Cutlass Supreme. I had to park at the far side of nowhere in Walley's vast parking lot because it was packed with just about every citizen of Cannes and the three nearest towns. I had never been to Walley's, but I knew it was a huge box store, and I heard it sold packages of ten Hershey bars for a dollar.

"This is kind of exciting," I said, untying the rope that held my trunk closed. "It's like an event. I haven't gone out for a while."

Bridget took her sandwich board out of the trunk and slipped it over her head. "I'm excited, too. I haven't protested in weeks. Whoa, the sandwich board is tighter than usual. Maybe it shrank?"

"Everything's tight on me, too," I said. I closed up the trunk with the rope and we walked the long way through the parking lot to the store. The closer we got, the denser the crowd got. The diehard sale-hunters were already done and leaving the store with their carts piled high with discounted electronics.

"It's the Roman Empire, the later years," Bridget said.

"I might check out the chocolate."

"Don't let them suck you in with cheap chocolate, Gladie." She stopped walking and looked out into space. "On second thought, pick me up some while you're at it. I mean, they're open, anyway."

"Labor crimes!" she shouted into the crowd. "Exploitation!"

That was my cue. "I'll see you in an hour," I called and waved goodbye. I made my way through the crowd into the store. Walking in the middle of a wave of humanity, I almost didn't notice the mayor greeting customers. He was standing on a box, and he had a little dried blood by his lower lip, I assumed from chomping down on lightbulb glass at dinner.

"Hewo, hewo," he called out, smiling at the shoppers. Mary Trench was at his side waving, but I didn't see her husband. "Weemember to wote or me," he struggled to say with an injured tongue.

I walked by him, pushed by the crowd. He was a moron, but I had to hand it to him. Nothing got him down. He was eternally optimistic. I wasn't optimistic. My mother's words during dinner had sunk into my psyche and made me go back in time to the scared, insecure teenager I used to be. Was I sponging off my grandmother? Was I wasting my time, trying to become a matchmaker? What did I know about love, anyway? And what about Spencer? Whatever was between us was gone now.

I needed discounted chocolate in a bad way.

Walley's was packed with merchandise, even with the hordes of shoppers, ripping sales items off the shelves at record speed. I was swept along with the wave of shoppers with no idea where I was going. But somehow—maybe a miracle or the power of positive thinking—I found myself at Walley's chocolate section.

It was everything I had been promised and more. Hershey bars, ten for a dollar. Piles and piles of every brand of cheap chocolate imaginable. I grabbed handfuls of bags, kicking myself for not thinking to get a basket. When I couldn't carry any more, I tried to make my way to the cashier, but I was pushed and shoved by the increasingly excited crowd.

"Out of my way!" shouted a large woman, lugging a giant television box. She hit me with a corner of it, as she ran past, ramming me against a shelf. I clutched onto the shelf, trying to catch my balance. I managed to stay upright, but I knocked down a few items. When I bent down to pick them up, I noticed they were pregnancy tests.

"Buy at least three boxes," a massively pregnant woman told me, pointing at me as she looked at boxes of vaginal douches. "You won't be satisfied with only one answer."

"Oh, I'm not..." I began, but I stopped myself. Maybe I was. Maybe I should buy a pregnancy test or three, as the giant-bellied woman suggested.

She adjusted her wide girth and shifted the weight on her feet. She had a toddler in the basket's baby seat, and the basket itself was overflowing with diapers, toys, and clothes. "Don't do like I did. I took the test and then ran back to the store to get another. You know, just to make sure."

"I guess I should be sure?" I said like a question. Her belly was hypnotic. It gave her an authority, like she was able to fit an enormous lifeform in her gut so she had superhuman powers.

I didn't want superhuman powers.

"Three boxes?" I asked and stuck the boxes in my pocket next to Ruth's jar of peanut butter.

"Two-hundred dollar Xboxes! Two-hundred dollar Xboxes!" someone yelled, and there was a rush for the other side of the store. The very pregnant lady took off, waddling quickly, pushing her basket into the ankles of slower mortals. I looked down at my chocolate. It was a paltry haul compared to the other shoppers. Still, I was delighted at the prospect of taking it home and eating it in bed while I watched *I Love Lucy* reruns.

With the chocolate in my arms, I walked through the personal hygiene section to the children's clothes section, but I couldn't get past a large crowd that was surrounding a large table. "What's going on?" I asked a man, who was waving his hands at the table.

"Free samples. All kinds," he said, bursting with excitement.

"I like free."

I wasn't the only one. The air crackled with the euphoria brought on by large quantities of tiny free products. But the euphoria changed quickly to desperation and greed. The crowd grew increasingly aggressive, as time passed and they didn't reach the table, didn't get their share of the free goods. A worry passed around that the free samples would run out. Then they were pushing and shoving in earnest. Luckily, I was at the outer rim so I wasn't getting the worst of it. I stepped backward, away from the crowd, when a Walley's employee stepped up on the free sample table and began shouting.

"Get back, you animals! Get back!" she shouted. Her eyes were wild, and her hair had come out of her ponytail to stand up all over her head. She spat when she screamed, and she screamed really loudly. "If I had a gun, I would shoot you! Come any closer, and I'm going to kick you in the teeth."

Black Friday a day early wasn't for wimps.

Instead of scaring them off, the crowd rushed the table, decimating the supplies of free samples and running off to other sale items. The Walley's employee stopped screaming, but her mouth was still wide open. She wasn't blinking, and there was a good chance she was in shock. I looked down at my chocolate and the clear path to the registers and then looked back up at the employee.

"You're okay, right?" I asked her.

She finally blinked and seemed to notice me for the first time. "You're all animals!" she shouted. "You're all beasts!"

It had been a bad night for my ego.

"Well, if you're fine, I'm just going to take my chocolate and pay for it." I smiled and stepped away when the manager arrived.

"Nicole, get off that table!" the manager yelled.

"You're supposed to be in paper goods!"

Nicole took off her Walley's smock and threw it at the manager. "I quit! The money isn't worth this shit!"

She climbed down off the table and stormed toward the exit. The manager and I watched her go, standing side by side. "It's getting harder and harder to find reliable employees," he muttered.

"Really?"

"It's our busiest season, and now I have to replace her."

A little idea bubble popped in my brain. "I have some retail experience," I said.

"Really? Could you start tomorrow?"

Gulp. Black Friday.

"Yes, but let's discuss salary."

"No salary. Minimum wage," he said.

"Plus benefits?"

He handed me the smock. "This is Walley's," he said, as if that explained it all.

"Lunch break?"

"Thirty minutes. Come at seven tomorrow, and you can fill out the paperwork before you start."

"Seven in the morning?"

But he was gone, off to handle the riot in menswear.

My heart raced. What had I done? In an instant, I went from being a fledgling matchmaker to a Walley's employee with a hand-me-down smock.

I took a deep, healing breath and convinced myself

that I had done the right thing. I would show everyone that I wasn't a failure. I wasn't sponging off my grandmother. I would get a steady paycheck and pay my way.

Feeling energized, I decided to add a carton of ice cream to go along with my chocolate. There was a small cooler near the registers, and I fished around for a half gallon of chocolate chip cookie dough. It was hard to grab for it while holding the bags of chocolate and the smock in my arms up to my chin, but I managed to get one hand in and grab the first thing that I could reach.

But it didn't feel like an ice cream carton. For a moment, I thought Haagen-Dazs had issued a new kind of a container, but almost instantly I knew what I was holding. It was a large hand with five fingers and hairy knuckles, and it wasn't attached to an arm. I lifted it up to examine it more closely and double-check that I had really found another severed body part. My chocolate and smock fell to the floor, as I held it up. Yep, it was a severed hand.

Now that I was experienced with dismembered body parts, I held it together and didn't go into shock. Instead, I screamed and tossed the hand like a major league pitcher, throwing it halfway across the store. Nobody noticed my scream, since the store was filled with screaming customers, but I did get a lot attention when the hand flew through the air and hit the cashier in lane three right in the face.

The word got around Walley's pretty quickly about severed body parts flying through the store, and more than a few shoppers ran out of the store, taking their unpaid baskets full of merchandise with them. I flew out of the store, too, running full out with the stampede. Out of the corner of my eye, I saw the mayor get swept off his box, and he managed to take down Mrs. Trench with him when he swung his arms for balance. After that, I just tried to keep up with the tide and stay upright myself.

When I got outside, I grabbed Bridget by her sandwich board and kept running, tugging her behind me until we got to my car. "Look at them go," Bridget said, out of breath. "My protest really worked. They're running away from the labor criminals. It's a new dawn, Gladie."

I didn't have the heart to tell her they were running away from dead people parts and not minimum wage-paying management. Bridget had so few victories in her liberal crusade.

"You did great," I said.

"You can't go wrong with a sandwich board. It's a bit old school, but it never fails." She took it off and put it in my trunk. The sounds of sirens wailing were coming closer. "What's that?"

"Three police cars and one fire truck," I said. I had a lot of experience with first responders since I moved to Cannes.

"What did you do?" she asked.

"I might have found a hand."

"Oh. I'm hungry."

Damn. I left the chocolate in the store. "I got a job," I said.

"Like a real one?"

That's when Spencer showed up. He had some kind of radar when it came to me. While the rest of the cops ran inside of the store, he made a beeline for my car.

"Are you kidding me?"

"Do you have a wipe?"

"What is it with you? You're a trouble magnet," he said.

"She's a death magnet," Bridget said and yawned. "I don't know what's wrong with me. I'm bushed. Normally protesting invigorates me, but I could sleep for days. Must be the Thanksgiving food."

"I need to take her home," I told Spencer. I still couldn't look at him in the eyes. I fumbled in my purse for my key to unlock my door and the screwdriver to start my car.

Even though I knew Spencer wanted to talk to me, I got in the car and drove away with Bridget. She dozed on the way home, and I dropped her off at her condo. It had been quite a day, but it was only seven o'clock, twelve hours before I had to report to my new job.

I parked the car in my grandmother's driveway and walked into the house. The guests and the police had left, and the house was clean and quiet. Grandma was waiting for me just inside the house, dressed in her best blue housecoat and slippers with her hands on her hips, one eyebrow raised, clucking like a hen.

"What are you doing?" she demanded.

"I locked the door this time. I promise."

"Not that. You know what I mean."

"I didn't mean to find the hand," I whined. "I thought it was ice cream."

"Not that either. The job."

"Oh," I said. "Is there pie left?"

We walked to the kitchen. Grandma put on a pot of decaf while I got the pies out of the refrigerator. There were enough leftovers to last for a month. I sliced a couple of pieces of pumpkin pie, and we sat down at the table.

"You have the gift, dolly," she told me.

"No I don't. You have the gift."

"You've made good matches. Real matches."

"I've stumbled into them, like I stumble into dead people. Matchmakers don't stumble."

I finished the pie and slurped a cup of coffee with milk.

"Fine," she said.

I swallowed. "Fine?" I had figured my grandmother would have argued with me, forced me not to show up at Walley's in the morning and convinced me that I was born to be a matchmaker. If she gave up so quickly, maybe my mother was right. Maybe I was a failure, doomed to work at Walley's for the rest of my life.

"You're not doomed," she said. "But you have a little

more of a journey before you accept your destiny."

I thought about my destiny. Could it involve stretch marks and funding a college account?

I took a hot shower and was in bed by nine, dressed in sweats and a t-shirt, careful to set the alarm so I wouldn't be late on my first day of work. I was exhausted and thrilled to get a good night's sleep, but my mind wouldn't shut off.

Ignoring my problems with Spencer, Holden, and Remington, and even forgetting about the idea of growing a baby in my belly weren't that difficult, but the mystery of the body parts had my mind reeling. Bridget was right. I was a murder magnet. I was drawn to the mystery of gore and death.

Perhaps I was some kind of monster, but I couldn't clear my head of wondering why someone put a leg in my grandmother's trash or a hand in a cooler at Walley's. Who was the dead person and where was the rest of him and who killed him and chopped him up? I could ask Remington, but I was trying to stay clear of him while I figured out if I was his baby's mama and what role I wanted him to play in my life. I could also ask Spencer, but he frowned on me getting involved in his investigations, and he frowned on me in general these days.

Even though I had run into my share of murders while I lived in Cannes, it wasn't exactly a hotbed of crime.

There wasn't a lot of dismembering going on during the historical preservation meetings or knitting circles. What would make a person become a monster?

I had a bad feeling about this murder, not just because it was disgusting, but because I felt a foreboding about the nature of this killer. Perhaps not only was it a madman, but someone truly evil. I shuddered and pulled the covers up around my neck. I tried to sleep, but the thoughts of the murderer's victim prevented me from getting any rest. That's why I started my first day at Walley's without a minute of sleep.

CHAPTER 4

Surprise! Surprises are always good, right? Wrong!
Surprises are like a zetz on your head. A headache. You don't
believe me? Well, surprise, the IRS has decided to audit you for
your last ten years of taxes. How does that feel? You like that
surprise? Just kidding. I was playing a little joke. Just trying to
prove my point. So, understand what I'm telling you. Don't let
your matches surprise you. Knowledge is power. Learn everything
you can as soon as you can so you don't get a zetz on your head
and a pain in your ass.

Lesson 93, Matchmaking Advice from your
Grandma Zelda

It was a madhouse. Not only was Walley's packed
with Black Friday sales hunters, but everyone from the night
before who had run off after I threw the hand across the store

had come back this morning. I hated getting to work so early. Tea Time wasn't open yet, so I had to somehow wake up without Ruth's latte in my system.

I have had my share of early morning and night shift jobs in my life, but I hadn't put on a uniform this early since I worked at the *It's A Small World* ride doing maintenance at Disneyland for two months. I had found sixteen earrings, three dozen sunglasses, and enough condoms for the entire country of Ecuador to have safe sex for a year. It sure gave me a new perspective on humanity.

So did Walley's on Black Friday. There was an air of excitement, but it was pushed out of the way by the much stronger air of panic from shoppers that they wouldn't find the sale items still in stock. People walked quickly and unblinkingly toward their goals, most toward the electronics section of the store.

I walked to the customer service department, because I didn't know where the manager's office was. But once I found it, I filled out the paperwork in a couple of minutes and was handed a new smock with my own name badge. Glurpie Booger was written on the badge. I had been called worse in my life.

"You're in the kitchen utensils department until ten," I was told. "Be careful of the Ginsu knives."

"They're sharp, right?" I asked. I shuddered. There was a whole lot of damage that could be done to me with a Ginsu knife.

"No. They like to steal them. They're never on sale."

I was pleased to be in the kitchen utensils department. Sure, I didn't know the difference between a spatula and a whisk, but it was a relatively quiet area of the store. There wasn't a lot of sale action going on. I organized the shelves, laying out the wooden spoons by size. I was sort of proud of myself. I hadn't found any dead bodies. And I hadn't had any major disasters. Maybe Walley's was my future. It wasn't a very difficult job, but it was steady. Normal.

At ten o'clock, my shift at kitchen utensils was done, and I was allowed a ten minute break in the break room. The room was sterile and utilitarian, but the employees had brought in a crap load of leftover Thanksgiving desserts, which I attacked, since I hadn't eaten any breakfast. I managed to get a slice and a half of pecan pie in before my ten minutes were up, and I was transferred to checkout.

"I can't believe they gave me somebody to train on Black Friday," Sally, the cashier in Lane Five told me. Every checkout lane was open, and the lines were extremely long, filled with impatient people ready to get out of there.

"I know. What was he thinking?" I said, shrugging my shoulders, as if Walley's management was a bunch of imbeciles, and they probably were.

"Okay Glurpie," she said, obviously annoyed. "Just watch me for a while. The goal is to get them out as quickly as possible."

She was quick. Her fingers were like lightning on her register. *Beep. Beep. Beep.* Each item was passed through and dumped into a plastic bag in record time. I felt guilty just standing there, watching, so I helped by putting the plastic bags in the carts.

For the most part, it all ran smoothly. There was a lot of complaining about low stock on the sale items, but more often than not the shoppers went out with some big steals, like big screen TVs for seventy percent off.

I was getting the hang of it pretty quickly. I figured our lane was going the fastest, in part because I was helping. I started talking to each customer, smiling and asking them about their day and their children and how they were. It was smooth sailing. I was actually happy. I figured I really had made the right decision to quit matchmaking, which had been one mishap after another, to the easy, smooth world of Walley's.

The next customer put her items on the belt, and as the cashier put them in the plastic bags, I put them in the cart. That's when I saw the slithering green monster. A nasty, disgusting snake was in the cart.

I was filled with a sense of terror, but I also swelled with a feeling of heroics. In my new position at Walley's, I felt a responsibility to do my job properly, and the first thing to do was to save my customer.

"Snake! Snake!" I screamed. There was a general screaming from the other customers, and I took a bag of groceries and slammed it against the snake in the woman's cart as hard as I could. The cashier ran away and so did most of the customers, but I wasn't going to let them down. I continued to beat the snake into submission.

Until the shopper punched me in the face.

"What the hell do you think you're doing?" she yelled at me.

"Saving you!"

"Stop! That's my snake. That's my assistance snake."

"Assistance snake?"

It turned out that there were assistance snakes. The woman had an allergy to pet dander, and snakes didn't have any dander, whatever dander was.

"Do you know there's a mandatory fine of one hundred thousand dollars and six months probation for assault on assistance animals!" the manager yelled at me.

I was in some kind of Walley's jail. It was a room just off the employees lounge. It had two chairs and a poster with "Theft Affects You" printed on it.

"One hundred thousand dollars?" I asked. I tried to figure out how many Walley's hours I would have to work to pay that. A lot of hours.

"Not to mention all the money you lost us when those customers ran out before paying."

I didn't know if he was talking about when I threw the hand across the store or when I pummeled the snake, but I wasn't going to ask him to clarify, just in case he didn't know that I was the one with the hand.

"Is the snake all right?" I asked. It was a question I

never thought I would hear myself ask.

"The emergency veterinarian made a housecall and said it would be okay after therapy."

The snake needed therapy, and so did I. Where was I going to get one hundred thousand dollars?

"I hear they called META," the manager said.

"What's META?" I asked.

"It's a militant offshoot of PETA. PETA kicked them out for being too radical," he explained.

"Oh my God."

"Yes. I'm going to take a sick day. I don't give a shit that it's Black Friday. I'll never forget the run-in we had with META when our faux fur collar coats turned out not to be faux."

I looked at the door and back at the manager. He had a big gut and a comb-over. I was pretty confident that his athletic days were long in the past, but then again so were mine. Still, it was worth a shot trying to out run him. I didn't want to stick around to be arrested or worse, whatever META does to assistance snake attackers.

Before I could make a run for it, the door opened and two cops came in, followed by police Chief Spencer Bolton. I slapped my forehead. Really, I had the worst luck in the world.

"Officer," the manager told Spencer. "This is Glurpie Booger. She's the one who attacked the snake."

"Glurpie Booger," Spencer said. "Are you kidding me?"

"It wasn't my fault."

"You didn't attack a woman's snake with a bag of groceries?"

The policeman behind Spencer waved at me. I recognized him as Officer James. "Hello, Underwear Girl," he said.

I waved back. It was nice to be called Underwear Girl. Normally, I didn't like the name, but it was a lot better than murder girl, and Officer James was friendly, whereas META probably wouldn't be. But Spencer didn't like it. He shot Officer James a look that could kill.

"Sorry," Officer James said.

Spencer grabbed my hand and pulled me up. "Okay, Glurpie Booger. Let's go."

"I can't go. I have work until four."

Spencer knocked on my forehead. "Hello? Hello? Is anybody there? Look, Glurpie, you're not working here anymore." He shot a look to the manager, and the manager nodded his head, vigorously.

"But," I started. But then I remembered about META. Even if Spencer was arresting me, I didn't want to stick around.

"Okay. You can send the check home," I told the manager, as I followed Spencer out.

Outside I took a deep breath, inhaling the fresh air of freedom. Officer James and the other cop went to take statements, and Spencer walked me to my car.

"What's with you? What were you doing in there?" he

asked me. Spencer was one of the best looking men I'd ever met. He was wearing a perfectly tailored suit, as always. And he held himself with complete self-confidence. Sure, he was a womanizing jerk, but he was a sexy womanizing jerk.

"I didn't know it was an assistance snake, Spencer. I've never heard of an assistance snake before. Have you?"

"Of course, I've never heard of an assistance snake. Only in this crazy ass town, would there be assistance snakes. I'm talking about Walley's. I'm talking about this," he said tugging at my smock. "What were you doing in there? Are you going undercover? Because I told you not to get involved in this murder. I distinctly remember giving you a direct order not to get involved."

I poked his chest. "First of all, you don't order me to do anything. I don't take orders from you. You got that? Second of all, I wasn't here about the murder. I'm done with murders. Done with it all. So we never have to have these kinds of conversations again. I was working, like a normal worker person."

"You could never be a normal anything, let alone a normal worker person, Glurpie Booger."

I pushed him to the side and opened my car door. "Get used to it. This is the new me. I'm just a normal citizen. No more matches. No more murder."

Spencer blocked me from closing the door. He bent down and got in my face. His breath smelled like mint and peanut butter. I wondered if he was doing Birds' diet, like the rest of the town. Suddenly I remembered that I still had the peanut butter in my coat pocket, and the boxes of pregnancy tests that I had unwittingly stolen the night before. I worried that Spencer would search me and find them. But he was more concerned with other matters.

"Listen, Gladie," he said, still not calling me Pinky, as he usually did. Boy, he sure was pissed about me having sex with his subordinate. "I know you think you can just ignore me about these murders and continue snooping around, because that's what you normally do, but this time it's different. Do you hear me? This time is different."

"You think? Severed body parts found all over town? You think that's new? Don't worry, Spencer. I'm not getting involved. I've turned over a new leaf. I've quit being the old Gladie. I am reborn. I'm not the least bit interested in severed body parts, no matter how many I happen to find of this poor murder victim."

"Victims, Gladie. Plural. The hand belonged to one guy and the leg to another. So don't find anymore. This case is bad. You hear me?" He stared at me for a moment and sighed. "Oh God. You're getting that look."

"No, I'm not. I don't have a look."

"Yes you do. You've got the look you get when your brain is focusing on murder and mayhem."

"You're imagining things. I was thinking about lunch." I was thinking about lunch, but I was also thinking about the murders. A hand from one guy and a leg from another. To me that spelled one thing: serial killer. A serial killer in Cannes. That was a first.

"Were these girls? Were they locked up in a dungeon somewhere and then tortured and murdered and cut into pieces?" I asked.

"That doesn't sound like lunch. That sounds like you're sticking your nose in where it doesn't belong."

"Hey, you brought it up. And I should know because I'm a girl and I don't want to be locked up in a dungeon or tortured or murdered or cut up into pieces."

"They weren't girls. They were grown men. Good men."

"Good men? Did you know them?" I started counting in my head all the people that I knew in town. Was anybody missing? Had anybody I'd known gotten killed?

"Sort of. It was the manager and a trainer of a minor-league baseball team but don't go spreading that around. Do you hear me? Control your mouth." Spencer was a huge baseball fan, and I could imagine how upset he would be from their deaths. I touched his hand to console him, but he pulled it back quickly.

"Don't," he said. His lips tightened into a straight line. He was more than upset at me, I realized. Whatever he had felt was gone. Whatever relationship we had had was done. We had never been intimate or romantic, but now any chance of that happening was over.

"I won't get involved with the serial killer," I said and stuck the screwdriver in the ignition to start the car.

On the way home I stopped off at Tea Time for my latte. Inside, it was quiet, a lull in the day. Ruth was nowhere to be found. I walked up to the bar, slapped my money on it and called out her name.

"I'm coming," she called a moment later. "You try running when you're a thousand years old. Everybody wants immediate gratification. You're so used to that Internet crap you don't know how to wait for anything. Oh, it's you."

"I need a latte, Ruth. I've had a hard day, and I haven't had any coffee, yet."

"I heard about your day. They were looking for you, you know."

She turned her back to me and started to make my coffee. "Who was looking for me? I'm not in the matchmaker business anymore."

"Were you ever in the matchmaker business? It never seemed like you did too much on that front. But I don't mean singles. META was looking for you."

My heart raced. I was pretty sure I was having some kind of cardiac event. "META? How did they know to look for me here?"

Ruth's slapped the to go cup on the bar and took my money. "Who the hell knows? They're all a bunch of loonies. Like we're not supposed to eat meat. Who ever heard of such a thing? As far as I'm concerned, vegans can go straight to hell."

I was sort of in agreement with her about vegans. I tried to go vegan once but by lunch I was chowing down on a cheeseburger. "What did META want from me?"

"Something about making you an example. What the

hell did you do this time?" she demanded.

"I love animals. But I never heard of an assistance snake before."

"Assistance snake? Sounds like the dumbest thing alive. But I would watch your back, Gladie. They're out for blood."

I peeked outside before I left the shop, making sure that META wasn't lying in wait for me. But the coast was clear. I walked to my car and opened the door when I was almost run down. At first, I thought META had found me, but it was just a woman on a moped.

I rubbed my eyes, unsure that I was seeing what I thought I was seeing. "Hello, Mom," I said. She was riding a dilapidated moped, which spewed out smoke as she put-putted along. She was wearing a very short miniskirt and a see-through top with a push up bra. I'm not sure how she could have stood the cold dressed like that because it was freezing outside, but she seemed very happy on the moped, driving it one-handed, with one hand on the handlebar and the other hand holding a cigarette, which she sucked in and French inhaled.

She didn't react when I called out to her, probably because she wasn't used to anyone calling her Mom. "Luann," I called. She turned toward me sharply, making the moped swerve. She stopped in the middle of the street and tried to catch her balance. I ran up to her and held the bike while she fixed herself.

She looked at me, as if she was trying to place the

name to the face. "Nice bike, Mom. Where did you get it?"

She could've gotten it anywhere. She could've bought it, although as far as I could tell since she arrived at my grandmother's she hadn't actually paid for anything. She could've also found it and decided to borrow it or to steal it outright. On the back of the moped was a box, like pizza delivery guys had.

"Are you delivering pizzas?" I couldn't imagine her delivering pizzas. She wasn't much into food, and I couldn't imagine anybody hiring her to touch food.

"Why would I deliver pizzas?"

"Okay. So what are you doing?"

"I got a job," she said by way of explanation. I waited for her to give me more details, but she seemed intent on driving on. In any case, she was happy to be on her little moped and started to putt-putt away from me, even though I was holding onto the bike. I let go, quickly.

"You probably should wear underwear," I called after her. But she didn't hear or she didn't want to hear. My mother was giving the entire town a Lindsay Lohan experience on the cheap.

I got in my car and started it. My Cutlass Supreme was much better than my mother's moped. It had been silver at one time, but that was long before I owned it. Now, it was covered more in rust than paint. The upholstery was ripped and the stuffing was sticking out in places, and of course I had to start the car with the screwdriver. But at least I had a heater that worked, and I wasn't flashing my hoo-hah to half of Cannes's townspeople.

I wondered if my mother really did have a job, or if she was bullshitting me as usual. Normally, I wouldn't have cared, but since I just got fired from my umpteenth job and my mother had recently told me what a failure I was, I found myself slightly jealous that she was employed, even if she was freezing to death on a moped.

I arrived home two minutes later. Because of the holidays there was no class or clients, and the house was quiet. I snuck a peek next door where Holden used to live, and where he was temporarily living now, packing up and getting ready to leave. His truck was in the driveway, but there was no sign of him. I needed to speak to him, or at least listen to what he had to say, but I was a chicken. Besides, it was time to see if I had a bun in my oven.

I walked up to the front door, and grandma opened it. "Get in quick," she ordered, pulling me inside the house and slamming the door shut after me. "They've been looking for you, and they're on their way over here."

"META?"

"They're hell-bent on skinning you alive, bubeleh."

"Retail is dangerous work, Grandma," I said.

"I'm reheating leftovers. Bridget's on her way over to talk to you."

I went up to my room before I took off my coat. I didn't want my grandmother to see what was in my pocket. Not only was I a shoplifter, but I was possibly a pregnant shoplifter. I emptied my pockets onto my bed, took off my

74

smock, and changed into sweats and T-shirt and thick athletic socks.

Bridget burst into my room. "I don't know what's wrong with me. I'm eating. I'm throwing up. Then, I eat again. I'm sleeping all the time. I looked it up on Web M.D., and I'm pretty sure I have hepatitis C or tuberculosis."

I was hoping for hepatitis C or tuberculosis instead of what I feared I had. "Well, you look good," I told her. "Pretty. Kind of glowing. Must be the cold."

Bridget wasn't listening to me. Her attention was on my bed. "What's that?"

"Peanut butter."

"Next to the peanut butter."

"Well, you see, the thing is..."

Bridget set down next to my bed. "Does Lucy know?" she asked. Lucy was my other best friend, but she was away on a cruise with her boyfriend, Uncle Harry. She would've had some words of wisdom for me, but I would just have to deal with whatever wisdom I could scrape up between Bridget and me.

"No," I said. "And nobody else is going to know, either."

Bridget nodded. "Well, you know me, Gladie. I'm going to support you through all of this. It's your choice. It's your body. Your health. You do what's best for you. And if you want to have this baby, I will help you raise it. You'll be a fabulous mother. If that's what you want. No matter what, it will be fine. Don't worry about it. Don't give it another

75

thought."

"Okay. I'm good with not thinking."

I opened the first box and read the directions. I took the stick into the bathroom and peed on it. But nothing happened. Bridget read the directions and looked at it. "You peed on the wrong place," she explained. "See? You open it here. And pee there. Simple."

I had been so focused on my failures in life and my fear of META that I didn't realize just how scared I was at the pregnancy result. My hands were shaking, and no matter what I did, I couldn't take the test correctly. I peed on my hand and the floor…everywhere but where I was supposed to. It was one more failure in a string of failures.

"I can't even pee on a stick. I'm a complete idiot."

"Don't worry, Gladie. I'm here to help you. Let me show you." Bridget sat on the toilet, opened the stick, and showed me how to pee on it. Then, she stood up, and I sat back down and peed on my own stick. It was heartening to have a friend who would pee in front of me. I didn't feel so much alone in my time of panic.

We stood side by side, holding our sticks and watching the lines appear.

"See that?" Bridget said to me. "You were negative. Not pregnant. I told you there was nothing to worry about."

"Are you sure? Yours is totally different. So mine must mean that I'm pregnant. The little cross means not pregnant and the little line means pregnant?"

We rushed back to my bedroom and looked at the

directions. It was quickly obvious that either we got the test mixed up or Bridget had been eating for two. She stared at her stick and all the color drained out of her face. I put my hand on her shoulder. "I got more tests."

We each did another test, and it came out the same. Bridget was the one who was pregnant, and I only had to worry that I had hepatitis C or tuberculosis.

"Are you okay, Bridget? You don't look so good. Come and sit down."

I helped her to the chair next to my bed and fanned her with a magazine. She was in shock, and to tell the truth, so was I. Bridget was pregnant? She wasn't exactly a sexual dynamo. She did have a boyfriend who was a fellow accountant. Perhaps he was the father.

"I'm doomed," Bridget moaned. "Doomed. Doomed. Doomed."

"No you're not. I'm here to support you. It's your choice. It's your body. And if you choose to have a baby, it will be fine. I will help you raise it, and you'll do a great job. You'll be a great mother."

"Shut up, Gladie. That's a bunch of horseshit."

"But that's what you told me."

Bridget pushed her glasses up on the bridge of her nose. "I said that to make you feel better. This is horrible. What am I going to do? What am I going to do?"

"What do you want to do?" It was the only question I could come up with. There were other questions, of course, but I didn't think they would help much.

"I could go for something to eat."

"Grandma's reheating leftovers." That seemed to cheer her up. At the very least, there would always be comfort food at my grandmother's house.

We walked downstairs together. "Gladie, I heard the weirdest thing about you and a snake," she said.

"Whatever you do, don't tell META where to find me."

Downstairs, Grandma had warmed up and laid out all of the leftovers on the table. It was like having another Thanksgiving dinner but without the stress, except for the completely new kind of stress now.

"Eat some stuffing, Bridget," Grandma said. "It will make you think clearer."

We didn't actually tell Grandma that Bridget was pregnant, but we didn't need to. She just knew, somehow.

"What am I going to do after the stuffing?" Bridget asked her.

"I think you're going to do what you want."

"And what's that?" Bridget asked.

It was a contagious disease going around. None of us knew what we wanted, or if we did know what we wanted, we were too scared to act on it.

"You know what you want, bubeleh," grandma said to me. "You have the gift, and you like bringing love to others. And about the three penises, you know which penis you want."

Bridget dropped her fork. "Three penises? How did

you get up to three?"

I shrugged. "It just sort of happened."

"Well you don't need a man or a penis to make you happy, Gladie," Bridget said. "But if you were going to choose, of course you'll choose Holden."

"He's a good man," I agreed and looked at Grandma.

"He's a good man," she agreed. "He'll make some woman very happy someday."

"When does Lucy get back from her cruise?" I asked, changing the subject.

"Wednesday," Grandma said. "And she had a very good cruise. She has a surprise for you."

"I'm not sure I can take any more surprises. I have META after me and too many penises."

"I don't think I can take any more surprises either," Bridget said.

But we were going to get a Lucy surprise and a few others before it was done.

CHAPTER 5

Surrender, Dorothy! I remember the first time you watched Wizard of Oz. You covered your eyes every time the Wicked Witch appeared. You were sure that Dorothy was going to surrender, but she didn't! That little Dorothy sure was brave. A little pistol. She stood up to that witch and didn't give in. But surrender in love is good, bubeleh. No, I'm not talking about getting tied up, although under certain circumstances that can be good. No, I'm talking about giving in, letting yourself go, and allowing love to take you over. Some matches throw themselves in, surrendering when no one's asking them to, but others fight the surrender all the way. They push back against love with everything they have and then wonder why they're not happy. In these cases, explain to them that it's okay to surrender. It's okay to give in to love. Explain to them that it's safe to surrender…there isn't a Wicked Witch to worry about.

Lesson 48, Matchmaking Advice from your
Grandma Zelda

I did pretty well avoiding META. They had been distracted with fighting the town against its live nativity scene with real animals, which had been an annual tradition since cars were invented, and popped up every year on December first from five to nine at night in the little park in the center of the historic district.

But I was warned that they hadn't forgotten about the snake incident, and neither did Walley's. The lady with the snake filed a multimillion-dollar lawsuit against the store, and now I was persona non grata. I would never be able to buy discount chocolate again. It made me almost glad that I had shoplifted the pregnancy tests.

A week had gone by, and I hadn't found any more body parts. It was looking like I had not only avoided META, but I wouldn't be dragged into any murder mystery this time.

Spencer had disappeared, and once again I was trying to get used to not having him in my life. Sure, he didn't really like me and was always criticizing me, but I was used to him being around and I wasn't sure I liked him not being around. Remington had disappeared, laying low because I asked him to. I missed our rolls in the hay, but I wasn't ready to re-ignite that relationship. At least not now.

Because Holden was still there. He was still living next door to my grandmother's house. His truck was still parked in his driveway, and all of his belongings were packed and ready to go. He seemed to be waiting for something before he left, though. And I was that something.

Winter had come in earnest to Cannes. We had already had two snowfalls, and the second one had stuck. I wasn't good with ice, so I was staying home as much as possible. I didn't have a reason to go out, anyway, because I hadn't found another job. Word had gotten around about the snake, and even though there wasn't much love for snakes, nobody wanted a multimillion dollar lawsuit because of me.

Business was booming for Grandma, however, as people wanted to be in a relationship for the holidays. Grandma called it the most desperate time of the year, and she stressed the importance of being picky and not succumbing to desperation just because you wanted a date on New Year's Eve.

So the house was full all the time. Grandma added special classes, like Find The Special Someone For The Special Time Of The Year and Don't Kill Yourself Just Because You Can't Fit Into The Dress. She needed my help for the extra business, but I was being true to myself. I had decided that I wasn't going to fool myself any longer with trying to become a matchmaker and sponging off my grandmother. I was going to get any job I could.

It was Thursday afternoon, the week after Thanksgiving, and Grandma was in the parlor with her Decorate For The Season Decorate For Love class, while I was in the kitchen going through the want ads, when the doorbell rang. I opened the door to find Holden standing there. He was a beautiful man. Tall with a straight back. Muscular, but long and lean. He was wearing jeans, a plaid shirt, a leather jacket, and boots. He had explored the world and gone on every adventure imaginable, yet he was sticking around our small town just because of me. I couldn't imagine that I was more exciting than one of his adventures, but here he was on my doorstep.

"Sweets for the sweet," he said, handing me a large box of chocolates. "I have a day planned for us."

"Does it involve chocolate?"

"Sure. Get your coat."

Holden put his hand on the small of my back and we walked to his truck, which was parked next door. I noticed that he was careful not to kiss me and to not ask too much from me. He was treating me like a skittish horse that he was trying to tame. He opened the truck's passenger door and I hiked myself in.

"Beautiful evening," he remarked. It was. It was very cold but dry, and as we drove into town, I noticed that it was lit up, each house and building decorated for Christmas. Holidays were what Cannes did best. Even Grandma, who didn't celebrate Christmas, hung lights. She called it the happiness lights during the dark time of the year.

We drove through the historic district and up into the mountains. "Where are we going?"

"I thought you could pick out my Christmas tree for me, and then I could treat you to dinner."

"I like the idea of dinner."

We drove the rest the way up the mountains in silence. There was so much to say between us, that I didn't know where to start. When Holden returned about a month ago, he had a new name and his old life back. He had been stuck in witness protection, but he succeeded in finding someone to help him put his enemy in jail, and now Holden was a free man to do as he wished.

He turned off the main road onto the snow-covered dirt road. We drove for a few minutes before he parked. There were trees everywhere. Holden urged me to choose one. They all looked good to me, but I picked a large one about three rows in.

"Great choice," he said. He took an ax out of the back of the truck and whacked away at the tree. I bit my lower lip as I watched him cut it down. He was a beautiful sight to see. Strong and capable, like he enjoyed taking care of things. It dawned on me how much I would like to be taken care of. I had never been taken care of in my life, but I bet I could get used to it pretty easily.

The tree toppled over, as Holden shouted 'timber!' and laughed. I laughed, too. It was a moment of pure joy with no stress and no worries. Maybe I had it all wrong. Maybe Holden wasn't difficult. Maybe he was just complicated, and maybe complicated was a good thing.

I wrapped my arms around his middle and pulled

myself close. I looked up at him and melted. His eyes had grown big and dark, and all the waiting for me from the past month showed there. He might've seemed patient before, but that didn't mean he was without passion. He was loaded for bear when it came to passion.

He bent down until our lips were touching. He kissed me sweetly, with feather light caresses from his hot mouth, driving me crazy and wanting more. As if he aimed to please, the sweet turned darker, more passionate, and he deepened the kiss. Our tongues touched, coming together in an explosive chemistry. Remington was a good kisser, but when Holden kissed me there was something much bigger behind it. There was desire and something more that I had been running from.

His hand cradled the back of my head, and I pushed forward against his body. I could feel his arousal, and I wasn't doing too badly either. My head felt like it was going to burst with the weight of all my hormones igniting and exploding. I lifted a leg and wrapped it around his. There, in the forest kissing Holden, our bodies touching, I felt secure. I felt that as long as I was with him, I would be taken care of, made to feel special and beautiful.

We kissed for a long time until the forest grew very dark and I could no longer feel my hands. "Thank goodness," Holden breathed when we finally came up for air. "I thought I had lost you forever."

"You didn't lose me," I said. But I wasn't sure that I was being completely truthful. I also wasn't sure if he ever had me to begin with. But I was a fool to let him go. Anybody could see that. Holden was the best man I had ever met. And he was in love with me.

I shined a flashlight on him, as he picked up the tree and threw it in the back of his truck. He tied it down and then we drove off for the second half of our evening. We went further up into the mountains and finally parked at a large wood house, which turned out to be a beautiful new restaurant.

"I don't think I'm dressed for this," I said, looking down at my jeans.

Holden wrapped his arm around my waist and pulled me in close, as we walked up the path to the restaurant. "You'll be the most beautiful woman there," he said softly into my ear, making my toes curl and my insides melt into hot liquid.

Inside was just like the movies. Lots of rich people eating in a dark room with little candles on each table for two. A string quartet played softly in a corner and one wall was floor to ceiling windows overlooking a breathtaking view of the mountains and the holiday lights of Cannes below.

It was a lot nicer than my usual dining out places: Chik'n Lik'n and Burger Boy.

I recognized some of the diners. Mr. and Mrs. Trench were in the middle of their meal. The Mayor was at a large table with friends and constituents. And my best friend Lucy was sitting next to us at a table by the window with her boyfriend, who I called Uncle Harry, even though he wasn't related.

Lucy had been going out with Uncle Harry for the past month, and I had never seen her so happy. She was a Southern Belle, who worked in marketing, whatever that was, and she was very successful. Uncle Harry was a short man with no neck and very little hair on his head, but he made up for it on the rest of his body. He made his living in a dubious way, and he lived in a McMansion just outside of Cannes. I hadn't seen much of Lucy since they had gotten together, but that was okay. I enjoyed seeing her in love.

"Well, look what the cat dragged in," she said, rising to give me a big hug. "Should I say cat? I hear you've been having trouble with animal lovers."

"Hey there, legs," Uncle Harry said. "I hear you've been giving the town some trouble, as usual."

I shot a quick look at Holden. "No. No trouble. My trouble days are over."

Uncle Harry and Lucy burst out laughing, mistaking what I said as a joke. Uncle Harry insisted that the restaurant push two tables together so that all four of us could sit together. "On me," Uncle Harry told Holden.

"Where the hell is the cop, legs?" he demanded when I sat down. "You don't like the cop anymore?"

I could feel Holden's eyes on me. "I never liked the cop, Uncle Harry. He's a jerk."

Uncle Harry was close to Spencer, even though I had the feeling they were occasionally on opposite sides of the law. He leaned forward and gave Holden a heavy dose of the stink eye, probably feeling a need to help Spencer defend his territory. Holden didn't react. He was calm, relaxed, and in control. I had to hand it to him. Not many people remained calm under Uncle Harry's scrutiny. Lucy put her hand on Uncle Harry's arm, diffusing the tension.

"Such a pleasure to be dining with your tall drink of water," Lucy said to me. "You're not called Holden anymore right?"

"You could call me Holden, if you wish, but my name is Burton."

"Like Richard Burton, but you're so much better looking and about a foot taller." Lucy looked at me. "And Gladie could be your Liz Taylor. All she would need is a quick hair dye and a new wardrobe."

"And a new face and new body," I added.

I hadn't gotten into the habit of calling Holden, Burton, yet. Learning about his real identity was like meeting a new person, and it took some getting used to.

"And Gladie tells me that you are an explorer," Lucy continued. "I just find that so interesting. Are you a little like Indiana Jones?"

"I'm a lot like Indiana Jones," he said.

His voice came out dark and hot, like a slow-moving tidal wave of testosterone. I grabbed a glass of ice water and chugged it down, chewing on a mouthful of ice cubes.

"That was my water, darlin'," Lucy said.

"Are you like the guy who cut his own arm off?" Uncle Harry asked, taking a bite of his steak.

"Hopefully not, but I've hiked where he was."

I had no idea what they were talking about, but I was enjoying visualizing Holden in his hiking gear, climbing a mountain with his muscular thighs. Holden and I opened our menus. There weren't any prices, which made me break into a sweat just out of reflex. I had been cash poor since I could remember. I didn't recognize most of the items on the menu. They were in another language.

"The steak is pretty good," Uncle Harry suggested.

I searched my menu for steak, but I couldn't find it. I wondered if we had different menus. "The coq au vin is to die for," Lucy said.

I sighed. I closed my eyes and dropped my finger onto the menu. "Hom-Ard," I read.

Holden smiled. "Great choice."

"Here's your net."

The waiter handed me a net with a long handle. It turned out that "homard" was lobster. I had eaten lobster salad but never an actual lobster, and even though I worked on a tilapia farm in Mexico for three months, I never had to fish for my own dinner. That was all about to change.

After I ordered, the waiter escorted me to a huge fish tank in the back of the restaurant. There were lobsters on top of lobsters—at least fifty of them—and they were all alive. I gripped the net tightly.

"Pick which one delights you, and scoop it up. It's fun," the waiter said. He had an English accent and a pencil thin mustache. He looked a lot like a James Bond villain.

"I have a META problem."

"Some say the lively ones are tastier," he explained. "Catch a fast one."

I dipped the net in the tank. "I've never hunted before," I whined.

"It's not hunting. It's catching. We'll cook it. It's just like a carnival."

I had worked at a carnival for a summer in high school, but I had never hunted lobsters. I spotted Holden spying on me. He had climbed mountains, explored jungles, and paddled down rivers. What would he think about a woman who was squeamish around lobsters?

"Okay. What the hell." I moved the net around. I didn't want to target a specific lobster because no matter what META thought of me, I didn't have the heart to peg a creature for murder. So, I just tried to capture the closest one, but it was more difficult to grab than I thought. It was clutching onto another lobster. I yanked it up, anyway, determined to be done with the distasteful process.

"What is that?" the waiter asked.

"I think I caught a double."

"A double what?"

I looked closer at my catch. "He's deformed," I said. "Or he has a big tumor."

"Oh my God," the waiter moaned. His accent had

disappeared. Instead of sounding like a James Bond villain, he sounded like Murray from the auto shop. He pointed at my lobster in horror. I was slightly horrified, too. I should have ordered the steak. I wouldn't have had to pick my own cow.

"Do you want me to pick another one?" I asked him. He backed away. "Should I follow you?"

He took a few steps backward, and I followed him with the net. It was getting heavy, and the lobsters were moving. It was an awful lot of work for a meal, no matter how fancy it was.

"Could you take it from me?" I asked. "I can't carry it much longer. Come on, stop walking." It was like learning to swim with the teacher walking backward, making you swim a little more to get to him.

Instead of stopping, he turned around and ran full out to the kitchen. "Nothing in my life is normal," I said, watching the lobsters struggle in the net. I felt sorry for them and decided no matter how good lobster tasted, it wasn't worth all this. So, I went back to the tank to return them to the water. I choked up on the net's handle to get a better grip, but it was wet and slippery, and it turned over, sending one of the lobsters and its huge tumor falling to the floor.

"I hope META doesn't hear about this," I muttered. I bent down to scoop up the lobster, and that's when I realized that its tumor had two ears and a mouth.

And a buzz cut.

I dropped the net and backed up into the dining room. "I might have found a head," I said, pointing toward the tank. "A middle-aged one. With a five o'clock shadow. I'm not hungry anymore. I don't think I like French food."

CHAPTER 6

I've loved junk food my whole life. I can eat mayonnaise right out of the jar. I would rather eat ice cream for dinner than just about anything else...unless it's mashed potatoes. What can I tell you? I eat bad. Eating bad makes me feel good. Loved. I get desperate, sad matches ringing my doorbell all the time, who want to be loved. They don't care what kind of bad jar of mayonnaise loves them back, they'll take it. Don't give it to them! Bad love isn't good love, dolly. Take it from me, just because it tastes good on the tongue, doesn't mean it's good for your soul. There's not a lot of soulmate jars of mayonnaise.

Lesson 32, Matchmaking Advice from your
Grandma Zelda

I had gotten a chill, so I was wearing my coat, and Uncle Harry poured me a few cognacs. Because of the mood lighting, the violin music, and the generally beautiful ambience, it had taken a while for the restaurant's patrons to realize that there was a severed head on the floor.

Nobody had paid attention to me when I announced that I had found the head, so I went back to my seat and explained it to Holden. "When you say 'head,' what do you mean?" he asked.

"Oh, darlin', have you started again?" Lucy asked.

I nodded. Holden went over to inspect the head. That and the fact that the wait staff was huddled in the kitchen-- terrified that a decapitating killer was loose in the restaurant-- made the patrons start to question if something was wrong.

Then, it only took one woman walking toward the bathroom and spotting the head on the floor for there to be a wave of freakout in the restaurant, which was followed by a mini-stampede.

Standard severed body parts reaction. I was getting used to it.

"This is deja-vu all over again," I muttered. That's when Uncle Harry got me the cognac, and Holden called 911.

"I don't know what the fuss is about," Uncle Harry said, as we waited for the police, looking out at the view and sipping cognac. He didn't seem to be the least bit upset about dead people parts in the restaurant where he was eating dinner. Maybe it was his character or maybe it was similar experiences in his past, but he was totally at ease.

I was in shock. I didn't need a doctor to tell me that.

It took the police less than ten minutes to arrive at the restaurant. All the diners bolted before they arrived, however, except for the staff and our table. Even the mayor and his friends had run screaming, which surprised me because I didn't think much fazed him, but I figured he saw his chance to skip out on the check and went for it.

But all that was in the past, and frankly with all the cognac in me, even my name was a blur when the police raided the restaurant, and Spencer stormed over to our table.

"Are you kidding me?" he demanded.

"I can see my lips," I said, swatting the air in front of my face. Cognac packed a wallop. I was more stoned than the time I accidentally got injected with horse tranquilizers.

"Is there something innately wrong with you? How do you manage to do this every time?"

"I can see your lips, too," I continued, trying to focus on Spencer's face. "You have three of them, and they're huge. Like big, fleshy plates."

"Do you have a collection of dead body parts that you're distributing around town?"

"How dare you say my body parts are dead," I said, trying to stand. "My body parts are alive!"

I stripped off my coat, and I was working on my shirt, but I couldn't remember how to get it over my head. "Darlin' don't do that," Lucy said, pulling me down to my chair.

Meanwhile, Holden stood up and got into Spencer's face. "Are you accusing Gladie of something, because if you are, I think she should have an attorney present."

"How much is an attorney?" I asked. "I have five dollars and a coupon for shampoo in my wallet."

Spencer thumped Holden's chest with his finger. "Back off, Paul Bunyan. This isn't your business."

"It is my business. Gladie is with me," Holden roared.

Lucy patted my hand. "Oh, darlin', it's a shame you're not sober to watch this. It's like Cinemax At Night but with better looking men."

"Shoot him in the kneecaps," Uncle Harry told Spencer.

"Not fair," I said. "Don't play favorites. Hey, somebody stop the restaurant."

"Stop the restaurant?" Lucy asked.

"Yes," I said and passed out, landing face first onto the table, driving half of a loaf of French bread up my nose.

Cognac packed a much bigger punch than horse tranquilizers. At first it was all black—I'm pretty sure I died—and I was completely unaware of being moved from the restaurant to my bed. After a few hours, I moved from my coma state to exploring a psychedelic Narnia world of horrors. Lots of visions of my head exploding and wild lobsters eating my brains at the dinner table while a snake tried to worm its way into my pants.

Finally, I regained consciousness enough to throw up in my nightstand drawer and focus on my headache which had to be worse than childbirth or kidney stones or other wimpy ailments.

"Jackhammer," I croaked. And then it was all black again.

"Shut up," I whispered. Somebody was moaning, loudly, and they woke me up.

"That's you, dolly," I heard my grandmother say. "You're moaning like a porn star."

"Grandma, is that you? I can't see you," I said, more than a little panicked.

"That's because your eyes are closed."

I tried to open my eyes, but I couldn't work up the strength to lift my lids. "Take this," Grandma told me, putting four pills in my hand and a glass in my other. I swallowed them down and gave her back the glass.

"Let me die."

"You have a big day ahead of you," Grandma said.

"Bury me on a hill."

"Everybody wants a piece of you, today. You have to die another day." My eyelids popped open and I was surprised to see the sun shining through the window. "It's two o'clock, bubeleh. You've slept the day away."

Either the pills were starting to work or I suddenly had a grasp on reality. I sat up in bed. "What happened with the head?"

"Spencer took it when he took Holden."

"He huh what?"

"He was pissed off, dolly. Things have come to a head, no pun intended. You're going to have to decide."

I crawled out of bed. My muscles had turned soft like jelly and my legs were having a hard time supporting my weight. "I decided, Grandma. I'm going for stability and security."

Grandma shook her head and pulled her fake Ralph Lauren tunic down over her hips. "I don't deal in stability and security. I deal in love."

"But you're Jewish."

"I know. Weird, right?"

"Hello, Underwear Girl," Fred greeted me at the police station's front desk.

"Hi, Fred. Nice decorations."

The police station was relatively new with bright, shiny floors and big, bright windows. The police station had been rebuilt in the present location a little while before I moved to town. Before then, it was housed in a beat up old jail from the nineteenth century, which looked like it came right out of a western movie. The new police station was very clean and modern and bigger than we needed for our tiny police force.

The lobby was decorated with a large Christmas tree,

which was completely covered in lights, tinsel, and ornaments. Sergeant Fred Lytton was the desk sergeant and one of my clients.

"Thanks. I've been working on it all week," he said. Fred lived in a very Christmas-oriented house, and I figured he had access to a lot of tinsel. "The chief put the kibosh on real reindeer, but he's probably right. I think they would stand out."

"I think they would stand out, too."

"You would make a real pretty Mrs. Claus," He said, smiling. "Like a little piece of heaven."

"Thanks," I said. "Hey, I was wondering if you could help me find a friend of mine."

"Sure! A dead one?"

"Uh—"

"The head?"

"Well, no. Why? Do I know the head?" It hadn't looked familiar last night, but I wasn't good with faces. Everyone in town made it to my grandmother's house at one point or another, so maybe I did know the head.

"He was assistant manager of the Prickly Pears. Buck."

"Buck? Prickly Pears?"

"Don't say another word, sergeant," Spencer ordered, marching into the lobby. He was beautifully dressed as always, but he had a big shiner on his right eye. "That's classified information."

I stomped my foot. "What are you talking about? It

was in the newspaper this morning."

Spencer crossed his arms in front of him. "Ha! Nice try. Like you've ever looked at a newspaper."

"I've looked at a newspaper."

"The funnies, maybe. Maybe!" he shouted, shaking his finger in my face.

"Nobody calls them funnies. They're comics."

"Spiderman and Superman are comics. Garfield and Peanuts are funnies."

"I don't even know what you're talking about!" I shouted. Nobody made me angrier than Spencer. "Where's my—", I started and then bit my lip.

"Your what?"

"My—"

Spencer put his hands on his hips and leaned toward me, raising his eyebrow. "Your what? Your boyfriend? Your boyfriend?" His face turned red, and he punched Fred's Christmas tree, sending it flying against the wall.

"That was Fred's tree. You killed Fred's tree."

"It's the department's tree," Spencer said, straightening his tie. He struggled to pick up the tree, and scooped up some tinsel from the floor and threw it on the tree. "Sorry about that, Fred."

Fred stared at his tree, now bent and broken, standing at an angle with half of the ornaments rolling around the floor. I patted Fred's hand. "It doesn't look too bad. It just needs a little love," I lied.

Spencer looked appropriately embarrassed at his

behavior. He apologized to Fred, but I noticed he didn't apologize to me. In fact, he didn't say another word to me, didn't even look at me. He stared down at his shoes and walked out, a man dejected, angry, and sad.

My heart sank, watching him walk away from me. There was so much I wanted to say to him, but I didn't know what words to use, and as far as I could tell, he had no clue what to say to me. We didn't work right. We were a boat without a rudder.

Despite that, I almost went after him. But at that moment, Holden was released and appeared in the lobby. He looked exhausted, as if he had been up all night, and his hair was a mess and his clothes wrinkled. He also had a pair of black eyes, which looked a lot like Spencer's shiner.

"Oh my God," I said.

"Yep," he said and kissed me softly on the lips. "Thank you for picking me up." He wrapped his arm around my waist, and we walked out quickly before Spencer could change his mind.

As we were going out, Lucy and Bridget were walking in but stopped when they saw us. "Good, we caught you," Lucy said.

"What's wrong?" I asked.

"Time's a wasting. You need to come with us," Lucy said and then got a good look at Holden. "Oh, my. What happened to the tall drink of water?"

"You should see the other guy," he said, smiling.

But the other guy had only one black eye to Holden's

two, not that I was counting. Spencer was inside, hitting Christmas trees and cursing my name, while Holden was with me with his arm around my waist and love in his eyes.

I looked quickly behind me at the police station and felt a wave of sadness hit me. "I could go for a sandwich," I said.

"Me, too. And a slice of lemon meringue pie," Bridget said. I scanned her belly for signs of pregnancy, but she looked like her normal self, an average-sized woman in a blue suit, pumps, a down coat, and her usual round glasses. Her hair had grown down to her jawline in a cute bob after it had burned off in an unfortunate accident a couple months ago. She looked good, more relaxed than usual, and her skin had the stereotypical glow of a pregnant woman, which even glowed through her bright red blush and blue eye shadow.

Lucy was her usual put together self. Classy and elegant, even on the street in front of the police station in our small town. She wore expensive everything from her sable hat to her leather boots. Even though she was a businesswoman powerhouse, she seemed to have put work on the back burner since she got together with Uncle Harry.

"We have business to discuss," she said. "Ladies' business, darlin'," she said, pointedly to Holden.

Holden turned to me. "I'll let you go," he said, as if he was asking me. I nodded. I wanted some alone time, and I knew he must be dying to wash the jail off of him.

But before he left, he took me in his arms and kissed me like he meant business. With tongue. He pulled me against him, wrapping his arms around my back and squeezing me tight. His lips were hot and demanding, and the stubble on his chin scratched my skin and woke up my body down to my ankles, making my uterus whir into action like it was a racecar at the Indie 500 and ready to take on Holden's sperm.

Huge batches of sperm. Mountains of them.

Oh, Nelly, it was a good and dangerous kiss. When he finally let me go, my head spun, and Lucy had to grab my arm to stabilize me so I wouldn't fall flat on my face.

We watched Holden walk away toward his house, transfixed by his perfect ass, snug in his Levi's. He was tall and muscular and drop dead gorgeous. He was like a walking Tootsie Pop that I wanted to lick until I got to the center.

"Oh, my," Lucy breathed.

"How is he in bed?" Bridget asked.

"I'll bet a hundred dollars that he's great in bed," I said, even though I didn't have a hundred dollars. But I thought it was a safe bet.

Lucy turned away from looking at Holden's perfect ass and grabbed my upper arms. "What are you talking about?" she demanded. "You mean to tell me that you have not bedded that man?"

"Well…" I said, trying to avoid her eyes. "You see, it's like this."

"Shut your mouth. Shut your mouth!"

"Okay."

"No. That means 'keep talking' in Southern," she

explained. She was very excited, like she had discovered a money tree or the cure for body hair. "Tell us why you haven't slept with him. Not because he hasn't asked you, I'm sure."

He had sort of given up on asking me to sleep with him, since I had been making excuses to stay away from him while I slept with Remington on the sly. It was obvious Holden was waiting for me to approach him, until I told him I felt the way he did and allowed him to seduce me, like I was sure he was ready to do.

Lucy poked me in the chest. "Ohhhh…. You have it so bad for Spencer. That's why."

I shook my head. "That's not true."

"That's not true," Bridget agreed. "Holden is perfect. Spencer is a womanizing jerk. Gladie is too smart to have it bad for Spencer. She likes Holden."

"Thank you," I said. "Of course I like Holden." It was true. I did like Holden. He was much better for me than Spencer. I glanced back at the police station and gnawed the inside of my cheek.

Lucy hugged me hard. "I'm so sorry, darlin'," she whispered into my ear. "It's a hard break."

"I wouldn't mind a roast beef sandwich," Bridget said. "Or a Reuben. You think I could have both?"

We got a center table at Saladz, which was our usual

hangout when we had lunch together. It was a cute restaurant in the heart of the historic district. It was bright and cheerful, and the food was good, if you stuck to simpler items from the menu.

Today, it was packed with townspeople and tourists who had come in from the bitter cold. As soon as we arrived, Bridget ran to the bathroom and threw up. She came back out green, and we sat her down on a chair and put a cold compress on the back of her neck.

"I'm better," she said after a minute. "But I don't want a Reuben anymore. Do they have key lime pie?"

We sat down and looked through our menus. "I'm getting the impression that I'm missing something," Lucy said.

"You don't have the specials?" I handed her the list of specials, but she waved it away.

"No. No that. That," she said pointing at Bridget.

I shot Bridget a look. Her eyes grew wide, like a deer in the headlights. She obviously hadn't told Lucy that she was pregnant. I'm terrible with secrets and I turned bright red under Lucy's scrutiny and began to sweat bullets.

I mopped at my face with a napkin and clamped my mouth closed. The urge to spill the baby beans was nearly stronger than I was. Or stronger. Yes, much stronger.

"Where's the appetizers? Did we order nachos?" I asked.

"We didn't order anything at all," Lucy said.

"Nachos sounds good," Bridget said, craning her

head, looking for the waitress.

Lucy put her menu down. "They don't have nachos here. What's going on? You guys are hiding something from me. Gladie looks like she's about to explode."

I held my breath and shut my eyes and prayed that I wouldn't say anything. But I could only hold my breath for so long. So, I kicked Bridget under the table. It was up to her to say something, of course. It was her secret to keep or tell. Normally she told Lucy everything, but perhaps she was uncomfortable.

All of a sudden, I couldn't stand it anymore. The secret was too big for me to keep. I was already bursting with the secret about sleeping with Remington. Bridget's baby secret was one too many to hold inside of me. I jumped up.

"Pregnant!" I shouted.

The restaurant became completely quiet, like somebody had sucked out all of the sound. I guess that was me. I was the sucker.

With my pronouncement, every set of eyes in the place were locked right on me. Bridget blanched. I had committed the greatest girlfriend betrayal of all time. I was the worst friend, ever. I had broken the girl code.

But I didn't want to hurt Bridget for anything. My mind raced for a way to rectify my treachery. In my panic, I went from betrayal to stupidity.

"I mean me!" I shouted, quickly. "*I'm* pregnant!"

The entire restaurant was paralyzed, staring at me wide-eyed and unblinking. Diners held their forks in the air, halfway from their plates to their mouths. Drinks were spilled, as customers missed their mouths. I was the main event, and no one wanted to miss a second of it.

Bridget was pretty nonplussed as well. Her eyes looked even bigger behind her hoot owl glasses. But nobody in Saladz was quite as shocked as police Chief Spencer Bolton, who had entered the restaurant right before my announcement, completely unaware that I was there.

If I had betrayed Bridget, I was the Benjamin Arnold of almost girlfriends to Spencer. He locked eyes with me, his face the expression of a man beaten, gutted, and tossed away. Tears sprouted in the back of my eyes, and I was desperate to explain myself to him, but of course I couldn't and not betray Bridget. In any case, it was too late. Spencer's mouth tightened until his lips disappeared, and he turned around and walked out.

Lucy tugged at my hand. "Time to sit down, darlin'."

I sat, and the restaurant's patrons slowly went back to normal. Bridget tapped my arm. "Thank you, Gladie."

"No problem," I tried to say, but my mouth had gotten dry, and I couldn't get words out.

Lucy signaled for the waitress and ordered for us. When I was finally given a glass of water, Bridget leaned forward and told Lucy the truth. "I'm pregnant, and I've weighed all of my options, and I've decided to have it."

Lucy nodded.

"I figure if it's a girl, I can empower her to be a strong female role model, and if it's a boy, I can raise him not to be a sexist jerk."

Lucy nodded again.

"And I want you and Gladie to be my coaches and be in the delivery room with me."

Lucy nodded. "Of course. I would love to."

"What do you mean the delivery room?" I asked.

"For my labor."

"Isn't that when a baby comes out of your vagina?"

"That's usually the way it happens," Lucy said.

I didn't think I could handle that. There would be blood and goop, and I was terrible with blood and goop. "I would love to," I said. It was the least I could do since I had almost ratted her out to the town.

"I'm going to keep it secret a little while longer. Just until I get to the twelve week mark. The doctor told me that was wise."

"When is that?" I asked.

"A couple of weeks."

"We should have a party," Lucy suggested. "We could do it at my place."

"Two weeks?" I asked. Two weeks was a long time to go around town saying I was pregnant in order to keep her secret. My heart sank.

Bridget smiled. "The doctor said."

We talked all about babies, not that any of us had any experience in that area. Babysitting was the one job I never did, and as far as I could tell, Lucy and Bridget didn't have much more experience than I had. Bridget was concerned about finding a nanny with similar feminist ideals, and Lucy touted the benefits of cashmere onesies. I didn't know anything about nannies or onesies, so I just smiled and nodded.

There was an air of excitement, but I couldn't get fully into it because Spencer was at that moment under the belief that I was the one with the bun in the oven. And it wasn't his bun.

I wondered who was responsible for Bridget's bun, but she wasn't forthcoming, and I wasn't about to ask until she was ready to tell me. She had had an on again, off again guy she dated, but I hadn't seen him around, lately.

We chatted while our food came, but I wasn't hungry, so Bridget ate my lunch. When dessert arrived, Lucy brought up the original reason for our lunch.

"I hear that Cannes has its first serial killer."

She and Bridget stared at me. "I don't know anything about it," I said.

Lucy laughed. "Yeah, right. Come on."

"I just found the body parts."

"I heard one of them was a golfer from Chicago," Bridget said.

"A baseball manager. And not from Chicago," I said.

Lucy pointed at me. "I knew it. You always know what's what."

"That's the only what I know. I know no more what's. I have to get a job. I'm unemployed again."

"I've got a client to see just outside of town. I can

drop you off at the employment agency, if you want," Bridget offered.

Lucy waved her hands. "Wait a minute. We're getting off target. What about the serial killer?"

"I don't know anything about it," I said. And I didn't want to know anything about it. I didn't want any more to do with murder, and I didn't want any more run-ins with Spencer. I just wanted to get a job and be a normal person again.

"Well, I do," Lucy said. "I've got a line on who the serial killer is. So, I'll drive you to the employment office myself, and then we can go check it out together. How about that?"

"No way," I said.

Lucy picked up the check. "How about if I pay for lunch?"

"Okay," I said. "We can go hunt for a serial killer. But just for an hour."

CHAPTER 7

You like those fakakta Star Wars movies? Feh! That's what I have to say about it. You know why? It's that Yoda. That Yoda doesn't know about love, dolly. He says, "Do. Or do not. There is no try." What a pile of dreck! Yoda could never be a matchmaker. Never. This old matchmaker is telling you to tell your matches to try. Try! They shouldn't sit like a bump on a log and let things happen. They should TRY and make things happen. You understand me? On the other hand... Try, but don't try too hard. If you try too hard to make it right at the beginning, you'll be crying in the long run. Because nobody can try every day for the rest of their lives. With love, try but give up if you have to try too hard. Otherwise, the love isn't real. You hear that, Mr. Yoda?

Lesson 41, Matchmaking Advice from your Grandma Zelda

elise sax

"What exactly are we doing?" I asked, sitting in the passenger seat of Lucy's luxurious new Mercedes in front of the Speedy Mart near Cannes Center Park. It was a dilapidated convenience store, which wasn't that convenient, since it was only open when the owner was in the mood, which worked out to about four days a week. Grandma didn't have a lot of use for Speedy Mart because it didn't sell slushies, so I had only been inside the store a couple of times.

Lucy handed me a pair of binoculars. They were bedazzled in pink and turquoise. "Take a look."

I looked through them. Inside the store, a pimply faced twenty-something with greasy hair picked his nose behind the counter next to a spinning hot dog machine and a rack of nudie magazines.

"What am I looking at?"

"Your serial killer, I'm betting. He fits the profile."

"There's a profile?" I asked, looking at him again through the binoculars. He had stopped picking his nose and had moved on to touching his acne. Blech.

"Yes. Quiet. A loner. You know, a Boo Radley type."

I handed her back her binoculars. "Are you kidding? This whole town is populated with Boo Radley types. Cannes should be re-named Boo Radleyville. By your reasoning, dead people would be stacking up in the historic district like firewood."

Lucy raised an eyebrow and pursed her lips. "Gladie, the death count has been rising, you know."

She was right. It had gotten dicey lately with murder more common than naked women on HBO. Could the Boo Radley mentality have turned everyone psycho?

"I'm afraid to ask this, but what do you want to do?" I asked.

"You're going to do your thing. You're going to Miss Marple the situation. Go talk to him."

"What?" I shrieked. "What if he's a serial killer?"

"Oh, please, Gladie. You've been around more murderers than any New York City homicide cop. It's mother's milk to you. Come on. You're in charge, but I'll have your back. I have pepper spray in my purse. I'll blind him if he makes a move."

She was giddy with excitement. While I had accidentally solved three murders in the past four months, Lucy had enjoyed every second she was involved. The thought of another murder mystery seemed to give her Bridget's pregnancy glow. I glanced down at her belly. It was flat as a board.

"I really have to get to the employment office. I need a job," I said.

"Yeah, right. Whatever. We'll just be a few minutes. You can fix your radar on him, and if he's the one, I've got the cops on speed dial."

Our town was waiting for a 9-1-1 call center, but for now, we had to call to the neighboring city if we had an emergency. We were just a sleepy town, known mainly for apples, antique shops, and fresh air. But maybe our reputation was going to change now that we were murder central.

"Why do you think this particular Boo Radley is the serial killer?" I asked.

"Uncle Harry told me that he lives up in the mountains, and where he goes, dead cats follow. You understand?"

My flesh crawled. Torturing and killing pets was one of the signs of an up and coming serial killer. I didn't want anything to do with him, but Lucy was right about my Miss Marple ways. I did want to know who had killed those poor people and carved them up like they were a Thanksgiving turkey. I did want to prevent the psycho from doing it again. I had the Miss Marple bug real bad.

But I wished Holden was with me. Or Remington. Or Spencer.

Sigh. Spencer.

"Do you know how to use that pepper spray?" I asked her.

She took it out of her purse. It was nestled in a pink, bedazzled case, attached to her makeup bag with a faux fur strap. "It's got a one-button super sprayer. It can stop a bear at one hundred paces."

"You have no idea what a pace is, do you?"

"No, but it sounded good, right?"

We walked single file into the Speedy Mart, with Lucy behind me, like a high-class bodyguard in three inch boots. "I can't believe I'm doing this stupid ass thing," I muttered, as I opened the door, which made a bell ring to announce our presence.

Inside, the heat was on full blast. The store was very small, without any customers. There was a good supply of candy and beer, but the store looked unloved. Half of the refrigerators were empty, and the shelves were thick with dust.

We stopped at the front counter, and the serial killer looked at us, dully. I had no idea what I was supposed to say to him. Was I supposed to ask him if he had chopped up any baseball players lately?

"Uh," I said.

He squinted at me. He had a couple food stains on his polyester uniform and lines of dirt under his fingernails. "I know you."

"I don't think so."

He wagged his finger at me, excited. "Yeah, yeah, I know you. You were at Walley's. You killed that snake." He smiled big, and for a moment I thought he was going to ask me for my autograph.

"*Injured* the snake," I corrected. "It's not dead. It's recovering at the animal hospital in San Diego."

"I saw it happen. You pulverized it."

I began to sweat, and I wiped my forehead with the back of my hand. "It was an honest mistake."

"It was lights out for that snake. You were a beast. Your eyes turned red. You were all kinds of 6-6-6 shit."

The conversation had gone in a bad direction. He was

making me sound like the serial killer, not him.

Lucy pushed me out of the way and pounded the counter with her delicate fist. "Where were you Thanksgiving weekend, Boo Radley?"

He stumbled backward, surprised. "What?"

"Cut up any baseball players lately?" she continued.

"What?"

"Holy cow," I said. Her hand played on her purse, tapping at it, her fingers obviously itching to pepper spray him. "Cool down, Wonder Woman."

"But…" she started.

"How did you know I was a baseball player?" he asked.

"What?" I said.

"Well, I used to be. I played for the Prickly Pears. Short stop."

The Prickly Pears. It sounded familiar. My brain took a minute to remember that the head I found came from the manager of the Prickly Pears. My skin prickled with fear.

"What did you do to Buck?" I breathed. "Did you hurt him?"

"Buck the manager? Did something happen to him?"

He was honestly curious. And there was no way he was a serial killer. He couldn't even keep the shelves clean, let alone mastermind mass murder. He was nowhere near anal enough to be a serial killer. Perhaps he was a great actor, but I didn't think so.

"Buck met with an untimely end," I said. "Did you

know him well?"

"I guess so. I mean, he was a great manager. He knew his stuff, you know? But he didn't let me play a lot and cut me after half of a season. He was always talking about making the Pears a winning team, you know?"

I didn't know minor league baseball had winning teams, but I understood the need to be successful in a career. I had wanted to be successful, but I hadn't come anywhere near to success.

"I gotta go," I said to Lucy. "I need to get a job."

"You want a burrito?" the guy offered. "Fifty percent off because they're kinda old."

He pointed at a glass case with some sad, dried out burritos in it. It looked like a bad case of E. coli. Since I had moved in with my grandmother, my tastes had adapted to hers, and I ate way too much junk food. I had a pooch that I couldn't get rid of. My hand went to my coat pocket, but I had left Bird's peanut butter at home. I promised myself I would start eating it just as soon as I got back.

"Sure, I'll take the burrito," I said and signaled to Lucy to cough up the fifty five cents. It was the least she could do since she was making me go around town to hunt a serial killer.

On the way back to the car, I let her have it. "No more picking people at random and accusing them of murder," I said while I chewed a bite of burrito.

"You have to admit that he was creepy, and he had a connection to one of the victims. How about that?"

Actually, he had a connection to all three victims. They had all come from the Prickly Pears team, but I didn't want to tell her that. She wouldn't have let me go to the employment office if she knew. She would have insisted that we keep searching for the culprit. But I was done. I had a lot of other things to think about.

"I don't care," I said, putting my seatbelt on. "I don't do murder anymore."

"Darn. I love when you do murder."

While she drove me to the employment office, I looked over at my southern friend. She seemed very happy and not just because she was trying to investigate a murder with me. I remembered what Grandma told me about Lucy having something to tell me.

"So how are you and Uncle Harry?" I asked.

Lucy swerved the car but righted it, quickly. I held on to the handle above the window. I hadn't had good luck with Lucy's driving. And nothing rattled Lucy like Uncle Harry. She was ga-ga for him.

"Good," she giggled. She didn't give me any more information than that. Grandma was never wrong, though, and I was sure Lucy was holding back. Something big was happening between them.

Jane Hartsfield ran the employment office, which was nestled between the Weight Watchers and Bernie's Rib

Shack. The office was about the size of my bedroom with an old, utilitarian desk, two chairs, and wall to wall file cabinets and stacks of files on top of the cabinets. It didn't look like Jane had entered the technological age, and it didn't look like she cared.

She was about sixty-five years old. Her hair was salt and pepper and cut very short. She wore a polyester suit that looked like it came out of the early eighties with a polyester blouse, which had a built in bow tie. I sat down on the chair at the desk facing her. I dug my resume out of my purse and handed it to her.

She looked at the resume for a couple of seconds and then looked back up at me. "Your resume is twenty-three pages long."

"That's good, right?"

She riffled through the pages. "There's over a hundred jobs here in less than a two-year period."

I bit a nail. "That many? Are you sure?"

"I know how to count, Miss Burger."

"You could say that I have a lot of skills and talents." Or that I got fired a lot.

She squinted and pointed her pen at me. "Aren't you the woman that Walley's is suing?"

"No. META is suing Walley's because of me. I can see how you got that confused."

"The snake, right?"

"Who ever heard of an assistance snake?" I laughed, but she wasn't laughing with me. She was still squinting and shaking the pen at my face.

"And the head, right? You did something with a severed head?"

"I thought it was a lobster," I squeaked.

"Holy crap! You're the woman who drove through Ruth Fletcher's tea shop!"

"It wasn't me! I wasn't driving!"

"I know exactly who you are, now. You're Zelda's granddaughter. You find the dead people."

"Well…" I started. "If you want to get technical."

She handed my resume back to me. "Sorry. I can't find you a job. My liability insurance won't cover you. You're a disaster."

She stood and put her hand out. I stood, too and shook it. "Disaster is a little harsh," I said. "I'm very good with data entry. And I got very few complaints as a seating hostess at Denny's. Four or five, tops."

She pushed me toward the door. "You should probably leave before you burn down my office."

"I resent that. I've never burned down an employment office." She pushed me harder and opened the door for me, waving me outside. "I'm not bad with food. I could be some kind of taster."

She leaned in and got in my face. "Listen young lady, nobody will ever hire you in this town. Do you understand me? One whiff of your trouble-making, and they'll head for the hills. You're the jinx of minimum wage jobs. You get me?"

"I'm happy to work for more than minimum wage," I offered. But it was too late. She closed the door on me and locked it to make sure my bad luck self couldn't infect her employment files.

What was I going to do? I had worked every job in America. I had run into a brick wall. And not just the one I ran into when I was a chauffeur in Los Angeles for three days. This was an employment brick wall. I was persona non grata for anything with a paycheck. I was doomed.

I closed my coat and lifted my collar against the cold. With no prospects of getting a job, I walked slowly through the town toward my grandmother's house. I had about five dollars in my purse. I could get a latte and a half of a scone from Tea Time or a hot chocolate and a half of a piece of pie from the pie shop. Either would make me feel slightly better about being a failure and a sponge, as my mother would say. But the latte would come with a big dose of abuse from Ruth. So, I decided on the pie.

Cannes is a beautiful town, especially in the winter. Peaceful. Cannes's historic district is a large rectangle of houses and shops located in the center of town, which is quaint and western dotted with upscale antique stores and American cuisine with indoor and outdoor seating.

It was a real winter wonderland in December, and the town did Christmas up right, just like it did all the holidays. There were lights on every building, a Christmas tree on every corner, and enough holly and tinsel to cover an area ten times the size. Christmas music played from speakers on Main

Street from seven in the morning to nine at night.

I willed the charm and fresh air to lighten my mood, but being told I was a walking disaster had really affected me. I was worried that my mother had been right about me.

Yep, I would need pie.

As I got closer, however, the peace vanished. There was something going on in the little park on Main Street, and the crowd spilled out into the street and onto the sidewalks, drowning out the Christmas music. Bird's hair salon patrons had come outside to see what the commotion was about, some in smocks and curlers and others with their hair covered in foil packets and tint.

Bird stood out front, leaning her hip against the side of the building. She held a jar of peanut butter in one hand and a spoon in the other, and she scooped up a generous amount of peanut butter and put it in her mouth.

"What's going on?" I asked her.

"Darth Vader," she explained. "He decided to do some campaigning at the live nativity scene. He wants to get the Christmas vote."

"What's the Christmas vote? Shoppers?"

"I don't know. He keeps playing his theme music. And he's wearing a Santa hat over his helmet."

I craned my neck, but I couldn't see him above the heads of the crowd. As if on cue, his theme music started to blare over the Rudolph the Red Nosed Reindeer song.

"See what I mean?" Bird said, spooning more peanut butter into her mouth. She scanned my body. "Are you eating that Skippy I gave you?"

"Uh, well the thing is…"

"That's fine. Maybe your grandmother will share her clothes with you."

I stumbled backward. What was it with people lately? Did I have a bulls-eye on my forehead? "Ouch, Bird. That really hurt."

"The truth hurts, Gladie. Where are you headed now? To get some pie?"

I sucked in my stomach. "I was not going to get pie," I lied. "I was going to yoga class."

There was no way Bird would ever believe I was going to yoga class, but Darth Vader's music got louder and distracted her.

The crowd oohed and aahed. I took a couple of steps closer to see what was going on. It's not every day that a man dressed as a Star Wars character runs for mayor, even in Cannes, and I had to admit it sparked my curiosity.

I squeezed my way to the center of the park where the action was really happening. The mayoral candidate had his usual entourage of stormtroopers around him, but there wasn't enough room for both them and the live nativity players. None of the horses, sheep, goats, and pigs were very happy. They were complaining pretty loudly and pulling at their handlers, who were dressed as Mary and Joseph and the wise men. Baby Jesus, thankfully, was at daycare and didn't show up today.

"What a town, right?"

At the sound of his voice, my body grew hot, and I unbuttoned my coat. Remington Cumberbatch was standing next to me in his pea coat, jeans, and boots. His tall, imposing body was close to mine, and I wanted to jump him right there and then. He was a very sexy man.

"Yeah, what a town," I said, stupidly.

"I've got a bet with the other cops about when this shit is going to turn. I'm guessing another ten minutes."

"I think you're an optimist," I croaked. Geez. I really was a whore. I had just mourned over Spencer and pretty much committed myself to Holden, and now I was ready to get naked with Remington in the middle of the street, even though the freezing temperatures could freeze off some of my important bits. Frostbite be damned.

He must have sensed my mood change, because he looked down at me with an expression that told me he was working with the same level of desire. He took my hand in his and gave it a gentle squeeze, which turned my insides to mush.

"Holy hell," I muttered. His hormones were shooting out of him right into my uterus. I knew that with one word from me, he would leave his post watching the phony Darth Vader, and he would take me to his apartment where we would bonk like rabbits under his real Star Wars poster.

"You're one dank woman," he growled, his voice thick with manly goodness and his body turned toward me. He let go of my hand and pulled me close. I was so out of it that I didn't think that he was about to blow our cover and turn our top secret tryst into Cannes' circular's top story.

"Is dank good?" I asked. But I didn't get the answer, and I didn't have to worry about anybody noticing that I was slobbering over the large, dark man of the law because right then and there, Darth Vader launched an intergalactic war.

CHAPTER 8

When I was a little girl, my mother was a big fancy matchmaker lady in this town. The biggest. The fanciest. You should have seen her. Then, one day, she went blind. Not with her two eyes. You know…with her third eye. It wasn't a one day thing. It went on for months. You can imagine that she was hysterical, out of her mind scared about being blind. She lost her ability to help matches find love, which made her feel useless. A failure. It got so bad that she wouldn't get out of bed. She wouldn't even put on makeup. It was like all the doors had shut in her face. Then, a miracle happened. It was just like the parting of the Red Sea. A little glimmer of light shined through. She could have ignored it because it wasn't exactly her sight returning, but she grabbed onto that glimmer with both hands. Slowly, the glimmer got brighter until her third eye was seeing better than it ever had before, and ta da! She was back to being a big fancy matchmaker lady. Make your matches grab onto their glimmers, bubeleh. No matter how dim the glimmer might be, make them use it to light their paths to love. Don't let the glimmer go.

Lesson 8, Matchmaking Advice from your
Grandma Zelda

I was distracted by Remington's muscles, so I didn't catch the buildup to the disaster, but it was pretty easy to figure out what was going on. Darth Vader and his stormtroopers had spooked the manger residents so bad that they escaped their handlers and went after the mayoral candidate like they were the Rebel Alliance and the Force was with them.

"It's a stampede," Remington said, obviously aghast. I figured he hadn't bet on this much of a disaster. The entire farm of animals escaped Mary, Joseph, and the wise men and jumped all over Darth and his entourage. They screamed bloody murder and tried to run, but they were taken down pretty easily by the goats.

Capes and helmets went flying into the air, as if the pigs had sprouted opposable thumbs and were capable of de-robing a man while they chowed down on his limbs.

"It's a race riot!" someone yelled in the crowd, which started the actual stampede of townspeople. People ran in every direction. It was chaos. In the melee, the nativity scene got the worst of it. Manger props, hay bales, and Christmas lights went flying.

It was a war zone.

Remington looked from the rioting people to me and back, again. He shrugged and picked me up, cradling me in his arms, as if I was no heavier than a child. "You okay?" he asked, looking down at me with his gorgeous face.

"You're my hero," I said like I was Marilyn Monroe.

But even though he decided to save me, his law enforcement other half was still active. "Lock down the scene!" he shouted to his subordinates. There were about three other cops in the park, and I didn't think they had a shot in hell of locking down the scene. They were way outnumbered and the farm animals were angry.

I spotted Fred in the crowd, crouching down with his arms over his head, trying to protect himself from flying laser guns and Christmas ornaments. Officer James was a little bit away from him, yelling, "shoo!" at some large geese.

Remington sighed and walked toward the melee without putting me down. He sidestepped screaming townspeople, as they ran for their lives. As we got closer to the real action, I noticed that Darth Vader had been reduced to his normal Irving Schwartz, his costume chewed to bits, showing his *I Love New York* boxers and Hanes white undershirt. His stormtroopers had fared better, running down the street along with the crowd with the goats in hot pursuit.

Like a miracle, the Christmas music began playing, again, and it seemed to calm the animals down, waking them out of their rabid reverie.

Or they were just tired or sick from eating too much

cape.

Joseph had run down the street after his goats, and Mary was shell shocked, hiding in the manger, but two of the wise men had gathered their wits and had begun to corral some of the animals.

Irving Schwartz, aka Darth Vader, was on the ground in a fetal position.

"You okay, dude?" Remington asked him. He moaned in return. "Dude, you need a doctor?"

"I think it's fairly certain he needs a doctor," I said.

The crowd had more or less dispersed, and it had quieted down. Fred approached us, wiping his brow on his sleeve and shaking his head, as if to say the world was going to hell.

"Hello Underwear Girl. Why is the detective carrying you? Is it because of the baby?"

Time stopped. The earth stopped rotating. I could feel Remington's heart pound in his chest and then fall quiet. He shifted on his feet and let me slip down from his arms.

"Uh," I said.

He wasn't blinking. The blood drained from his face, and I had the urge to yell 'timber!'

"You're going to be a beautiful mother," Fred continued. "Like an angel. I think I see the baby bump." He stared down at my stomach with glee.

"It's not a baby bump," I said through clenched teeth. "I don't have a bump, and besides, I'm wearing a coat. You see a bump through my coat?"

I was panicked. Had Grandma's junk food habit given me that much of a gut? I patted my stomach, desperate to get some peanut butter in me, quick. Remington was back to blinking, but now he was blinking a mile a minute, staring directly at my midsection.

"I don't have a bump," I told him.

"B-b-b…" he stammered.

It was heart-breaking, watching his cool completely leave him. The prospect of his casual sex buddy becoming his baby's mama, made him lose his swagger.

I had de-swaggered him.

He was so altered in that instant that I wasn't sure I could fix him with a dose of reality. But I had to relieve him quickly and let him know I wasn't pregnant, while protecting Bridget's privacy.

I snapped my fingers, trying to move his focus from my belly to my face. "Remington, the thing is…" I started, but before I could get more words out, the half-naked Darth Vader came to.

"I will start an intergalactic empire!" he shouted, but without his helmet and back up stormtroopers, it came out much more Irving Schwartz than Darth Vader. It was also hard to concentrate on what he was saying because his boxers had shifted and his Mr. Happy had escaped.

And he had the biggest Mr. Happy I had ever seen. Ever. Even in movies…not that I watched those kind of movies.

"Dude, adjust yourself," Remington said, snapping

out of it.

"Intergalactic!" he shouted back at Remington, but his mouth clamped closed when something behind us caught his attention. I turned around to see a group coming our way. They were wearing META t-shirts, and they looked supremely pissed. A couple were walking some goats that they must have caught down the street and collared them.

"Are you the man responsible for this?" one of them asked Darth Vader. I don't know how he figured the little man with his shlong hanging out was responsible for anything, but I wasn't about to say a word. I was trying to be invisible. If META realized they had the snake abuser in their midst, I was a goner.

I hid behind Remington and peeked out, looking for the right moment to escape.

"Didn't we make it clear that a live nativity scene, especially in the middle of winter, is unacceptable? It's abuse!" the META guy yelled.

It was unclear who he was talking to since the nativity players were long gone, except for the two straggler wise men, who were loading up the remaining farm animals in the back of a truck.

Cannes' version of the manger was decimated. The Christmas tree had been pulverized by the stampede and laid on its side in a pile of pine needles and broken ornaments. Twinkle lights had stopped twinkling, and there was a general look of World War Three where the seasonal spirit used to be.

"Nothing to see here, folks," Remington said, waving his hands at the animal rights activists. "It's all over. Time to go home."

Luckily, Remington was right. There was nothing to see. Darth Vader had put away his pecker and stood shivering in his boxers and torn clothing. Even though his Irving Schwartz was showing and his Darth Vader was long gone, he was still imbued with the attitude of a man with superpowers. He stormed over to the META members, his tiny five-foot-four frame ridiculous against them. Still, he didn't back down.

"How dare you!" he shouted.

"How dare *you*!" the META leader shouted back.

They how dared you back and forth for a while. It looked like I was in the clear. Nobody mentioned me or the assistance snake.

"Time to disburse," Remington said in his deep baritone.

"Hey there, Loretta," Fred called, waving to a middle-aged woman, who pushed her way through the group. She was a dead-ringer for Santa's wife. She was average height, with exceedingly wide hips, and she wore a white wig and red bonnet, a Christmas tree dress that fell to her ankles in triangular points with real colored lights and ornaments, and pointy green elf shoes. Little half-moon glasses hung at the tip of her nose, and her nose and cheeks were rouged in red circles.

And she was pissed.

I had never met her before, but Loretta Swine was the owner of the year-round Christmas store and Fred's landlady. I had visited him at her house, which was decked out all year with more Christmas decorations than Santa's Village.

"What the fuck did you assholes do to my motherfucking decorations?" she said, adjusting the spectacles on her nose. She took stock of the damage, tapping her pointed shoe on the ground and crossed her Christmas tree arms in front of her.

"I will shit down the throat of the one responsible for this! Do you hear me? I donated these cocksucking decorations. Do you assholes know how expensive that was? Whoever robbed me is going to get their dick cut off and rammed so far up their ass that they're going to look like Pinocchio. Are we clear, asswipes?"

Everyone took a step back, away from the scary Mrs. Claus.

"What's going on here? You okay, Loretta?" Mayor Robinson came out of nowhere, tall and dashing. His tongue was mostly healed, and now he sounded like he just got braces. Gold cufflinks peeked out from the sleeves of his long camel cashmere coat. He put his arm around Loretta's shoulders, like a friendly uncle, and scowled at what was left of Darth Vader.

"These fuckers destroyed my display," she told him.

"Now, now, I'm sure it wasn't the nice animal lovers," he said, smiling at the META delegation. "It was him, wasn't it?" He pointed at his arch rival, the man he was running against for mayor in just a couple of weeks. "Why don't you arrest this so-called man for indecent exposure, detective?"

Remington shot a look at Darth's crotch. "He tucked it back in. So all I could arrest him now is for ugly knees. And the chief hates paperwork. Sorry, mayor. I was going to break up the party, though."

The mayor blinked. "Ugly knees? I don't know that statute. Is it on the books in Cannes?"

"But this isn't resolved," the META leader insisted. "You still have an annual live nativity scene. You're exploiting animals!" He was furious, yelling at the top of his lungs. Suddenly, he stopped and pointed at the mayor. "Hey, aren't you the one with the donkey?"

"What?" the mayor asked. His arm dropped off Loretta's shoulder, and his hand flew to his chest, as if he was having a heart attack.

"Yes, that's you. You're the mayor with the donkey."

"Don't you dare go near Dulcinea."

The META leader wagged his finger at him. "You forced your donkey to fly over the town. What kind of madman are you?"

It was a reasonable question. The mayor was kind of a madman but only in a moron sort of way. He had a pet donkey named Dulcinea, with whom he had an unnaturally close relationship. Dulcinea did fly over the town several months ago, but it wasn't his fault. In fact, I heard that the mayor was so traumatized by the event that he built a special security barn for his donkey and had hidden her away for her protection.

"I didn't force her. She was assaulted, and it wasn't my fault," the mayor said.

"You're a criminal!"

"I am not. Why are you persecuting me? *She* killed an assistance snake!"

He pointed right at me with his long arm outstretched. Everything froze, as if the earth had stopped spinning. All eyes cut to me, and the META guys' mouths dropped open with the shock of finally finding the culprit they had been hunting for over a week.

The snake killer.

"I didn't kill it. I only injured it," I squeaked.

After the initial shock wore off, the group of META members came after me. I didn't know what they were going to do to me once they caught me, but I didn't want to find out. To his credit, Remington shouted at them and blocked a few from getting to me, even while his men just stood around trying to figure out what was going on. But in the end, it was potty-mouthed Loretta Swine who came to my rescue.

She pulled me behind her Christmas dress, shielding me from the snake-lovers with her industrial strength polyester-blend outfit. "Come on, let's get the hell out of here," she said.

She took off like a jack rabbit, pulling me behind her. I huffed and puffed, trying to keep up, and I didn't dare turn around. If I was going to be tarred and feathered, I didn't want to see it coming.

But I didn't need to fear with Loretta in charge. She pulled me through gaps in fences, and we crossed through backyards into long forgotten alleyways not used since Wyatt Earp was there. It was as if Loretta had an escape route planned out. She was incredibly fast. I wondered if her pointy elf shoes had arch support.

Just as I thought my lungs would explode from exertion, we arrived at Loretta's shop. *Christmas 365* was located in a ramshackle house, left over from the town's short gold rush period in the 1800's, when squat wooden structures were built quickly and just as quickly abandoned when the gold ran out. *Christmas 365* had three warped wood steps leading up to a warped porch, and the entire building leaned to the left, making it pretty clear that Loretta hadn't done any structural renovations to the building.

But she had done every other kind of renovation. Her shop glowed with enough Christmas lights and neon to signal ships from sea, and Cannes was sixty-five miles from the ocean. The house itself was painted red and green. The posts on the porch were wrapped in candy cane ribbons. Out in front, there were at least fifteen mechanical reindeer and Santas hanging around. Christmas music blared from a large speaker on the roof, with someone crooning about wanting a white Christmas.

As if on cue, it began to snow. For a second I thought it was part of Loretta's decorations...somehow she made it snow on customers, but it was real snow, light flurries at first, which quickly turned to a heavy snow, whipped by on a hard wind.

"Come on in," Loretta instructed, stepping up on her creaking steps. "Don't you love Christmas?"

I couldn't stand Christmas. It had taunted me my whole life, highlighting everything that was wrong: My dysfunctional family, not enough money, being alone. I took a deep breath. I didn't think "no" was the answer Loretta was looking for.

"Yes. I can't get enough of it. I love…tinsel."

"Well, you'll get your share in here," she said, opening the door to her store. I had never been inside, but it was pretty much how I pictured it. It was like Santa Claus had thrown up all over it, and it smelled like nutmeg, gingerbread, and pine. Everything that had anything to do with Christmas was crammed into the shop. Most of the house's interior walls had been knocked down to create a warehouse of holiday spirit.

"I've never seen so many Christmas trees," I noted.

"Fabulous, right? There's twelve. All real. I don't cotton to fake trees. Cookies?" She offered me a platter of sumptuous holiday cookies with frosting in the shapes of reindeer and snowflakes.

The waistband on my jeans were digging into me. "I think I'm supposed to be eating peanut butter," I said.

"Half of the motherfucking town is eating peanut butter," she complained. "How about some peanut butter cookies? I've got some big Christmas tree peanut butter cookies."

"Okay. That probably counts."

The door opened with the jingle of a reindeer bell, and a mother and her two daughters walked in.

"Ho. Ho. Ho," Loretta said, welcoming them. She sang the first two verses of "Rudolph the Red Nosed Reindeer," which thrilled her customers to no end. She offered them the plate of peanut butter Christmas trees, and they each took one.

"Do you have the glow in the dark Harry Potter advent calendar?" one of the little girls asked.

"Ours got eaten by the dog," the other little girl said.

Loretta smiled. "I have three kinds. Glow in the dark. Glow in the dark that plays music. And glow in the dark 3-D."

Of course she did.

They went for the deluxe model, a Scooby Doo ornament, and a set of flashing lights. I helped bag their purchases, while Loretta rang up the sale. She waved them away, and they left happy as could be.

"You did that well," she said. "Most people are bastards, do everything half-assed. So, those people were out to get you, huh?"

I took another cookie. "It was an accident. I didn't know it was an assistance snake."

"I don't give a shit about snakes. Snakes aren't Christmas. I don't give a shit about anything that isn't Christmas."

I wondered if she had Tourette's syndrome. She

talked like a sailor but managed to turn back into Mrs. Claus when a customer walked in.

"I'm not a big fan of snakes either. But don't let that get around," I added.

"I don't think it's right that Walley's fired you. I don't think it's right that nobody gives you a fair shake. What the hell's wrong with fucking people?"

She waited for an answer, but I didn't have one to give.

"I think you'll fit into the costume just fine," she said.

"Excuse me?"

"I can't give you more than thirty hours a week, but you can start today. All the cookies you can eat. Free."

It took me a minute to understand that she was offering me a job.

"I'll take it!" I shouted. I grabbed her hand and pumped it, like I was expecting to draw water out of her mouth.

"Don't drool over me, for shit's sake. It's not the damned lottery. The uniform is hanging on the peg with the Frosty head in the backroom closet on the right."

The reindeer bell rang, again, and a man walked in. Loretta started singing at him, and I snuck away to get my uniform.

Tables with Christmas merchandise were cram-packed in the store, and I had to side-step most of the way to the back. I found the uniform on the Frosty peg, just where she said I would. I closed the door and stripped out of my clothes. Loretta was right about it fitting, but there wasn't much to it.

The uniform was a red velour dress with white faux fur trimmed collar, hem, and cuffs. The dress didn't cover my ass, but that was fixed by the second part of the uniform…tight frilly underpants, like a Little Bo Peep porn star. The toppers were a little Santa hat and my own version of Loretta's green pointy elf shoes.

"No way," I said, turning my head to study my frilly rear. I didn't think the uniform was optional, and I didn't want to quit the only job I would most likely ever be offered again, but the thought of being humiliated in front of every Cannes resident and tourist purchasing Christmas ornaments, made my stomach twist and my heart sink.

The door burst open, slamming against the wall. "Did you grow roots?" Loretta yelled. Then, she studied my frilly butt for a second and smiled. Pleased. "Oh, it fits perfectly. This is going to work. Get the hell out there, and I'll train your ass."

The training took an hour and was mostly memorizing the location of the different inventory. It was impossible to learn everything, but she explained it was a hunt and peck operation. People liked to search through the mountains of stuff. It was part of the charm of the place.

She had me study the decorations with a duster in my

hand, cleaning as I went. There was a steady stream of customers, with the door opening about every ten minutes and blowing in a cold wind and snow. Most of the customers were good at trying to ignore the frills on my behind, but more than one husband and teenage boy ogled outright. It was all I could do not to beat them over the head with Santa's Village commemorative snow globe.

But Loretta seemed to be pleased with my work and even more pleased by the influx of young male customers. When the shop was ready to close at seven, I hadn't set anything on fire, hadn't beaten any animals, and didn't get one complaint.

I was a hit.

The reindeer bell rang, and I turned around to see Detective Remington Cumberbatch walk in. He took up most of the doorway, his massive body blocking the cold air and snow. He was a breathtaking man, a tattooed part-time UFC fighter with muscles on top of muscles and a talent for oral sex.

I was crazy stupid for calling it quits with him. He locked eyes with me, and I read one thing in his: panic.

"Oh my good goddamn," Loretta breathed and touched her head, making her cap slip off. Staring at him, she stumbled backward and grabbed onto a gingerbread house display for balance and knocked it to the ground.

Even though she had seen him before, it must have been Remington framed in Christmas with his head touching mistletoe that sent her over the edge. He was the one gift for

Christmas that she never thought to stock, and it was too much for her to handle.

I was worried that his testosterone was going to see me out of a job. "How did you find me?" I asked.

"I heard talk about a fine ass, and I put two and two together. We've got to talk."

I nodded. "Back here."

He closed the door behind him and followed me to the back of the store. He was so big that he knocked into tables as he walked and had to right merchandise before it fell to the floor. When we made it to the back room, he nudged me against the wall and put his hands on the wall on either side of me. He bent down and looked me eye to eye. Serious. Hopeful. Scared.

"I'm not pregnant," I said.

"But you said at Saladz…"

"I can't tell you why, but it wasn't true. I'm not pregnant. Not even a little bit."

His head dropped, and he breathed loudly, like he had been holding his breath a long time and just got a dose of oxygen.

"Relieved?" I asked.

"Oh, thank Christmas."

He pressed his lips on mine, hot and urgent, and his fingers trailed across my frilly underpants. I didn't know where this was going, but it was going fast.

CHAPTER 9

Yes, we often have to dress our matches because they dress like a shlump. But even a shlump in sweatpants can be well dressed with one single accessory. I'm talking about a smile. A smile is so easy, and yet so many people forget to wear it. Rule number one for a first date is to smile. Tell your matches that. While you're at it, tell them not to get spinach caught between their teeth.

Lesson 29, Matchmaking Advice from your
Grandma Zelda

The reindeer bell rang and without looking up, I started singing "White Christmas." I didn't actually know a full Christmas carol all the way through, but Loretta only required that I sing one or two verses to each customer as a greeting, even though Christmas music blared both inside and outside the shop at all times.

I had sung "Frosty the Snowman" and "Rudolph the Red Nosed Reindeer" a million times in the past week, and it just seemed like time for White Christmas, especially since we were having the largest snowfall in Cannes history, and every Christmas-happy resident and tourist were traipsing in the white mess to get to the store, and I was the one who had to mop it up with the glitter encrusted mop.

"Do you have a set of Grinch dishes?" the man asked.

"Bone china or ceramic?" I asked, finally taking a look at him. He was short, no more than five foot with a ponytail and goatee. He had small brown eyes, set very close together, and he wore a long coat down to his ankles.

And around his neck, he wore a pair of tighty whities. They were too big for him, and the waistband sagged down to his chest.

"Uh," I said.

"China, I guess?"

"Uh," I repeated.

"The underpants?" he asked.

I nodded.

"They're much warmer than a scarf, I've found. Would you like to try them on? Very comfortable. Don't worry. They're clean. No skid marks."

"Uh."

I tried not to make eye contact or look anywhere near his underpants-covered neck. I wrapped the set of Grinch dishes and rang it up. I wondered if he was right about underpants being warmer than a scarf. As Loretta would say, it was "colder than a witch's tit" outside.

She was in a stellar mood, brought on by the most Christmasy weather Cannes had ever seen. She was in such a good mood that she volunteered to clean up the remains of the live nativity and was re-decorating it, herself. The whole town was in on the Christmas mood. Normally, holidays were what Cannes did best, but this year, they had pulled out all the stops.

Everything was going pretty smoothly. META had even moved on, filled with the joy of rumors of animal abusers in Colorado. I was doing great in the store. I had been there a full week without a problem. Loretta often left me in charge. It was like I was born to work in a Christmas shop. I had been searching for a place to belong for years, and here it was, a year-round Christmas store, dressed in a slutty Christmas outfit.

I was imbued with optimism that I hadn't felt since I took my grandmother up on her offer to live with her and to work in her matchmaking business. I felt mature and grown up, like I had my life together. I had a steady job with a real paycheck, and my romantic life was back on track, too.

Last week, Remington had me in the backroom, my back pushed up against the wall, his knee separating my legs so that I rested on his muscular thigh, my core hot and liquid and ready for him. His hands cupped my face and he kissed me passionately, possessing me with the tongue I knew intimately. Passion turned to need to possession and then finally to what I knew had to happen. With one last world record amazing kiss, we were saying goodbye.

If I had realized it before, the pregnancy scare must have clinched it for Remington. We were not made to be serious with each other. Our relationship was based on pure sexual attraction, animal magnetism, and burning hot sex. But we had gotten to the point of put up or shut up. And it was time to shut up and move on.

It was hard to part, especially since he had a monster sized erection, and I was ready to inaugurate my Christmas uniform with a major bonking up against a wall, but we had to satisfy ourselves with a kiss.

He took a step backward and caught his breath. His mouth curved up in a small smile. "I'll see you around, Gladie. It's been fun."

"A lot of fun," I agreed, my voice cracking, as I tried to come down off my hormonal tidal wave. As much as I was sorry to let go of my easy hot sex with a kind and thoughtful hottie, I was relieved to be free of one complication in my life.

Since then, I had seen Holden every day. We held hands, made out, and I worked hard to appreciate him as part of my new mature and responsible way of life. He didn't make a secret out of his wish to make our relationship permanent and serious. He was packed up and ready to go, and it was obvious he wanted to take me with him. I hadn't told him how I felt, one way or the other, but tomorrow we were having dinner at his house, and I knew we were finally going to seal the deal. I wasn't going to push him away any longer. I was going to give him a chance. And that involved getting naked together. I bet his naked was really good.

I wasn't even thinking about Spencer's naked. I didn't care that I would never see his naked. He was aggressively ignoring me and refused to help Loretta with our recent problems of teenage boys peeking through the windows while I did inventory. So, as Loretta would say, Spencer could go straight to hell.

The underpants customer left, and I went back to sifting through the town's destroyed nativity decorations, looking for things to salvage. But almost as soon as the door closed, it opened again, and this time Lucy walked in. She looked sublime in head to toe expensive faux fur and high heeled boots and leather gloves with a clutch purse, wedged under her arm and a gift box in her hand. She was glamour, personified. I wanted to grow up to be Lucy. I wondered if I would ever have enough money to do it.

She closed the door and stomped her boots on the Merry Christmas mat to get rid of the remnants of snow and handed me the gift box. "Harry's gift for your baby," she said. I tossed it behind the cash register on the pile of baby gifts I had gotten since I worked in the shop. I was going to have to return a lot of gifts, but I was hoping I could just transfer them to Bridget when the secret was finally revealed.

"He's very excited about your baby," Lucy said. "He's hoping it's a boy and you'll name it after him."

"Harry Burger?"

"Yeah, well, I'm going to have to hold him when he hears you're not preggers."

"You're holding him a lot these days." Lucy usually traveled a lot for business, but lately she and Harry were tied at the hip. She hadn't left town since she went away with him on vacation.

She blushed, her face bright red against her white hat. "I like holding him," she giggled. I remembered what Grandma said about Lucy needing to tell me something, but she was taking her time about it.

"I haven't been spending all my time holding him. I've been doing some serious serial killer hunting," she continued, her eyes big.

I walked away and began to organize a table of wreath napkins and holly napkin holders. I was afraid her sleuthing was contagious. I had been down that road before, gotten bitten by the mystery bug, and I wasn't going to let it happen again. I had moved on to normal. Serial killer hunting wasn't normal.

"I've got some leads on some good Boo Radleys," she continued, helping me with the napkins.

"I've got Boo Radleys coming through that door every five minutes. Sit on the life-size Santa in the corner and watch the Boo Radleys parade by as they shop for 'You're my favorite Ho Ho Ho' dolls. I think you're wasting your time. Don't let yourself get stuck down the rabbit hole. It will mess up your career."

"The thing is I don't exactly have a career any longer,

darlin'."

I looked up, surprised. Lucy and Bridget had been steadily working ever since I met them. "Did you get fired?"

"No, darlin'. I quit. I am most happily unemployed. Don't look at me that way. I've got enough money socked away to be happy the rest of my life, and I'm all about the happily ever after right now."

"Happily ever after for as long as you both shall live?" I asked.

Lucy blushed and nodded. I gave her a big hug. She had had a crush on Uncle Harry since the beginning of time, and I was thrilled that they were finally together.

"I'm so happy for you," I said. Tears of joy flowed down her cheeks, and just like sleuthing, they were contagious, and I wept, too.

"But it's a secret for now. Just like Bridget, but in my case, I won't get fat. So, change out of that Barbie Christmas outfit, and let's track down this crazy psycho," she said, dabbing her eyes.

"I don't think I want to get close to a crazy psycho. I've put murder behind me."

Lucy crossed her arms in front of her and gave me her best Scarlett O'Hara pout. "You can't put it behind you. You have the gift, remember?"

I moved back to the pile of nativity decorations, throwing the unsalvageable pieces into a large trash bag. "I don't have any gift. Not murder. Not love. I sell Christmas. That's all that I do."

Lucy kissed my forehead. "You'll come around. You always do. I have complete faith. I'll see you later. I have a lead on a man who talks to cats."

She headed out the door. I didn't have the heart to tell her the cat-talking guy was Fred Lawry, and he was the town's cat psychic. I heard he brought in seven figures last year telling folks that their cats wanted more catnip and to sleep on the Lazy Boy recliner. Grandma had fixed him up with Gina Frankel, the owner of the pet daycare just outside of town. Fred was way too rich to be a serial killer, as far as I was concerned.

Lucy opened the door and tried one more time to draft me. "Don't you care that three members of a baseball team's management were murdered and hacked up into pieces?"

"Not a bit," I said, but my brain was racing. All three were part of the local minor league baseball team's management. That didn't spell serial killer to me. That spelled a targeted killer, and I had an idea about it that was hard to keep quiet. In fact, I had a strong urge to go with Lucy and follow my hunch.

But I kept my mouth shut because I was serious about putting murder behind me. I had a good thing with my new job and new relationship. I was finally on the right track, and I wasn't going to jeopardize it.

After Lucy left, I went back to tackling the rest of the nativity decorations. The stampede had destroyed a lot and made a jumble of the rest. I worked on detangling lights for fifteen minutes when the reindeer bell went off, and a woman walked in. She was middle-aged and in better shape than I was.

She was looking for a present for her husband, something Christmasy and cheap. There was a lot of that in the store, and she preferred to look around rather than have me help her. I didn't blame her. There was a treasure trove of kitsch and gaudy that couldn't be resisted. The woman was captivated by the decorations, and after a few minutes came to my table to see what I was doing.

"Are these clearance items?" she asked, pointing to the pile of decorations.

I shrugged. "I guess so." I was pleased with myself. I was going to sell items that Loretta had thought were unsalable. She would be impressed with my entrepreneurial skills. It was more proof that I was where I should be, destined to succeed.

The customer sifted through the ornaments while I worked. "Look at this," she giggled. "What a crazy whimsical ornament. I love it."

She lifted it up and showed it to me. "I just love the kitschy fun stuff you have here," she gushed. "You make Christmas so edgy."

I squinted and leaned forward, trying to get a better look at what she found. "What is that? Is that an ornament?"

"Of course. What did you think it was?"

I knew what it was. It was a very hairy big toe, and I had seen its twin during Thanksgiving dinner when I took out the trash. I was totally sure of it. For a moment, I thought I would try to play it off as an ornament. Maybe put a hook through, charge the woman $4.99, and let her hang it on her tree, just so that I could continue with the peace and quiet I had grown to appreciate.

My stomach clenched, as I realized that this toe ornament wasn't going to end well. I tried to grab it from her and toss it in the trash or gift wrap it, when she did a double-take, bringing the toe up closer to her face.

"What the..." she started. I knew her look, well. It was the look that people got just as they realized they were holding dead body parts. It was my go-to expression, lately.

"The thing is..." I started and then shut my mouth. What could I say? How could I explain to her that she was holding a toe in her hand? A toe that wasn't connected to a foot.

But a second later, I didn't have to explain a thing. She screamed like it was her own toe that had been cut off. She had amazing lungs, like an opera singer, able to maintain a note for a crazy long time.

Still holding the toe in her hand in horror, she flew backward into a Christmas tree. She held the toe out far from her, as she tried to regain her balance but ran into the dancing Santas display.

"Let me help you," I said, trying to help her up. She continued to scream and punched me square in the jaw with her toeless hand, sending me flying across the nativity decorations table and into another Christmas tree. I struggled to my feet, just as she finally managed to release the toe, throwing it across the store and hitting me in the chest, where it stuck to my velour-covered left boob. I screamed and swatted at the toe with both hands making it fly back at her.

It got bad from there.

I was half-aware that the reindeer bell dinged, but I was too caught up in the action to give the door any attention. The toe had made the rounds between us two more times before it fell to the floor in a heap with at least seventy-five percent of the store's inventory. I tripped and fell over Christmas toys, candy, decorations, and train sets, and the woman did the same thing. As we struggled, more tables fell over and more stock tumbled off shelves.

"You're sick!" she shouted at me, clinging to the giant Santa for dear life. "You're a sick psycho, crazy, lunatic, nutjobber! I don't care if you're a destitute pregnant single mother. You chop up people. You chop them up! Being pregnant doesn't mean you have the right to carve up people!"

I tripped over some packages of tinsel and managed to scramble up to stand, leaning against a wall. "I don't chop them up!" I shouted back at her. "I just find them, but I didn't even find this one."

"You're sick! You're a psycho!" she continued to yell.

"You're fired!" came another voice near the front door. It was Loretta. She was the maddest Mrs. Claus I had ever seen.

The good news was that no one was permanently injured, except for the poor guy with the missing toe. Loretta was so angry that her Christmas spirit left her entirely. She threw her wig on the floor and tore off a couple ornaments from her dress and threw them at me. I was cornered against a wall, barricaded in by the fallen stock without a way to get out.

Loretta yelled a lot of things but settled on "smut fucker" as her preferred word to describe me and what had happened to her beloved shop.

"Smut fucker!" she shouted, taking a direct route through her trashed inventory, shuffling through it like a cross-country skier at the Olympics. "You're a smut fucker!"

I had no idea what a smut fucker was, but I didn't dare ask. Besides, I figured it wasn't good. Definitely not a term of endearment. I shielded my head with my arms, in case she was going to attack me.

Meanwhile, the customer had run out, still screaming, and there would be no witness, if Loretta, wearing an acrylic, Christmas tree-shaped Mrs. Claus outfit, killed me. I resigned myself to dying on a pile of Season's Greetings shot glasses. After all, I was now jobless and blackballed from every employer in a two-hundred mile radius. I was a leper. A pariah.

I wondered if I could get unemployment insurance.

Loretta shook her fists above her head. Her face was red, and not just because of the red rouge circles she had painted. She was determined to beat me to death. I wanted to say a prayer, but all I could remember was the lyrics to "Frosty the Snowman," and I didn't think she would appreciate being reminded of the once upon a time joy of Christmas.

"Smut fucker!" she yelled and let her fists fly. I flinched and closed my eyes, preparing for impact.

But it never came.

"No you don't," I heard a familiar voice say. I opened my eyes. Loretta's arms hung in the air, a few inches from my face, suspended by Spencer's strong hands.

CHAPTER 10

When I was little, I wanted to be a ballerina. You know I have a weakness for fashion, dolly, and those tutus! I've always loved those tutus. I still have one in my closet, if you want to know the truth. When you bury me, wrap me in pink tulle. It will make me happy for eternity. Anyway, I wanted to be a ballerina, so my mother took me to ballet class. Stop laughing, bubeleh. It's true that I don't have such gorgeous legs. It's true that my knees look like there's two pumpernickels strapped to them. But believe it or not, I had a certain grace in my tutu and ballet slippers. I could have grand jete'd forever. But on the first day of class, I saw something in my teacher's heart. It distracted me from a world of pink tulle. In fact, her heart spoke so loud to me that I couldn't focus on anything else. I pulled her aside with my little hand and asked her if she was sad about Charlie. Who was this Charlie? I didn't know, but I did know that he belonged at her side and not just in her heart. She cried on my little shoulder. She told me about her love. Well, that was that. Ballet was gornisht. I couldn't stop until my teacher was with Charlie, happily ever after. You will do the same. When you're making your matches, dolly, don't give up, no matter how much pink tulle gets in the way.

Lesson 26, Matchmaking Advice from your
Grandma Zelda

"Big breath," Spencer instructed Loretta, and she lowered her hands.

"Look what this half-wit bitch did to my store! My livelihood! Look!" she shouted. She had a point. The store was decimated. Even the sound system wasn't working properly. Frank Sinatra was singing at half-speed.

Spencer shot me a look and raised his eyebrow. I looked down at my feet and felt my face grow hot. How humiliating. He was always around when I screwed up. He side-stepped Loretta and helped me out of the store.

We stood on the street while three cops helped Loretta survey the damage. "She brought sonofabitch dead body parts in here!" I heard her yell from inside the store.

"Are you kidding me?" Spencer said, but I didn't think he wanted a response this time. It was more of a half-hearted, exhausted kind of "are you kidding me", as if he had lost patience with me. I didn't blame him. I had lost patience with me, too.

I studied the street and kicked at the asphalt. It was

doubtful that he would let me go until they found the toe, and it was doubtful they were going to let me help find the toe. Not that I wanted to.

"I want an ice cream sandwich," I mumbled.

"What the hell are you wearing?"

I clenched my jaw. My clothes and shearling coat were hung up in the back room in the heated store. I was outside in the snow in frilly underpants, a mini-dress Santa outfit, and felt elf shoes. I was freezing. Meanwhile, Spencer was wearing slacks, thick-soled boots, and a down parka. I noticed he didn't offer me his coat like a gentleman. Holden would have offered it to me. One more reason I was glad that I hadn't given my heart to Spencer.

"I'm wearing my uniform. You know, for my job."

"Smut fucker!" Loretta screamed from inside the store.

"I don't think you have a job anymore," Spencer said. His eyes flicked to my midsection, and he groaned. He took off his coat and handed it to me. "Put that on. You have no common sense. You shouldn't catch a chill in your condition."

At first I thought he was referring to the weight I couldn't lose, but he was more upset than that. He stomped at the ground and couldn't make eye contact with me any more than I could make eye contact with him.

Good.

I was glad he was miserable. I was more than happy to let him think I was pregnant. Let him stew in that misery.

Officer James walked out onto the porch with his arms full of wrapped presents. "She says they're yours, Gladie. Presents for the little one."

Spencer growled. "Put them in the back of my car. I'll take her home."

"Found it!" a young cop shouted, walking outside, holding the toe between his thumb and forefinger.

"Bag it, you idiot," Spencer said. He had arrived in Cannes a couple months before I did. Before that, he was a hotshot cop in Los Angeles. Being chief of police in Cannes was a definite promotion, but he was saddled with a completely inept police force, except for newcomer Remington, and it tried his patience.

With the toe found and the immediate excitement over, Spencer opened the passenger door of his car, and I got in. He walked around to the other side, sat in the driver's seat, and started it up.

"Hold on!" Fred shouted, running out to the car. "You forgot this, Underwear Girl." He handed Spencer a large box through his window, and Spencer tossed it in the backseat.

"What the hell is that?" Spencer asked.

"A Diaper Genie," I said.

He pounded the steering wheel a couple times. His face looked like it was going to blow, but he managed to contain himself after a few seconds. "Fine. Okay," he muttered to himself, as if he was trying to convince himself, and I hoped he was right.

He took a deep breath and exhaled slowly. After readjusting his body in his seat, he put the car into drive and left the curb, but he immediately slammed on his brakes.

"What the hell?" he said. I watched as my mother put-putted by us on her moped, narrowly missing getting hit by Spencer's car. At first I thought she was bottomless, but she was wearing a very short pink mini-skirt, and a low-cut black sweater with a push up bra and high heels. She must have been freezing, but she was smiling ear to ear.

She recognized me as she passed. "I knew you would get knocked up," she shouted, delighted.

"Was that your mother?" Spencer asked.

"I'm still waiting on the DNA results."

"You have her legs."

"I have nothing from her. Nothing."

My mother took a left at the next block and put-putted away with a puff of nasty exhaust. "Then you got your crazy from someone else in the family?" Spencer asked and drove down the street.

Spencer visibly debated with himself whether he should help me inside with the packages or if he should just stay in his car and watch me make a few trips from car to Grandma's house. He came out on the side of chivalry but pouted like a five year old while he took out the gifts.

"I'm not carrying the Diaper Genie," he said, handing

it to me.

"Fine. Take the breast pump, then."

He loaded his arms with presents, and Grandma opened the front door before we had time to knock. "Just in time for lunch," she said.

She was all smiles for Spencer, and I knew he had her vote for Mr. Burger. She loved his company and didn't give a fig that I wanted no part of him.

"I can't stay," Spencer said, dropping the boxes in the entranceway.

"Ribs from Bernie's. I have a six pack of root beer, too. And coleslaw, of course." She was playing dirty. Despite Spencer's perfect physique, he had pretty much the same diet as Grandma.

Spencer stopped and cocked his head to the side. "With potato chips?"

She nodded. "Sour cream and onion or barbecue. Your choice."

I gave Grandma my best killer stare, but she smiled back and put her hand around Spencer's back, completely ignoring me. He was under her spell of greasy, fatty foods and seemed to forget that he wanted to be far away from me.

But I remembered, and it was a very awkward moment. I was pissed that she was making me live through it. I followed them into the kitchen and sat at the table. She had put out quite a spread. There were piles of ribs, a vat of coleslaw and potato salad, and various other snack foods.

"Oh, pickles," I cheered, letting the excitement of

food override my anxiety about being with Spencer. He was distracted by the food, too, shoveling a couple helpings onto his plate. He tucked a paper towel under his collar and went at it, gnawing through a beef rib with his elbows planted on the table on either side of his plate.

"You got root beer?" he asked with his mouth full.

"In the refrigerator. Dolly, get it for us, please," Grandma said.

I shot her the killer look, again, but it had no effect. I took the six pack out of the fridge, pulled a can out of its plastic loop, and smacked it hard down on the table in front of Spencer. He put his rib down, wiped his fingers on his napkin and flipped the can open, pointed in my direction, spraying the front of my Mrs. Claus outfit.

"Hey! Put your dukes up, pal!" I shouted, but he ignored me. He took a swig of root beer and got back to decimating his rib. It looked so good. My stomach growled, and I sat back down, spooning potato salad onto my plate.

"You're looking very well," Grandma told Spencer. She pushed the coleslaw away from her, probably because it was too healthy for her tastes, and took a barbecue chip out of the value-sized bag.

"Thanks. New suit from Nordstrom."

Spencer was a confirmed metrosexual. He was better dressed than Cary Grant. "How are you doing these days? Keeping busy?" she asked him.

"Yep," he said, tossing me a glance. "Never felt better. Playing the field suits me great. Take for example tonight.

I've got a date with a model named Svetlana. Keeps me busy and in shape."

He smirked his usual annoying smirk right at me and grabbed another rib. I grabbed a rib, too, and took a bite. It was delicious. Greasy and smothered in sauce. Some sauce dripped on my uniform, but I didn't care. Served Loretta right for firing me if her precious uniform was stained. Besides, she still had my clothes and my good shearling coat.

"It's probably wise to use a double condom with Svetlana, sweetie," Grandma told Spencer. "Call it a hunch."

Spencer choked on his rib, and I slapped his back extra hard. He took a swig of his root beer and belched.

Grandma opened another can of root beer. "There's a lot of playing the field happening tonight. Your nice Detective Remington will be out with four ladies glomming onto him. Very impressive."

Spencer dropped his rib, again. "I'll kill him."

"You will?" Grandma said, innocently. "Why?"

"Why?" he asked a little too loudly, making it echo off the kitchen walls. He pointed at me. "He's two-timing your granddaughter in her present condition."

"Oh, geez," I said, stuffing a handful of sour cream and onion chips into my mouth.

"What condition is that?" Grandma asked.

"Her condition! Her condition! You know."

"I know?"

"You know. Inside her."

"Inside?" she asked, torturing him. The color had

drained from his face with the effort to not say "pregnant" while getting his point across. His forehead had a slick layer of sweat that dripped into his eyes and made him blink fast, as if he was a girl, flirting.

"With child," he whispered, finally.

"Gladie isn't pregnant," Grandma said, putting him out of his misery.

Spencer's head whipped toward me so quickly that he was sure to get whiplash. I slopped more potato salad on my plate and shrugged.

"She was never pregnant," Grandma continued. "It was a mistake. A miscommunication that spread like wildfire, just like everything spreads in this town."

Spencer was stock still, his napkin blowing lightly up and down on his chest. I could practically hear the gears of his brain crank and spin, trying to understand the situation.

"I'm not pregnant. Sit down. You're dripping barbecue sauce off your chin," I said. It was a lie. His face was completely clean with only a light five o'clock shadow dusting his cheeks and chin over his perfect bone structure.

The jerk.

He sat down, considerably more cocky than he was a minute ago. "And Remington is fooling around with four other women?"

A huge smile grew out of his cocky smirk. He was riding high. Relieved. He was a new man, which was his old self that he had lost for a while.

He dumped some chips onto his plate with flair. The

old Spencer was back big time. He was thrilled that I was barren and being fooled around on by my recent boy toy.

I had wanted to make him suffer a little longer, to make him think that I was pregnant with triplets from my hottie lover, but it was good not to have him hate me for a little while. It was almost nice having him around. The three of us ate in silence for a few minutes, except for the sound of our chewing, like hogs at feeding time, inhaling large amounts of fatty food.

"No more body parts!" Spencer yelled, suddenly, wagging his fork at me. "What's with you and the body parts?"

Damn. The old Spencer really was back.

"It wasn't my fault! I didn't even find this one. It was the lady customer. She thought it was an ornament."

"Trash, lobsters, ice cream sandwiches, and ornaments," he said, counting on his fingers. "What's with you?"

I slammed my fist down on the table. "Nothing! Nothing! It's not my fault. I was minding my own business."

He wiped his face with his napkin and put his dirty plate in the sink. "Body parts is not your business, Pinky. Keep your nose out of my murders. I know you think you're Miss Marple, but you're not."

"I don't think I'm Miss Marple."

He adjusted his suit. "Thank you, Zelda, for a delicious dinner. Where'd you put my coat, Pinky? It's Ralph Lauren, and it's cold enough outside to freeze my balls. And we wouldn't want that, would we?" He winked at me and smirked his annoying smirk. It was all I could do not to smear barbecue sauce all over his precious suit.

"I don't care about your balls," I growled. "Come on."

He followed me out of the kitchen and into the entranceway. I had thrown his down coat onto my baby presents. I was going to miss it. I was coatless, and his was amazingly warm. He picked it up, dusted off the baby cooties, and slipped his he-man arms through the sleeves.

He leaned in against me. With one finger under my chin, he tilted my head so I was looking right into his big dark eyes. Gone was the hate and the disappointment and they were replaced by the same Spencer I had known in the past few months.

"I know you care about my balls," he said, smirking.

I kept a straight face, but I wanted to wrap my leg around his waist, hoist myself up, and stick my tongue down his throat. "Only if they're served with spaghetti and parmesan cheese," I croaked.

"For you, Pinky, that can be arranged." I stepped backward and tripped over the baby presents. "Be careful. That Diaper Genie can be treacherous."

I flipped over on all fours, scooting some packages aside with my foot. Spencer gurgled behind me. "Stop looking at my ass," I said.

"I've always been a thong man, but you're converting me to frilly bikinis."

I leaped up. "Shut up about my underpants. Not one word. It has nothing to do with you. Not even a teeny bit. And shut up about your balls, while you're at it. I'm not interested in anything about you below the waist."

He put his arms around me and pulled me close to him. "So your pupils are dilating for my brain, then, huh?"

I slapped at his hands, and he dropped them by his sides. "Don't worry about my pupils. Worry about your Soviet, Stalin, red, commie, pinko model girlfriend, Svetlana," I said, drawing out the name Svetlana like it had thirty-six syllables and I was a pissed off high school cheerleader from the Valley.

It wasn't my finest moment.

"Svetlana was born way after the fall of the Soviet empire. Way after." He zipped up his coat and opened the front door. "And don't worry, she doesn't wear frilly underpants. Come to think of it, she doesn't wear any underpants."

I threw a baby present at him, but he ducked out the door before it hit him. Grandma appeared next to me.

"If I were your age, I would drag him back in the house and ride him like I was going for gold at the rodeo," she said.

I studied her to see if she was joking or not. She wasn't cracking a smile. She was staring at the door where Spencer had left with a wistful expression on her face.

"I don't think Spencer is the relationship type. He's a love 'em and leave 'em type," I said.

elise sax

"Perhaps. But it might be worth the leave em' to get a dose of his love 'em. Come back in the kitchen. Jersey Smith brought me over a strudel as a thank you for fixing her up with John Smith."

"Smart. She won't have to change her monogramed towels."

The strudel was delicious, even better with vanilla ice cream and coffee. Grandma turned down the vanilla ice cream, which was a sure sign that something was troubling her.

"You know what I want to talk to you about, don't you, bubeleh?"

There was a whole list of things, from Remington to Holden to Spencer to dead people to my frilly underpants. I scooped some ice cream into my mouth.

"You have the gift," she continued.

"The gift for catastrophe," I said.

She put her hand on mine. "No. You have the gift. Same as me. Same as my mother and hers before her. I know you have it, just like I know the sky is blue or that the mayor is going to have a nervous breakdown when he opens the suggestion box he put out next to the live nativity scene in the park."

"I bet there are some doozy suggestions in that box," I said.

"Worse than any Twitter hashtag you could think of," she agreed.

I put my spoon down. "Are you sure I have the gift? I

don't feel it at all."

"You don't have to feel. I feel it for you. Do you trust me?"

Of course I trusted her, but this was a stretch for anybody to believe. Still, what was my alternative? I was broke with nowhere to go and no prospects.

"You've made four good matches, even though you're just a beginner. How many matchmakers have been so successful?" she asked.

"Three, not four."

"You're not counting Lucy and Harry. You did that," she said, poking my arm with each word.

Actually, I just pushed them together, but maybe that's what matchmaking was all about.

"I did that?" I asked.

"And just think how many more love matches you're going to make. You're going to be famous."

"I think I'm already famous," I said, thinking about the dead people I'd stumbled onto since moving to Cannes.

"No, dolly. You're infamous. Famous is different."

I bit my lip. Famous. I wasn't sure I wanted to be famous, but it had to be better than infamous.

"More important than that, bubeleh, there's the heritage to think about. The dynasty," she continued. She took the ice cream out of the freezer and scooped out two scoops and plopped them on her strudel.

"What dynasty?" I asked.

"The Burger women dynasty, of course. The

matchmaking heritage. You're the last in line. After me, who will take my place? You, of course."

It was a lot to put on my shoulders. A dynasty. I was a high school dropout with a twenty-three page resume. What did I know about dynasties? My mother's words hit me: A sponge. A failure. I dropped my spoon into my bowl. My appetite was gone.

"Your mother doesn't have the gift," Grandma said. "She doesn't have anything. She's a hot mess. You have the gift. No more jobs. No more frilly underpants. Do we have a deal?"

"I guess so?" I said like a question, terrified at promising her to hold up my so-called heritage.

Grandma clapped her hands together. "Good! I have a big assignment for you."

Even though I had enough baby supplies to outfit three babies, Bridget didn't want my presents. She insisted that I return them when her secret would be revealed and that she would get her own presents and buy her own baby supplies.

Bridget was also conscious about buying things that were fair trade, fair labor, and non-gender specific because she wanted her child to be a non-sexist, ultra-progressive super-baby.

It was hard to shop for a super baby. We went to

every store in Cannes, but none of them complied to Bridget's demands.

"I have a lot of protesting in front of me, Gladie," she said, outside of Jenna's Knitted Sensations.

Jenna had been taken aback when Bridget informed her that her yarn was made by child slaves. "What are you talking about? This is wool. Sheep made this wool," Jenna said, confused.

But Bridget couldn't be dissuaded from her crusade to start her child off correctly in our unjust world. She jotted down the name of Jenna's shop on her list of establishments that needed to be picketed.

We hopped into her Volkswagen Bug and drove to her OB GYN. It had been only three days since I decimated Loretta Swine's Christmas shop, but a lot had happened. Thankfully, Loretta wasn't suing me, but she was holding my paycheck and my shearling coat as hostage to pay for the damage. Not only was there a lot of inventory that had to be tossed out, but the police department had thrown fingerprint dust on every square inch of her store.

Grandma loaned me her winter coat, since she never left the property and didn't need it. It was warm enough, but it was a yellow and orange knee length coat from the sixties with a fur collar that was shedding and was giving me a ring of hives around my neck.

I was glad to get into the doctor's office so I could take it off. Bridget had chosen the most woo-woo, la-la OB GYN she could find. The office was located above the ice cream shop in the heart of the historic district, which I thought was the perfect place for it. I bought two scoops of apple cinnamon in a homemade waffle cone before we walked the flight up to the doctor's office.

"Dr. Sara is not a doctor," Bridget explained, in the waiting room. It was lit solely with lavender and vanilla-scented candles, and the windows were covered in black star cutouts which sent a stream of star shapes onto the walls. Tibetan monk chanting filled the air and every once in a while, the receptionist would come out from behind her desk and hit some chimes.

"She's not?"

"No, Gladie. The medical field is rife with male domination. It's completely geared to male health. No one gives a fig if you're a woman. You could live or die, and no one cares unless you have a penis."

It occurred to me that her baby might have a penis, but I didn't want to freak her out.

"Dr. Sara is a midwife and a doula. She's all about the vagina," she continued. "And uterus, of course."

"Of course." I finished the first scoop of ice cream and started on the second.

"And the baby, I guess," she whispered, staring at a star on a wall. I put my hand on her knee.

"It's going to be great," I said. Actually, I had no idea if it was going to be great or a terrible disaster. But Bridget was better off than most. She had a good job as the bookkeeper for most of the town. She owned a cute townhouse and probably had money socked away. She was also a good person who wanted the best for humanity, and I was sure she would spread that message to her offspring.

"Ms. Donovan? Dr. Sara will see you," the receptionist said. She was a pretty young woman, just barely old enough to vote, with long, straight blond hair covered in a wreath of flowers. She wore a short, floral dress, even though it was the middle of a freezing winter. She had perfect teeth, and she was showing pretty much all of them, smiling like she was the happiest woman in the world, and we should be happy too.

I was happy that the back was lit with more than just candles. It looked more like a regular doctor's office, but with rich wallpaper and Bob Dylan piped through a speaker system. The receptionist brought us into a little room, covered with pictures of babies, uteruses, and vaginas. Pink oven mitts covered the metal stirrups on the exam table.

I got woozy. "Maybe I should wait for you outside to give you more privacy," I said.

Bridget grabbed my arm with surprising strength. "Don't you dare. I'm not doing this alone."

"Of course you're not. I'll be there every step of the way." I tossed my ice cream in the medical waste trash can and took a seat, facing the vaginas on the wall but away from the stirrups.

The receptionist was also some kind of nurse, and she took Bridget's vitals. "Don't I know you?" she asked me.

"Me? No, I don't think so."

"She's Zelda's granddaughter. She's a matchmaker," Bridget explained.

"Hi, I'm Daisy. No, that's not it."

"Yes, she's a matchmaker," Bridget said, sitting straighter on the exam table.

"Oh, I'm sure she is, but that's not where I know her from." Then, it hit her. She blinked hard, opening her eyes wide to make sure that she was seeing what she thought she was seeing. Her smile left her, and she stumbled backward with the blood pressure cuff in her hand.

"You," she said, pointing at me.

I waved. "Me."

It wasn't a totally abnormal reaction to recognizing me, lately. I had gotten a reputation.

"What did you do to her?" Bridget asked me.

I shrugged. "Did you buy any Christmas decorations, lately?"

"My cousin's head," she breathed.

"You bought your cousin's head?"

"Well, this is awkward," Bridget said.

"My cousin's head," she said a little louder. Her cousin's head. I put two and two together and came up with the head that I fished out of the lobster tank.

I scanned the exam room for weapons. I wondered if Daisy could do permanent damage to me with a speculum. I shuddered.

"It wasn't her fault," Bridget said, taking my side like a good friend.

Daisy walked toward me, and I braced for impact. I wasn't exactly ready to meet my maker. But she had other plans. She bent down and gave me a big hug. "Thank you for finding him," she said. "It's been a terrible ordeal for my family."

It turned out the head belonged to her cousin and the assistant manager of the Prickly Pears, Buck Rogers. He had gone missing a few days before I went out for lobster.

"I think it's a psycho fan who murdered him," Daisy said. "Think about it. Three men from the management team of the Prickly Pears are murdered and dismembered. What does that say to you?"

It said a lot to me. I had kept pushing back the now-familiar itch to solve the mystery, but it was getting stronger than my resolve.

"Uh oh. You're getting that look, again," Bridget said. "You're off in Sherlock land."

"What does that say to you, Daisy?" I asked her. "Besides the fact that it's a crazed fan."

Daisy thought about it for a minute. "I'll tell you this. The Trenches are sweating bullets."

"The Trenches?"

"You know, the owners of the team."

"The Trenches own the team?"

As much as I wanted to, I didn't have a chance to talk about murder any longer because Dr. Sara walked in and got to work, examining Bridget. She poked and prodded and spoke in great detail about PH factors. But it was all worth it when she turned off the light and turned on the ultrasound machine and introduced us to Bridget's baby.

"Thirteen weeks gestation," Dr. Sara announced.

"Thirteen weeks?" Bridget exclaimed, almost jumping off the table to study the ultrasound screen more closely. "Are you sure?"

"Thirteen weeks, and you have a little boy. You want to see his pee pee?"

Bridget's shock over giving the world another male was far outweighed by her shock over the fact that she got knocked up more than three months before. Dr. Sara handed her a 3-D photo of her son and gave her an appointment time in a month. I slipped my arm through Bridget's and helped her out of the office and down the stairs.

"You okay?" I asked.

"I thought I got pregnant a month ago." She counted on her fingers. "I got pregnant in September, Gladie. Do you know what this means?"

I didn't know what it meant, and she didn't tell me, but from her reaction, I realized it was something important. Something big. She was too shocked to drive, so I took the keys, and she sat in her passenger seat, staring at the ultrasound photo.

"Don't take me home," Bridget said. "Go somewhere else."

She didn't have to tell me twice.

It was easy to get Mary and George Trench's address. They lived in a mansion in the same gated community as Uncle Harry, further up into the mountains. Even though Bridget's baby was her main topic of conversation during the past couple of weeks, she now deflected all of my attempts to talk about it. So, we talked about murder, instead, which seemed to relax her from her thoughts of what she was doing three months ago to make a baby.

"I like the idea of someone targeting a minor league baseball team instead of a crazed serial killer being on the loose," Bridget said, as we climbed up higher into the mountains.

I thought of the charming Mr. Trench. "Maybe it was revenge."

"What do you mean?"

"Against Mr. Trench. Hit him where it hurts."

Bridget thought about that idea for a minute. "He's a jerk. I was his bookkeeper for a hot minute. Mrs. Trench was the one who hired me, but he said I was too small potatoes to work on his books."

"What an asshole."

"He was probably right. He's got a ton of holdings. A big accounting firm was more appropriate, not some local bookkeeper."

Bridget was modest. She was a CPA, and she had an

MBA from UCLA. With all those letters, I would have let her handle my books...if I had books.

The security guard stopped us at the gate and called Mrs. Trench, who was reluctant to let us in. Luckily, Grandma's name carried a lot of weight, and eventually, she had the guy open the gate for us.

"Well, so far they've never surprised me," I said to Bridget.

"Yep. Grade A jerks."

Their house was one of the largest in the development. Three stories with a huge driveway, which was long enough to land small aircraft.

"Uh oh," I said, parking.

"Isn't that Spencer's car?"

"A lot of people have blue sedans," I said, but I knew it was his car. Drat.

We left the car and got halfway to the front door when it slammed open and Spencer stormed out. "Get back in your car!" he shouted.

"It's a free country!" I shouted back, stomping my foot on the ground.

"I'm hungry," Bridget said.

"What the hell is going on here?" George Trench said, peeking his head out of the door.

"Hello, Mr. Trench, we just came to talk," I said, side-stepping Spencer. I skipped quickly to the door before Spencer could hold me back or arrest me for being nosy.

Bridget was on my heels. "I smell honey mustard

pretzels. Am I right?" she asked, pushing me out of the way.

The inside of the Trench mansion looked like Laura Ashley had a seizure in it. Different floral prints covered every surface from sofas to window treatments to tables to the wallpaper. A giant television took up one wall and there was a boxing match playing. We had obviously interrupted George Trench watching the fight. Two cans of beer and bowls of chips and pretzels were sitting on a small purple and yellow cloth-covered table next to his recliner. I wondered if the chair had a massage setting.

Bridget walked straight for the chair, flipped it back to recline, put the bowl of pretzels on her lap, and went to town.

George was incensed. He was wearing sweats and a white t-shirt, and our visit was not a good kind of surprise. "Why are you here and when are you going to leave?" he demanded.

"Hi. I'm Gladie."

"She's the one who digs up dead people," Mary Trench explained. She was dressed for comfort, too in a muumuu and slippers just like my Grandmother's that clacked on the tile floor when she walked.

"I don't dig up dead people."

"What do you want?" George demanded.

"Yes, what do you want?" Spencer demanded, standing with his arms crossed in front of him. He hated me sleuthing more than he hated me screwing his subordinate.

I ignored Spencer and spoke only to the Trenches. "I

was thinking that this rash of killings is not the work of a serial killer. I think your team's management was the target."

"Oh, that," George said, unimpressed.

"We were just talking about that," Spencer said, smirking.

"Yes, but…"

"Can I have my chair back?" George asked. "Are you done? The police are on the case. I just want to sit back and relax. I work very hard. I deserve to rest once in a while."

"But I wanted to talk to you about the three men."

"No, Pinky. You're not going to talk about the three men," Spencer said in his I'm-in-command voice. Screw his I'm-in-command voice. I needed to get answers.

"But…"

George Trench hovered over Bridget. She took the hint, finishing off the pretzels and giving him back his chair. "I think we better go, Gladie," she said, licking the pretzel dust off of the tips of her fingers.

George sat down and reclined back. He was a stereotypical snobby rich man who didn't concern himself with the little people.

"I just want to ask you a few questions about Buck Rogers," I said. George turned up the volume on the television, and Mary scowled at me, like she had discovered mold on her wall.

"Pinky," Spencer said.

"But…"

Bridget took my hand. "Let's get going."

She squeezed my hand, giving me support while I skulked out. Mary Trench closed the door as soon as we left. We stood outside on the driveway. "You okay?" Bridget asked me.

"She's in shock that someone didn't want her nosing around in their business," Spencer said.

He was right. I had been completely rebuffed. I had just begun to investigate, and I was derailed. Mysteries weren't supposed to go like this. It was all wrong, like the universe had exploded or imploded or just not worked right at all.

"They were rude," Bridget said. "They didn't offer me something to drink. Would an iced tea have killed them?"

I tapped my nose with my finger. "Suspicious. Very suspicious."

"No, not suspicious," Spencer insisted.

"They must be hiding something," I continued, still tapping and looking out into space, as if I could find the solution to the mystery, floating in the air on a speck of dust.

Spencer grabbed my arms, firmly. "Is it out of the realm of your imagination that I already interviewed the Trenches and have all the information I need?"

I arched an eyebrow and pursed my lips.

"The man lost a ton of money with these murders, Gladys," Spencer said, leaning down and getting in my face. His breath smelled of coffee and sweet holy sexy wow.

"Don't call me Gladys. How did he lose money?"

"His management was murdered. It stopped him

cold, and it's not easy getting volunteers to take their place and perhaps get hacked up into pieces. Right?"

I thought about it. It sounded logical. Someone was targeting the Trenches, hacking up their business, just like they hacked up Buck Rogers and the others. It was a brutal way to attack someone, financially, but it was efficient. Could someone hate the Trenches that much? Probably. I almost hated them that much, and I had just met them.

"I don't like how she looks," Spencer told Bridget.

"Like her brain is spinning so fast it's going to explode," Bridget agreed.

"Stop thinking," Spencer commanded me.

"I don't think she can," Bridget said. "She's got the murder bug real bad. Maybe we should stand back out of range."

Spencer grabbed my arms and gave me a little shake. "Stop thinking," he repeated. "These people have suffered enough. Besides, they're meaner than spit, and they won't see your snooping as helping."

"I'm not snooping."

"You're snooping."

I shrugged off his hands. "I'm not snooping."

"Maybe just a little snooping," Bridget said.

"No amount of snooping," Spencer growled. "Not even a little."

I wasn't listening. Instead, I was planning on giving Spencer the slip and grilling the Trenches for any information they could give. They must have accumulated a million enemies, but I would track down every one of them before they cut up another innocent baseball player.

"No more snooping. Scout's honor," I told him, holding up two fingers.

Spencer raised an eyebrow. "Yeah, right. Like I believe that."

"I swear!"

"He's got a point," Bridget said.

"Shut up. I swear." I didn't even believe myself. But why did I have to answer to Spencer anyway?

"Listen, Pinky, stay away from them. And stay away from the team's management and their families. Do you hear me?"

There was a *ding, ding, ding* chiming in my head. "What did you say?"

"I said stay away from them."

"Of course. Why didn't I think of that before?"

Spencer stepped back and rubbed his forehead. "What?"

"Right?" I asked Bridget.

"I guess so. Can we stop for a sandwich?"

"What are you playing at?"

"I'm not playing. I just realized that I shouldn't be bothering with the Trenches. I need to investigate the team. Figure out who wants them dead."

"No."

"You don't own me. You don't tell me what to do. I'm not one of your Eastern European mail bride prostitutes,"

I said.

He took his shield off his belt and shoved it in my face. "See this? This shiny gold shield means that I tell you what to do. It means I own you. So, stay away from the team. Don't talk to them. This has nothing to do with you. Nothing. Not one thing. Not even one thousand degrees of separation. Not even a million."

His cellphone rang. He checked his phone and put his finger up in the air, telling me to shut up while he took the call. "What? Are you kidding me?" he said into the phone. "I'll be right there."

He clicked off the phone. "Come on," he said, tugging at my coat. "You're coming with me."

"Why should I?" It was just like him to kidnap me to prevent me from snooping, but nothing he could say could prevent me from driving off with Bridget to interview the rest of the team. I was determined, and I wouldn't be swayed.

Except for one thing.

"Because your mother just got arrested," Spencer said.

CHAPTER 11

Life would be easier if you could just knock on someone's head and the crazy would come out. 'Cause there's crazy in everyone, bubeleh. Whole busloads of crazy in people! It might be better to find out about the crazy before you fall in love with them. So, here's my handy dandy list of things to watch for on a date…just to make sure your match isn't sharing appetizers with Jeffrey Dahmer. 1. Does he make eye contact? No? He could be shy, but he could also have his own Grandma Zelda locked up in a closet somewhere. Next! 2. Does he ask all kinds of personal information about you, but doesn't say a word about himself? He could just be interested in you, but more likely he's hiding his crazy. See ya later, crazy man! 3. Does she tell you her ring finger size? Offer you a puppy? Take selfies with you in the first five minutes? Run, don't walk, to the nearest exit. I like commitment, but this will wind up with a bunny in a pot, mark my words.

Lesson 31, Matchmaking Advice from your
Grandma Zelda

"What are you wearing? You look like a giant bumblebee."

"I resent the word 'giant.'"

Bridget drove herself home, and Spencer forced me into the passenger seat of his car and was driving me down the mountain to the police station. He was keeping quiet about why exactly my mother was arrested, but I had a feeling it was something big.

"Where's your regular coat? Did Lucy trick you into buying that?" he asked.

"I don't have money to buy a coat. This is my grandmother's. My coat is being held hostage by my previous employer. Hey, can you arrest her for that? Maybe get my coat back?"

"Are you kidding? You're lucky she didn't have *you* arrested. If all it costs you is a coat, I would call it a wash."

I really liked my coat, but he had a point. I had never been arrested before, and I didn't plan on starting now.

He parked in the lot behind the station. A large group of officers were hovering by the back door of the precinct. As we walked by them toward the door, I could tell that they were all wearing gloves and masks, and they were taking apart my mother's moped.

I couldn't imagine why my mother's moped was so interesting, but I was afraid I was about to find out.

Spencer opened the door for me, and I walked in. I followed him past his office to an interrogation room that I had never visited before. Remington was standing guard outside, all business and muscles. Spencer motioned for Remington to come with him, and they talked quietly down the hall from me. While they spoke to each other, I watched my mother through the two-way mirror.

She was sitting on a metal chair with her bird-legs wrapped around each other. She was still dressed like she was going to a party at Studio 54 in the 80s. She wore a hot pink miniskirt with a slit up to her crotch and a white camisole. She was biting a fingernail, like it was corn on the cob. Her hair was wild and tangled, but her makeup was perfect... if she was singing backup for David Bowie at the Odeon.

"Why am I here?" I asked Spencer when he returned.

"Don't you want to talk to your mother in her time of need?"

"No."

"I need you to talk to her. This is serious."

I gnawed on the inside of my cheek. "We don't really talk. Normally she just gets drunk and tells me that I'm a failure. It's called 'new parenting.'"

Spencer leaned his shoulder against the wall. "Don't you even want to know what happened? Why she got arrested?"

"No," I lied. "I have an appointment to get to. I'm a professional, you know."

"That's a laugh, Pinky. If I had been drinking milk, it

would have shot out my nose all over you."

"I am a professional. My grandmother told me. I'm part of a dynasty."

Spencer raised an eyebrow. "Dynasty. Ha."

I sighed. Spencer wouldn't let it go, no matter how much I didn't want to deal with it. "Did she cut off someone's head? It's that, isn't it?" I said, voicing my worst fears. "My mother's the serial killer. She never did like baseball, and now's she's chopping up baseball players. How am I going to live that down? Finding dead people is one thing…"

Spencer touched my shoulder. "She didn't chop anybody up, as far as I know. She was in a shady business."

"Oh, well," I said, relieved. "That's not a new one. She sold illegal cigarettes when we lived in Glendale. There was a steady stream of constipated old ladies coming to our apartment, looking for a smoke."

Spencer shook his head. "Bigger business. Bigger smoke. Way more constipated."

Marijuana? I couldn't believe that. My mother never gardened a day in her life. She wouldn't even make a salad. Her idea of greens was olives in her martini.

"It would help me out a lot if you would talk to her. Get the low down," Spencer said. He was almost vulnerable. He was asking me for help. It felt good. I wondered if I held out a little longer, if he would cry or offer me money or free movie tickets.

"Fine," I said finally. "If you really need me."

But the minute I walked into the interrogation room, I changed my mind. I wanted out. It wasn't the fact that my mother was arrested for something "big," or the fact that the lighting was terrible, but it was just the simple act of talking with her. She wasn't exactly Mrs. Brady. There was no nurturing, maternal instinct in her.

I mean, she was a bitch.

My mother looked up when we entered and squinted as if I looked familiar, but she couldn't quite place me. But she recognized Spencer all right. "Get away, pig!" she shouted. "I told the good-looking one I wasn't talking, and sure as shit I'm not talking to *you*!"

"I think she was talking about Remington when she said the good-looking one," I told Spencer.

"Yes, I picked up on that. Go ahead and talk to her."

I sat down across from my mother, careful to scoot the chair an arm-swinging length away from her. "Hi, Mom," I said and shot Spencer a victorious look.

"Go away," my mother growled.

"Okay," I said and jumped up. "I tried," I told Spencer.

He scowled and pointed at the chair. "Sit back down. Try again."

I would have rather gotten a lobotomy with a shrimp fork, but I sat back down. "Mom, what did you do?"

"I was minding my own business."

"And what was your business?"

"I'm not ratting out anybody. They'll cut my thumbs

off," she said.

I turned toward Spencer. "Can you speed this along? At least tell me what she was arrested for?"

"Her moped is a mobile meth lab. She was selling meth," he explained.

"It what? She what? Is that even possible?" I asked.

"Yep. Her moped was a mobile meth lab."

"Genius, right?" my mother said, positively glowing with pride.

"My mother is Breaking Bad?"

"She won't say who she was working for," Spencer said. "Ask her who she was working for."

"Working in the meth business, couldn't you have afforded a lab with doors?" I asked. "Something a little warmer?"

"I like the cold, and it had great gas mileage," she said. "And I told you I'm not ratting out my employer. If I have an employer," she added, biting another nail.

"You have an employer?" I asked. How perfect was that? My mother had more job stability driving a mobile meth lab than I did doing anything.

"My lips are zipped," she said. She flicked her eyes at Spencer and back at me.

"Can you leave us alone for a little bit?" I asked him.

"No."

"Five minutes."

"Don't do anything stupid," he said, as he left. I didn't know if he was talking to the woman who drove a moped mobile meth lab or the woman who threw a severed hand across a box store.

"You've got to get me out of here," my mother commanded as soon as the door closed.

"They have guns."

"I don't mean break me out. I mean, bail me out."

Emotion built inside me and burst out in an explosion of laughter. I laughed so hard that I cried. I snorted, and my nose ran. She wanted me to bail her out. It was the funniest thing I had ever heard. My mother was not amused, however. She sat back in her chair, her skinny body wrapped in on itself.

"I can't afford to bail you out," I said finally.

"It's only a hundred grand."

I snapped my fingers in front of her face. "Earth to Luann. Earth to Luann. I have four dollars in my bank account."

She cupped her hands around her mouth and whispered. "I have three hundred grand under my bed."

"Excuse me?"

"I'll give you five grand if you dig out my bail money and get me out of here."

"I think I heard you wrong. I might be having hearing problems," I said. Three hundred thousand dollars sitting under my mother's bed didn't compute in my brain. I couldn't understand her.

"Fine. If you want to play hardball, I'll cut you in for ten grand. But hurry up. I gotta get out of here. I have places to go."

"And meth to deliver? Check, please!" I shouted, and Spencer opened the door.

"Well?" he asked.

"I need to go home," I said.

"Yes, she needs to go home," my mother echoed.

I left the room and went straight to the back door and out to the parking lot without even glancing back. I tried Spencer's car door, but it was locked. Spencer was right behind me. "What did she say?" he asked.

"You mean Walter White? Not much."

"I need to know who she was working for. She doesn't strike me as a chemist and a business mastermind."

"She rode a moped mobile meth lab," I pointed out. "Does that spell mastermind to you? Take me home."

I put my hand on my knee to stop my leg from bouncing up and down. I was itching to get back home and search under my mother's bed, but I thought Spencer would get suspicious if I jumped out of his car and ran full out.

In five minutes, he was driving up our driveway, and I opened my door before he came to a full stop. "Thanks for everything," I said, hopping out of the car. "See you later. I love you."

I ran to the front door, and Grandma opened it.

"Hi, Grandma," I said and bolted up the stairs.

Mom's room was next to mine, but in the nearly two months that she lived there, I hadn't entered it because I was scared what I would find inside.

I never figured I would find three hundred thousand dollars.

The door was locked. I took a paperclip out of my purse and jimmied the lock, but it wouldn't open. "Try this," Grandma said, appearing at my side with a key.

I took it from her and unlocked the door. I stood outside and let the door swing open. "I'm scared," I said.

We peeked our heads through the doorway. The room looked pretty much as I expected. The floor was covered in a foot-thick layer of dirty clothes. A large container of boxed wine—probably empty—was on her nightstand and two others on the chest of drawers. Surprisingly, her bed was made, and her pillows fluffed. Her curtains were drawn, but the window was left open, blowing a freezing wind into the room.

"I don't see any rats," I said.

"I thought I saw one duck under a pile of dirty clothes, but it was just the wind blowing," Grandma said.

"I guess I should go first since she's my mother," I said.

"That's brave of you. I should shout 'save yourself' and go in first. It's my house, after all."

Despite our pronouncements of bravado, neither of us moved a muscle. Our feet were rooted in the hallway floor.

"We could toss a coin," I suggested.

"This is silly. There isn't a monster in there."

"You're right. The monster is on ice at the police station."

I took a deep breath and took two steps inside the room. Nothing crawled on me. Nothing jumped out at me from behind the door.

"I think it's safe," I said.

I shut the window, scooted some dirty clothes aside with my shoe and dropped down on all fours to look under the bed. "I will kill her if I get fleas," I said.

"We'll both need a shower after."

There were two trash bags stuffed under the bed. I pulled one out and opened it. "No way," I breathed. I sat cross-legged and dug my hands into the bags, pulling out handfuls of money. "Do you think it's real?"

"Yes, which is bad. This is bad, bad, bad."

I had never seen so much money, and it was all fifty-dollar bills. "She wants me to bail her out with it. She offered me a cut if I will," I said.

"We need to get rid of it. It's bad money. It will bring bad mojo to this house." Grandma was dead serious. When she knew things, she knew them. It wasn't wise to fool around with Grandma's third eye.

I dropped the money back into the bag. "Worse mojo than finding a leg in the trash? Oh, God."

Grandma helped me take the trash bags out of the house and pack them into the trunk of my car. "Sister Cyril is waiting at the church. Put the bags in the second confessional on the left, and she'll get it," she instructed.

"She's not worried about bad mojo?"

"When ill-gotten gain is filtered through a charity, it erases the bad mojo," she explained, helping me tie the trunk closed with the piece of rope.

It seemed like a convenient loophole in the mojo rulebook, but my grandmother looked convinced. "The house feels lighter already," she continued.

"Three hundred thousand dollars lighter," I said. It was complete insanity to give away all of the cash. I had no money at all. My car was running on empty, and I couldn't afford to fill it up. And I wasn't thrilled with looking like a giant bumblebee. I wanted my coat back. It was nice, and there was no way for me to scrounge enough money to get a new one.

I wondered how much bad mojo I would get if I took a handful or two of cash from my trunk. The bad mojo might be worth a new coat. Or a new car.

But Grandma was scared of the bad mojo money, and if she was scared, there was reason to be scared. Grandma was always right about mojo.

I punched my steering wheel in frustration. Damn. I couldn't catch a break. I was going to be poor forever. I was never going to hold up the dynasty. I was going to fail my heritage.

Cannes's small Catholic church was located right in the heart of the historic district. It was a beautiful small nineteenth century building, built during the gold rush. I hadn't been near it since there was a shooting inside it in August.

As I drove, I realized that *Christmas 365* was on the way to the church. With two Hefty trash bags full of Ulysses S. Grant in my trunk, I felt a burst of courage. It wasn't my fault Loretta's shop was ransacked. I deserved to have my property back. I wanted my coat, and I was going to get it. I was tired of looking like a bumblebee with hives on my neck. I was going to get my coat back no matter what. With my decision made, I took a quick left and parked in front of Loretta's store.

As soon as I got out of the car, I knew something was terribly wrong. There was no Christmas music blaring from the speaker on the roof. Half of the lights were off, and Dasher and Prancer were knocked over on their sides on the lawn.

I took my screwdriver out of my purse and held it in a defensive posture. "Loretta?" I called in a whisper. My biggest worry was that Loretta had offed herself in sympathy with the life-sized Santa that bit the dust in my tangle with the toe.

With the screwdriver raised over my head, I knocked on the door. "Loretta?" I called and almost peed myself when the door swung open. I stood for a minute, waiting for any kind of response, but it was dead silent. Even the wind had stopped.

"Hello?" I croaked. My mouth was completely dry. It was totally possible that Loretta decided to close for the day, but since she had never closed the shop—ever—I thought there was more of a nefarious reason for the quiet and the open door.

With my flight response raised up to mach ten, I was shocked when my feet walked me inside the shop. It was the opposite direction of running away, which my brain was insisting I do.

"Hello?" I called, softly. The store was neat as a pin. There was no sign of the disaster from the week before. I took a look around, but it was evident the place was empty. It was a miracle. Loretta was nowhere to be found, and I could sneak in and sneak out without getting caught. I had a clear shot to the backroom to get my shearling coat. Ripping Grandma's bumblebee coat off me, I skipped to the back of the store.

My shearling coat was right where I left it. I had thought that Loretta had sold it or burned it, but it was hanging on the Frosty the Snowman hook in perfect shape. I slipped it off the hook and put it on, caressing the soft fabric with my hand. Yum. I didn't have money, but at least I had a pretty coat.

"No bad mojo," I said out loud. "I feel like things are looking up."

But I was wrong.

Like really wrong.

There was an ear-splitting crash overhead, and I

jumped backward in time to narrowly miss a set of stairs open from the ceiling and drop to the floor with a loud creak. Loretta Swine flew down the stairs, dressed in a red dress with neon ornaments hanging from it, her usual pointy elf shoes, and a large CDC-grade mask with a toxin filtration system on her face.

Her eyes grew enormous when she saw me through the mask, but after she hit the floor, she ran past me without stopping.

"Get the fuck out of my way! Run for your motherfucking life!" she shouted through the mask.

"What's happening?"

A rumbling above me answered for Loretta. There was a loud clanking of metal against metal and then a series of crashes with sound of glass breaking.

"Uh oh," I said.

Loretta was running full out in her elf shoes. "Run the fuck away!" she shouted again as she reached the front door and bolted outside.

"What's happening?" I asked again, stupidly. The noises above me were getting louder. It sounded like a freight train. My feet were stuck to the floor. I willed them to move, but they were stubbornly ignoring me. The freight train noises above me were joined by the sound of sirens coming closer. I closed my eyes like the wimp I am.

In a couple seconds, heavy footsteps burst into the store and came right for me. I opened one eye to see Spencer running in my direction. He hit me like a linebacker at the

Superbowl. I doubled over his shoulder, and without stopping, he carried me out that way, as the top of *Christmas 365* began to burn.

Spencer ran outside and jumped off the porch. He continued to run across the street with me draped over him where he dumped me in to a snowdrift and fell over my body in order to shield me. I struggled against him.

"Get off me. I can't breathe. I don't need you to protect me," I complained.

He shifted his weight just enough so that I could see Loretta's house go up in flames.

Then, the explosions started.

Have you ever had a day like this?

They started off small. A little *kaboom* at one side of the house and a *kapow* at the other. But the shock and awe wasn't far behind, and suddenly, the entire upper half of the store went up in a giant explosion.

"Are we being droned?" I shouted. Spencer didn't answer me, and he didn't get off of me. We watched as the flames shot up in a fireball into the sky, hitting a tree. The heat was unbearable, even on the other side of the street buried in a snowdrift.

But the heat near the house was much worse. Loretta and the other cops had run for their lives, and it was a good thing they did, because the buildings' explosions were contagious, spreading to the cars parked in front.

"My car!" Spencer shouted, as his sedan exploded, jumping into the air and landing on the back of a cop car. It was like dominoes. One car after another went up in flames. *Boom! Boom! Boom!* They were like jumping beans, flying up in the air and exploding. I knew what was going to happen next, but I couldn't quite believe it.

One, two, three, the cars became an inferno, and then it was my car's turn. My poor, beat up Oldsmobile Cutlass Supreme that had survived since Bill Clinton first became president caught fire. Sure, I had to start it with a screwdriver and keep the trunk closed with rope. Sure, it had more rust than paint, and the interior upholstery was ripped. But it was my car. It worked. It got me where I needed to go.

Well, not anymore.

The hood caught fire first, and then it was only a matter of minutes before it traveled to the back of the car. With one last explosion, the trunk popped open, and three hundred thousand dollars flew into the air, like it was New Year's and the confetti was scorched fifty dollar bills. They exploded upward and then rained down on us, like we won a lottery from heaven.

"Oh my God," I breathed. "Talk about bad mojo."

CHAPTER 12

Is that all there is? Remember that song? No, of course you don't. I have bras older than you. You think Cary Grant is a takeout place. Anyway, is that all there is? Maybe a match will come to you and ask you that. This is a very important question. Difficult. It's like a King Solomon question. It's a question about the meaning of love. Am I really in love? Is this what love feels like? Where are the violins? Where are the harps? You got to help them with this, dolly. You're the love barometer. You measure the love. If they don't know, it could be a bad sign. But maybe they don't understand love. Maybe love just is. Like a solo act. It doesn't always have orchestral accompaniment.

Lesson 57, Matchmaking Advice from your
Grandma Zelda

"Sit down and don't talk," Spencer ordered. I did as

he said and sat down on the chair in his office, facing his desk.

"No, don't talk," he repeated. "I see your mouth twitching, Pinky. Don't say a word. I can't be held responsible for my actions if you say anything at all."

I clamped down on my lower lip. He was right. I wanted to say a lot. The left sleeve of my beautiful shearling coat was singed black. My ears were ringing from the blasts, and I needed a drink. But what I wanted to say was, "What the hell happened?"

With half of the police force's cars destroyed, it took some logistical gymnastics to get back to the station. They put me in one car and Loretta in another. She looked great, completely unscathed. The firefighters arrived just as everything was blowing skyward, and they put out the fire before it spread to the rest of Cannes's historic district. The paramedics did a cursory check for injuries, but Spencer didn't let them take too much time because he was eager to get everyone to the police station.

Obviously, Spencer thought I was to blame for the explosion. Otherwise, why would he be so angry? I really needed a drink. A bottle of bourbon. And a vat of margaritas. And maybe six or seven martinis. Yes, that would hit the spot, I thought, sitting back in the uncomfortable chair.

There was a scuffle outside the office.

"Let me in to see her," I heard Holden order in his deep voice. "Don't get in my way. I have the right to see her."

"Haven't you gotten the picture?" I heard Spencer

say. "She doesn't want you."

"Who said?"

"She said. She told me. She…"

I jumped up from my seat and ran out of the office. There in the hall, Holden and Spencer were squaring off. Holden was a couple of inches taller than Spencer, but Spencer was bulkier. They were like two bulls, pawing at the ground and blowing smoke out of their noses, standing face to face and ready to do damage.

I couldn't believe that Spencer would lie to Holden about me. Telling him that I said I didn't want him was the ultimate betrayal. It was over the line.

"I said no such thing!" I shouted.

Spencer flinched, as if I had hit him. "But you said…"

"Liar. Shut up. Leave Holden alone. Stop terrorizing innocent people."

Spencer got in my face. He went from hurt to angry. "But you know what you said. You said it."

"What the hell are you talking about? Did the explosion give you a concussion? Should I call the men in white coats to take you to the funny farm?"

He arched an eyebrow and crossed his arms in front of him. "Is that how we're going to play it?"

I twirled a finger by the side of my head. "Rubber room. That's what you need."

"You have no right to arrest her," Holden said.

"She's not under arrest," Spencer said.

"I'm not?" I asked. I was surprised. I had been sure I was under arrest for all kind of things. Like blowing up police cars for one.

"No, you're a witness."

"Oh," I said, relieved. "I'm a witness. Yes, I witnessed everything go to hell, including my car."

Holden stepped around Spencer. "Are you okay?" he asked me. He cupped my face with his hands and studied me. "Do you need medical care?"

"Would they give me valium?"

He smiled. He was awfully good-looking. The definition of ruggedly handsome in his coat and plaid flannel shirt. He was James Franco hiking before he chopped off his arm. "I don't have valium, but I know where I can get you a stiff drink."

"I like the sound of 'stiff.'"

Spencer put his arms between us and separated us. "I'm sorry to break up this Nicholas Sparks moment, but I have a lot of work to do, and I need Gladie to stay for a while. So, hit the road, Paul Bunyan."

"Two literary references. Impressive, Jughead," Holden shot back.

It was getting heated, again. I had had my fill of violence lately, but I couldn't deny the idea of watching the two hottie muscle men get physical sort of turned me on. There was a definite cloud of testosterone and heated cologne in the hallway that I found intoxicating.

"You need help, boss?" Remington appeared behind

Spencer, massive and perfectly formed in jeans and a hoodie. The three of them in the narrow hallway was too much hormones for the small area. It was like Gladiators Gone Wild. My pulse was going a mile a minute. I bit my lip and thought of getting naked. The thought made my pulse go even faster.

"Just cleaning up," Spencer told Remington.

Holden turned to me. "Are you okay? Tell me you're okay."

"I'm okay. I'll see you later?" I needed him to leave. If he stayed, I didn't know what would happen, but it could get pretty bad if the three of them went at it. It might be like the Hadron Collider in Switzerland. Elements colliding so we can see through time and space. Perhaps we would fall into an alternate universe. Actually, that last part didn't sound so bad. Maybe I had a car in an alternate universe.

I felt Remington's and Spencer's eyes on me. Awkward. Very, very awkward. My breath hitched, and my saliva went down the wrong pipe, making me choke. I stuck a finger up in the air.

"I'm o...kay," I choked out, hacking loudly. I turned away from the three hunks and ran back into Spencer's office to hide. I closed the door behind me and grabbed a half-used bottle of water off Spencer's desk and swigged it back.

It worked. I stopped choking. The door opened, and Spencer walked in. He was more relaxed. Obviously, Holden had cleared out of Spencer's territory. I sat down in the uncomfortable chair.

"Smooth, Pinky. Real smooth."

"You are such a troublemaker."

"What were you doing at the Christmas store?" he asked, standing too close to me.

"I was picking up my coat." I looked down at my singed sleeve. No car. No coat. No valium.

I was having a terrible day.

He threw a handful of smoky cash on his desk. "Do you usually carry that much money with you?"

"Uh," I said.

He put his hand out palm forward. "Stop," he said. "Don't say anything." He took a seat next to me. He leaned over and shot me a benign smile. He was patient and nice, all of a sudden.

It panicked me.

"What are you doing? You're making me nervous," I said, inching away from him.

"I just want to talk to you."

I gasped. "Oh my God, you lied. I *am* under arrest. I can't go to jail, Spencer. I can't pee in front of people. I already feel claustrophobic. Open a window. I can't breathe." I clutched at my throat and pulled at my sweater.

He put his hand on mine. "You're not under arrest," he said softly, oozing kindness and consideration for my feelings.

I swatted his hand off and squinted, trying to read him. "You're being way too nice. You've never been nice to me before."

"You wound me, Pinky. I can be nice. I'm great at nice. I'm the nicest at nice. Did you want me to be nice to you?" he added, smirking his annoying little smirk and scooting his chair closer to me.

"No," I said, unconvincingly.

"Before you say anything about the money, let me give you some background information. Your mother cut a deal."

"Is that like cutting the cheese?"

He smiled. "Why Pinky, I'm impressed. You engaged in juvenile humor."

"You've rubbed off on me," I said.

He raised an eyebrow. "Would you like more of me to rub off on you?"

"Ugh. You're five years old."

Spencer leaned back and straightened his legs out in front of him, crossing them at the ankles. Relaxed.

"Your mother cut a deal. She gave us information about her boss, and we gave her one year at a luxury farm and a promise not to prosecute her for other crimes having to do with this meth operation."

"Luxury farm? What's that? Is it like a spa?"

"That's what you took from that conversation?"

"I can't even believe we're having this conversation," I said. "It's all Charlie Brown's teacher to me. Blah. Blah. Blah."

"I'm telling you that it's safe for you to tell me what you were doing with at least one hundred thousand dollars in the trunk of your car. It won't get your mother into more trouble."

"I didn't have one hundred thousand dollars," I said. He was way off. Did that mean that two-thirds of it burned?

"What were you doing with it?"

I thought fast. I was pretty sure that Spencer wouldn't have been down with taking my mother's ill-gotten gain to Sister Cyril. Not that he was anti-charity, but he had a pesky belief in the law.

"I was taking it to you. My mom has a deal, right?"

He nodded. I would have to take him at his word.

"I might have found it under her bed. But I was taking it to you. Cross my heart," I said crossing my fingers behind my back. Crossing my fingers or crossing my heart... What's the difference?

"And you just stopped at Loretta's to get your coat, right?"

This time I really did cross my heart. "Yep. What's happening?"

"Loretta is your mother's boss."

"Huh?" I asked. "My mother was selling Christmas tchotchkes? I thought you said she was driving a mobile meth lab."

"Strange town, right? Loretta was the chemist. Not a very good one because she exploded her store."

I was working in a front for a meth operation? "Are you sure? Are you punking me? Is there a hidden camera in here?"

Right on cue, Loretta started to scream in the hallway. "You motherfucker, cocksucker, dickwad, ass shit balls!"

Spencer and I jumped up and went to see what the ruckus was about. Loretta was there, still dressed in her Mrs. Claus outfit and elf shoes. Her mask hung off her neck, and her hands and feet were shackled. She was being forcibly escorted down the hallway by men in bulletproof vests marked DEA and FBI.

"She's right about them being dickwads," Spencer told me. "The DEA and FBI have taken over the case. Pushed me out. I'm just instructed to sit back and let them do whatever they want. It's like my badge isn't worth a thing. I might as well hang a Marriott sign on the front door and forget about being a cop.

"Are you sure that Loretta is a chemist? I've never seen anyone love Christmas so much."

"I think there's a lot more money in meth than there is in Christmas ornaments. She's already confessed to working for a Mexican cartel, and maybe you should sit down for the rest."

"What do you mean? Is the rest worse than my mother arrested and my boss taken away by the feds?"

Spencer put his hand on the small of my back and led me down the hallway behind Loretta. "It seems her cartel connection here in Cannes was Danny Fieldstone, the murdered trainer from the Prickly Pears."

I punched his chest. "Get out of town. No way. Are you saying this has all been some kind of drug war?"

"Yes, Miss Marple. Are you disappointed? I know you had your heart set on snooping, but this mystery is tied with a bow. Neat and tidy. Done. It was all a cartel thing. What the hell is this world coming to when baseball management is dealing drugs, huh? It's America's pastime! You hear what I'm saying?"

I wasn't hearing what he was saying. I was focusing on the fact that the mystery was over. I had planned to talk to the victims' families, to investigate the whole team, to figure out why they were murdered. I had a plan. I was going to look for motives and opportunities. I was going to have a list of suspects and cross them off one at a time.

But the mystery was done. Tied with a bow. Neat and tidy.

Murdered for drugs was anti-climactic. Simple. Uninteresting. A letdown. I was itching like a heroin addict because my mystery-solving was ripped out from under me. I felt like I no longer had a purpose.

It was a real downer.

Spencer and I turned the corner just as the feds brought in a short little man with a scar down his face. "I didn't do nothing! I didn't do nothing!" he shouted.

"They arrested the next man on the totem pole, above Loretta," Spencer explained to me. "It's like a pyramid, but we don't know how far up it goes." He pointed toward the interrogation room. "Would you like a moment to say goodbye to your mother?"

I could see her through the two-way mirror. Someone

had given her a cup, and she was drinking from it. I hoped it was liquor, because she probably needed it. For the first time in a long time, she looked small and helpless, not the mean-spirited person that I knew. She was about to go away for a year, and even if the prison was a so-called "luxury farm," I felt sorry for her.

"Okay. I guess so."

Spencer unlocked the door for me, and I walked inside and took a seat across from my mother. Her eyes grew big. "You didn't give them the money, did you?" she demanded. She was frantic, and I didn't see the need to stress her out more.

"I didn't give it to them," I said, which was the literal truth. I never actually gave it to them.

"Good. I need you to hide it away. Somewhere where they can't find it."

"I don't think they'll ever find it."

I didn't have the heart to tell her that most of her money had gone up in a cloud of meth smoke and the rest was charred bits, now in the hands of the authorities. Later, when she was a safe distance away in her luxury farm, I would send her a letter telling her that her retirement money was long gone.

"It's a shame about Loretta," she said. "That was a good job."

"If you don't count the getting arrested part."

"Oh, please. They're sending me to a luxury farm. I could do that time standing on my head. It's like going to a spa, except they don't let me smoke."

"It might be a good thing to not smoke or drink for a year, Mom," I said. Maybe a year of clean living was exactly what she needed. A year where she was forced to live on the straight and narrow and clean up her act might turn her around.

"Gladie, if I could sell meth on a moped, I can find Jell-O shots at a luxury farm," she said, shooting down my plan to fix her life.

But it was the most we had spoken since I was twelve years old, and it wasn't exactly a sweet moment. There was no hug goodbye when I got up to leave. In fact, she was more interested in studying a hangnail than she was in saying goodbye to her only child.

I didn't expect more than that. Any distant memories I had of a loving mother went out the window when my father was taken from us. Just as my grandmother could never bear to leave her property again, my mother could never bear to be in a family again. My father had lost his life, but he took a chunk of ours with him.

I knocked on the door, and Spencer opened it to let me out. He took my hand and gave it a little squeeze. Behind him, two federal officers approached. They were wearing DEA and FBI jackets, and both looked very pleased with themselves.

"Okay, Chief," the FBI guy said. I figured he was in his fifties. He had slicked back hair, cut short, and his face was clean shaven except for the three hairs growing out of the mole on his cheek. "That was easy. In fact, this is the easiest case we've ever had. Everybody is snitching on everybody. I love when that happens."

Spencer perked up like a puppy given a bone. "Oh yeah? What did he say?"

The FBI guy glanced at me briefly, but I guess he decided I wasn't a threat and that he could talk in front of me. "He threw the cartel boys under a bus. He said that they wanted to do away with Fieldstone because he was getting too big for his britches, and they killed the other two guys to take the suspicion off of them. Make it look like a serial killing. Stupid, right? Nobody would think that was a serial killing."

I pawed the floor with my foot. I had been fooled. I thought it was a serial killing, at least for a while. But it made sense. Fieldstone was the point man for the cartel and when he got too power hungry, they offed him and killed the other two guys to take suspicion off of the cartel.

"What did you give him to make him turn over like that?" Spencer asked.

The DEA guy stepped forward and scowled. "He's only going up on drug trafficking and not taking the rap for the murders. He's also going to a minimum security farm in northern California under a different name so the cartel can't find him. He'll be out in ten years, probably."

Everything was solved, neat and tidy. It could've been wrapped in one of Loretta's fancy red ribbons, and it left me feeling sort of sad and alone. "I'm going to walk home," I said.

"We're going to take these three off your hands," the FBI guy told Spencer. "Where can we do the paperwork?"

Spencer looked from me to the feds and back to me. He stuck a finger up in the air. "You can take my office. I'll be right there." He grabbed me by my arm and pulled me away. With my back up against the wall he leaned in and studied my face.

"Are you all right? Do you want me to take you home?"

"I'm fine. Look at me. Not a scratch on me."

Spencer cocked his head to the side and raised an eyebrow. "Well…"

I put my hand up, palm forward. "No. Really, I'm fine. I want to walk myself home. Get some fresh air. It will do me good. Besides, my grandmother has given me a big assignment, and I can't let her down. She put me in charge of the Romance for the Holidays event at the Cannes Mountain Ski Resort. I have a lot of planning to do. I think it's my coming out party as a matchmaker."

Spencer smiled. "Good. Throw yourself into your work. Make a lot of couples happy. This is great news. No more murders. I think things are looking up, Pinky."

I tried to smile, but I felt worn out and a little down. I waved goodbye and left through the lobby. Fred was working as the desk sergeant, and he didn't look any happier than I was. He had his elbows on the desk, cradling his chin with his hands and staring out into space, as if someone had just shot his puppy.

As I passed, he didn't even greet me with his usual, "Hi, Underwear Girl".

"Are you all right, Fred?" I asked.

"Oh, hi," he moaned. I put my hand on his shoulder, and he shuddered.

"What's wrong?"

"I'm a drug addict. A drug trafficker. I'm a Czar."

I took a step back. I didn't think I could take one more shock today. It wasn't that hard to imagine my mother riding a mobile moped meth lab. It was harder to believe that the Christmas lady was breaking bad, and that the Mexican cartel had all but overrun our bucolic town. But Fred? Fred was a dopey innocent, someone who had always had a crush on me, and I couldn't believe that he would do anything illegal.

"I don't believe you, Fred. You're not any of those things," I said, taking a shot in the dark and trying to be positive. Fred was my first match. I couldn't let him go to the dark side.

He stood up straight. "I might as well be. All this time my landlady was a meth drug lord. And I happily lived in her house. I happily had a candy cane doorknob and a gingerbread closet. I didn't suspect a thing. I'm a failure at the very least, but I think I'm much worse."

Fred calling himself a failure struck a nerve with me.

"Loretta has been in this town for years, and no one suspected her, Fred. I didn't suspect her. Spencer didn't suspect her. Don't be so hard on yourself. You know what you need? You need to get away. Come next week to the Romance for the Holidays at the Cannes Mountain Ski Resort with Julie. It's going to be a lot of fun. I'll give you a thirty percent discount. Won't that be a nice change of pace?"

I regretted every word, instantly. As the words came out of my mouth, I knew I was being reckless and stupid. Romance for the Holidays was the biggest event I had ever done for my grandmother, and I needed it to be a success. The dynasty depended on it. But with Fred's danger prone girlfriend Julie there, it could mean all kinds of disasters. Perhaps another explosion. At the very least a fire. I made a mental note to ask Grandma about the ski resort's insurance policy.

My invitation perked Fred up, though, and he smiled again, which made my doubts wash away. I had done the right thing, no matter the danger.

"I do have some vacation days coming to me," he said. "Yes, that sure would be nice, Underwear Girl. I bet you're real pretty in a ski bunny outfit, outlined by snow up high in the mountains."

"Okay, then. I'll put you on the guest list. Come by the house tomorrow, and I'll give you the information."

Having something major to plan, something that I was in charge of and that people thought I could actually do, made me feel better. The sting of the explosion, my mother's arrest, and the mystery being solved without my help was dulled slightly, and when I left the police station, I enjoyed the cold air and the freedom of walking through town. After about fifteen minutes, I found myself back in the historic district, near Tea Time, and I decided to go inside for a latte.

The tea shop was enjoying a lull in the day, and I was the only customer. Ruth was busy cleaning off tables, and she barely glanced up when I walked in.

"You finished blowing up the town, so you thought you'd come in for some tea?" she asked. She walked over to the counter and studied my face, like she had never seen me before.

"No, I drink coffee after I blow up a town, but if you have any hooch, Ruth, would you consider putting it in my latte?"

"I'll make you a Kahlúa latte. You look like you could use it. But don't tell the cops. I don't have a liquor license." It was out of character for her to readily accept to make me coffee. She was a die-hard tea supporter.

I searched through my pocket for some cash and came up with three singed fifty-dollar bills. I put one on the counter. "Do you accept illegal money? I mean, just between us?"

Ruth pocketed the fifty. "I'm an equal opportunity American. If money got a little dirty, who am I to object? I'll put this toward your account."

I didn't have an account, but I guessed she was going to start one for me with the meth money. Boy, was I tired. With the first sip of the delicious Kahlúa latte, a wave of fatigue hit me.

"I can't believe it took this long for that woman to get

caught by the cops," Ruth said.

"You mean you knew?"

"Didn't the whole Christmas thing make your flesh crawl just a little?"

"I thought it was nice," I said, feeling charitable to Loretta for some reason. I had enjoyed working in her shop, and I was grateful that she had given me a chance when nobody else would.

"Whatever. Too much of a good thing is too much of a good thing, as far as I'm concerned, but what do I know? I'm just a successful businesswoman who survived through multiple wars and six Republican presidents."

I downed the rest of the latte in record time. Ruth took pity on me and filled my paper cup halfway with more Kahlúa and put a lid on it.

"Can I ask you one thing before you go?" Ruth asked. "What happened to your eyebrows? Is that a new look young people are sporting these days? You look kind of weird to me, but I've never been one for fashion. I've been painting on my eyebrows since my first hot flash."

"What are you talking about, Ruth?"

She pointed at my face with a long, bony finger. "You got no eyebrows, girl. It goes from your nose to your eyes and then it's forehead as far as the eye can see."

Ruth was a mean old lady, but she wasn't the type to make jokes or play tricks on people. That would take too much energy. My mouth got dry, and I took a big swig of Kahlúa. Very slowly I lifted my hand to my face and felt for my eyebrows.

Nope. There was nothing there.

Without another word, I ran to the bathroom and checked myself out in the mirror. I was eyebrowless. In their place were two little red strips where my eyebrows had gotten burned off by the meth explosion. Smooth as a baby's bottom. No waxing or laser treatment could ever get my face so smooth. No wonder everyone had been studying my face. Those finks. Why hadn't they told me I had no eyebrows?

It was just like people who don't let a person know when they have spinach between their teeth or that they tucked their dress into their pantyhose or that toilet paper was stuck to their shoe.

"Just perfect," I said to my reflection. "I might as well just shave my head and make it a match."

I skulked out of Tea Time with my Kahlúa to go cup. I kept my head down as I walked home, wishing for a hat or bangs or my eyebrows back. But it turned out that I didn't need to bother worrying about anyone noticing me, because Darth Vader and his stormtroopers were marching down the street with his theme music blaring, drawing everyone's attention.

I wondered if John Williams got a royalty every time the would-be mayor played his music. He looked none the worse for wear after his run-in with the stampede. He was back in his costume and shouting about Mexican drug lords, meth labs, and our mayor's complete failure to protect us from terrorist explosions.

He had a point, and I thought it was a good chance that Darth Vader was going to be the next mayor of Cannes.

Darth Vader and the Kahlua had distracted me so much that I had almost forgotten about my face by the time I reached home. I walked into the kitchen, looking for something to eat. Bird and her army of cosmetologists were there working on Grandma. She came every week to give Grandma a full beauty treatment, since Grandma couldn't come to her. Even if Grandma never left her property line, she always made sure to look her best. Today, she was wearing a knockoff Dior kaftan, which was one of the few loose-fitting outfits she owned.

Grandma sat on a chair with her hair in curlers. Bird was squirting permanent solution onto her head, while a young woman was taking a cheese grater to Grandma's heels. There was a full spread on the table, along with a half-eaten jar of peanut butter.

Bird gasped when she noticed me. I was a sight. A crime against cosmetology. A slap in the face of everything that she held sacred.

In other words, I was a mess.

It took a minute, but Bird finally regained her composure. "I'll teach you how to color on your eyebrows," she said, softly. "And here. Take this. It will help." She jammed a jar of peanut butter into the pocket of my shearling coat. She was taking pity on me. Pity on the woman with no eyebrows.

I sat down and sipped at my Kahlua. "Eyebrows are

overrated," Grandma said. "There are far more important things. Like love, for instance. And justice, of course. I'm glad Loretta's chemical experiment is over. We'll just buy our twinkle lights at Walley's from now on."

"I'm not allowed at Walley's either," I pointed out.

"We'll just have to widen our net," she said.

"But I don't have a car anymore."

"At least her eyebrows will grow back," Bird said. "I mean, they'll probably grow back. You're young. Don't worry about it. You'll learn to color them on. Not a problem."

"I need to get drunk," I said.

"I sensed you would," Grandma said. She instructed Bird to hand her the bottle of Jack Daniels and the glass that she had put on the counter for me. "Here you go, dolly. Get plastered. Now's a good time to tell you that Holden is planning on leaving, and he wants you to make a decision."

My stomach lurched. "I'm never making a decision again, Grandma," I said.

"Me neither, bubeleh. Decisions are for the dogs. That's why I like to feel things instead of think them. Go with my heart instead of my brain. It works for me."

I poured some Jack Daniels into a glass and took a sip. It burned all the way down. "Nothing works for me. Nothing at all."

"You have the Romance for the Holidays next week. It will be good. I feel like there's lots of love up in the snowy mountains."

Grandma was usually right about things that couldn't

be known. But even if she was wrong, I figured that the Romance for the Holidays couldn't be worse than a meth explosion.

CHAPTER 13

Happy. Happy. Happy. Did you know that the entire goal of Buddhists is to be happy? Not very Jewish, right? But happy is great, bubeleh. Happily ever afters are the best. But maybe it's not so wise to completely trust happy. Remember that happy has its ups and downs. There's a scale of happy. Sometimes you may be Disneyland happy, and sometimes you may be it's-not-raining happy. You understand? If your matches accept the sliding happiness scale, they'll be okay to be a little happy here and a little happy there and not go bananas if they're not happy all the time. So, when your matches come to you and complain about being sad, go back to them and tell them that they're not sad; their happy is just taking a break. See? Simple. Happy, now?

Lesson 14, Matchmaking Advice from your
Grandma Zelda

Heaven is room service.

And a complimentary pillowy robe.

And success.

I had all three. I was sitting in the luxury suite at the Cannes Mountain Ski Resort, an upgrade perk the management awarded me for bringing thirty paying customers with me to the Romance for the Holidays event that Grandma had organized. I was sitting in a gorgeous white chair with my feet propped up on the ottoman, and I was sipping coffee out of a fine china cup.

It was the morning of day two of Romance for the Holidays, and it was going without a hitch. Grandma had organized every day for me so I only had to follow the instructions. We had singles and couples attending with all kinds of activities, such as cocktail hours, marshmallow toasts, sleigh rides, and skiing.

The ski resort had its own staff for events, and they never dropped the ball. The thirty participants all seemed happy, and two singles had already become a couple. I was basking in the glow of success. Maybe Grandma was right. Perhaps I had the gift, and I was just as Dynasty as shoulder pads.

After the coffee, I took a vanilla-scented bath in my enormous sunken Jacuzzi bath, while I watched Brady Bunch reruns on a television built into the mirror on the marble wall and ate a giant-sized Toblerone from my mini-fridge.

I got dressed in jeans, a sweater, and boots. I blow-dried my hair and was careful with my makeup.

I was feeling great.

I arrived downstairs at the ski resort's restaurant in a special dining room reserved just for our event. Ten guests had already showed up and had started on their breakfasts. Uncle Harry was seated at one table, and Lucy was at his left. They were holding hands, and Lucy had a glow around her, as if she had swallowed a flashlight.

I made a round of the other tables, saying good morning to the other participants. I had felt strange at first being in charge, but now I was in my groove. This had always been my grandmother's role, while I was just the matchmaker-in-training and Zelda's granddaughter standing in the corner. Now at Romance for the Holidays, I was the one who gave out the advice.

So far, though, my advice was limited to lunch choices and how to make the perfect s'more. Group activities were just that... social events. But this morning started a series of workshops on finding love and keeping it, relationship advice, and generally how to keep the love alive. Grandma had prepared the classes, organizing everything in a binder, which I carried wherever I went. It was a big test for me.

"Dolly, you have the gift," my grandmother told me before I left. "But it doesn't hurt to have backup. Matches are just like the Wild West. I mean, Wyatt Earp had Doc Holliday to back him up. Remember that, bubeleh."

My Doc Holliday was a purple binder with eight, multi-colored dividers and bullet-point lists for each workshop. The first up was "Stumbling into Love," for the fourteen singles of the group. Grandma had given me topics, questions, and bios of each single.

I was nervous about running my first workshop, but with one successful day behind me, I couldn't help but believe that it would go without a hitch.

"Isn't it a beautiful day?" I cheered, as the dining room filled with more people.

"Gorgeous," Bridget agreed, sitting down. "There's French toast, right?"

Bridget had attended the Romance for the Holidays as a couple because, according to her, she was two people. "I want to show my son love, and I don't want him to grow up thinking he deserves love and doesn't have to give it," she had told me as she drove us up to the ski resort in her Volkswagen.

She was determined to raise the perfect man, and that was starting in utero. Every few minutes, she would direct the conversation to her unborn child, talking directly to him about the importance of women's rights and universal healthcare, among other progressive priorities.

I sat at a table with one couple and three singles, and I ordered pancakes and sausage links. "We're having a marvelous time," Tracy Ross, one half of the couple told me.

"Me, too," I said, smiling.

"It's just the right amount of romance, fun, and relaxation," she said.

It was life-changing being complimented on my

competence. And a first. "I'm so glad you're enjoying yourself."

If only I could have frozen that moment in time. The moment of my triumph. The moment where I could throw off a lifetime of temporary jobs and embrace my calling as a well above average matchmaker.

If only.

Unfortunately, it was a brief moment and destined not to last. In fact, I was the embodiment of proof that all good things must come to an end. Especially in my life. I just wished the good thing could have lasted a little while longer.

"Looky here! Looky here!" a familiar voice shouted in our private dining room.

"No," I breathed. "No, no, no, no, no."

A big hand slapped my back. "Careful of your breakfasts, Cannes residents! Remember, breaking wind is illegal in town limits."

"Well, I never," Tracy Ross said, clutching at her chest.

"Don't worry. What's done is done. Just don't let it happen again."

I turned around. Mayor Wayne Robinson was standing there in all his glory, dressed to the nines in a custom made suit and his signature camel coat. He smelled of high-priced cologne and stupidity.

And he was happy, smiling ear to ear. Delirious, even. He had brought an entourage with him, including George and Mary Trench, and they stood next to him, waiting for the mayor to tell them what to do.

With all the talk of farting, my table cleared out pretty quickly. The mayor and the Trenches took a seat next to me and ordered breakfast.

"This is a private event," I said.

"The more the merrier," the mayor said.

"You should be happy the mayor is visiting your group," Mary Trench sneered. "He gives it class and prestige."

"That's a load of donkey pucks," George Trench said, knocking back some coffee.

The mayor and his entourage seemed determined to stay, and there was no way for me to kick them out without making a scene. I was upset, but I reminded myself that it was just for breakfast and then I would have my group back, again. After this hiccough, all would go smoothly, I told myself.

"I'll have a double-stack of pancakes and bacon," George ordered.

"No. He'll have the oatmeal," Mary told the server.

George's face turned redder than normal. Hot air came out of his nose, as if his head had turned into a locomotive or a really pissed off bull. I scooched a little bit away from him on my chair. I had experience with explosions, and I wanted to be out of the range of shrapnel when his head exploded.

'Cause it looked like his head was going to explode. Mary Trench looked totally unconcerned, however. She barely gave him any notice at all. This seemed to enrage George Trench all the more. He harrumphed and tossed his napkin on the table. He stood, took out a packet of papers from his jacket pocket, and threw them at his wife.

"Mary Trench, you bitch from hell, you thorn in my side since the day I lost my mind and married you, I'm divorcing you," he announced, his voice rising above the noise in the room and quieting the other diners.

Mary blinked a few times, taking in the folded papers on her plate and her husband's triumphant expression, as he stood over us. Finally, he had gotten her attention.

"Because of pancakes?" she asked. Her voice had gone up an octave, and she was panting like a Chihuahua. It was like she had been struck by lightning, and in a way, she had.

"Because of pancakes, because of him," he said, pointing at the mayor. "And because I want to live before I die. Live! Live! Pancakes!" he shouted at the server and threw a wad of money at him.

He was meaner than spit and completely euphoric. He was a man reborn, ready to eat whatever he wanted and do whatever he wanted. I expected him to fart at any minute, just for spite. He pulled out a cigar from his coat and lit up. Nobody said a word about the no smoking rule in the resort.

In fact, nobody said a word about anything. Everyone's mouths were open, but no words came out. I got an eyeful of a half-dozen masticated meals. Even the mayor, who was so opposed to smelly farts, didn't make a peep about the smelly cigar smoke that filled the room.

"I'm going to eat whatever I want," George muttered under his breath. "I have balls, damn it!"

Mary's look of surprise morphed into vicious anger. Her shallow panting turned to heavy breathing, like her head had turned into a locomotive too, and it was speeding up. Now it was her turn to look like she was ready to blow, and I didn't want to be anywhere near her when she did. I was going to have to forfeit my breakfast.

"Remember singles, meet me in the lobby for 'Stumbling into Love' at ten while the couples have free time on the ski runs," I announced, hopping up from my seat and standing clear of the table.

I made it just in time. Mary jumped up and lunged for her soon-to-be ex-husband.

"And later, the Cannes Mountain Ski Resort's head chef is going to teach us how to make a hot toddy. Won't that be fun?" I continued, putting on a happy face.

Mary grabbed George's ears and pulled hard, as if she was trying to yank them off.

"Okay then," I shouted over George's screams. "Time to move the party outside and let the staff clean up breakfast."

I didn't need to tell them twice. It was getting ugly. Mary was going after George with a vengeance. The mayor was chewing on a fingernail, probably unsure what to do about his best campaign contributor going bonkers.

My singles and couples fled the room, and I followed them without looking back. I figured the mayor's entourage could get Mary under control and save George's ears. Besides,

I was pissed that they had invaded my peace and harmony and blown it all to hell.

Back in the lobby, I took deep healing breaths. I could barely hear George's screams from there, and I tried to clear my mind and get my mojo back. My group didn't seem too traumatized.

Bridget squeezed my arm. "I'm going to take a nap. I'll come to the Hot Toddy class, though. I'll make a virgin one, of course. Come on, son. Let's get some sleep," she told her stomach.

As she left, Uncle Harry and Lucy walked toward me. "Never a dull moment with you, Legs," Uncle Harry told me. "But you're slowing down. No dead people this time. Kind of boring."

"What do you think, Gladie? Is there going to be a murder?" Lucy asked with way too much enthusiasm.

"No. Of course not. This is Romance for the Holidays."

I gnawed the inside of my cheek. Was there going to be another murder? Was I going to find a body part and ruin the whole event and destroy my budding career?

I shook my head. No, this was just a blip. There were five more days at the ski resort, and there was no reason to believe that they wouldn't be as great as the first day. Just because Mary Trench was in the next room trying to kill her husband, didn't mean that Romance for the Holidays was a failure. It had just taken a slight detour.

Bridget left to take a nap in her room, and Lucy and

Uncle Harry left to do the dirty deed, I assumed. Things were already getting back to normal.

"Hey there, Underwear Girl!"

I whipped around. Fred was walking through the lobby, waving at me. His girlfriend Julie hovered by the door, looking up at the ceiling.

"Fred? I thought you couldn't come," I said.

He stopped a few inches from me, his tall lanky body casting a long shadow. "It turned out Julie didn't break a single bone, so we could come, after all. Hey Julie, come and show Gladie you're in one piece!" he called.

Julie shuffled her feet across the lobby. "Hello," she squeaked.

"Are you okay?" I asked.

"She practically bounced when she fell out that window," Fred answered for her. "It's like she's made of rubber."

I tried to swallow, but I had a lump in my throat. Julie might have been made of rubber, but she left a path of destruction in her wake wherever she went. My eyes darted to the sprinkler system on the ceiling and the various emergency exit signs, taking stock of the ski resort's defenses. Who was I kidding? There was no defense against danger-prone Julie.

"Are you two going to ski?" I asked, hoping they would take their disasters outside, away from the other guests.

"Aunt Ruth told me to stay away from pointy sticks," Julie squeaked.

"That may be wise," I said.

"I guess we should get checked in," Fred said.

"Good idea." I handed him a copy of the schedule of activities and sent a wish to the universe that Julie wouldn't set the guests on fire.

I took a deep, healing breath. It was still an hour before the workshop, but I noticed that the singles of the group were standing around the lobby, keeping to themselves in their shy single ways. They hovered, as if they didn't know where to go or what to do, and they focused on the ceiling or the walls, never making eye contact with each other. It was a matchmaker emergency.

I decided to take advantage of the moment and start the workshop early, which would also allow me to hide. While Fred and Julie checked in, I corralled the singles together and ushered them into the meeting room, which the resort had put aside for our needs.

They seemed relieved to be doing an organized activity, instead of left to their own devices. We sat in a circle, and I asked each single to introduce themselves and discuss a little about their dating experiences.

"My last boyfriend squeaked when we had sex," Moira Jones said, introducing herself. She was a forty-something apple picker with red hair. "He had two cheap hip replacements. The man wouldn't spend a dime even if he was threatened with death. So he refused the titanium and went for some scrap metal. Anyway, he squeaked. I don't want a squeaky boyfriend. Squeaky isn't sexy. It's such a turn-off. I want a guy who goes for the titanium."

I searched through the binder, frantically looking for words of wisdom about titanium, but I couldn't find a thing. I shuffled through the papers, past notes on orgasms, race cars, and threesomes, but there was nothing on replacement hips. In Moira's section, Grandma wrote "needs an accountant or a Teamster. Someone with job security… And a large penis."

I coughed and turned the page. Meanwhile, another single introduced himself.

"I'm Jimmy, and I don't squeak." He was a hedge fund manager, who had a vacation home in Cannes. He was a short man with a heavily pockmarked face. Moira shot him an approving look and smiled.

Introductions continued around the circle until it got to the last single. She was a young woman in a long shapeless dress and gray cardigan. There was no makeup on her face, and her long brown hair was tied back in a ponytail. She didn't make eye contact, and I got the idea that if she could make herself invisible, she would.

"I'm Fionnula Jericho," she half-whispered, talking into her chest. "My mother gave me this trip."

She didn't sound pleased with the gift. In fact, she looked pained to be there, not exactly a swinging single. Grandma's notes on Fionnula said that she was a grade A introvert and some kind of author, who wrote under a pen name and lived her life pretty much incognito. I wondered what she wrote, but it was obvious that she wouldn't welcome any questions. She was like a little mouse.

Mousy.

"You're going to fall in love next month," I heard myself say to her. "It's going to be a rocky road at first, but you're going to have your happily ever after. So don't worry at all."

I patted her knee. Her mouth had dropped open, and she made eye contact with me for the first time. My mouth had dropped open, too. I didn't know where the words had come from. It was as if I was channeling some other being, which spoke for me. But however I said it, I was completely sure I was right. I saw it clearly in my mind. Fionnula Jericho was going to fall in love in the next month.

Was this what my grandmother experienced on a daily basis? Could I really have the gift, just like she had been telling me for months? It seemed ludicrous. Impossible. It had to be some kind of fluke. I shook my head, trying to shake the surprise out of me, and I started the workshop.

"Stumbling into Love," I started. "Love is a mystical emotion. We can't plan for it. There's no strategy to fall in love. It's not D-Day. So, we stumble around and suddenly, we find that special someone."

I had no idea what I was talking about. Grandma had prepped me for the workshop, but I could have been reciting the Pledge of Allegiance, for all I knew. I knew nothing about love. Nothing. I knew that there was heartache and heartbreak involved, not to mention disappointment and resentment...all after an initial hormone-induced euphoria. But beyond that, I was clueless.

None of that mattered. They ate what I was serving. I was inspirational. I gave them hope. By the end of my spiel and the Q&A, they were all sure that they were going to "stumble into love" at any moment, probably by the end of our week at the ski resort. All except for Fionnula…now that she was finally giving me eye contact, she was giving me the stink eye. She didn't trust me. I had given her a crazy prophecy, and she was looking at me as if I was a side-show con man fortune-teller.

After the workshop, the singles filed out. I wanted to talk with Fionnula and redeem myself, but she left in a hurry. I struggled to catch up to her as she power-walked toward the elevators, probably to return to her room and hide. By the time I caught up with her, she was in an elevator and the doors were closing.

I pushed the up button and tapped my foot, impatiently. Christmas carols were piped through a speaker above the elevators, but suddenly the music was drowned out by Darth Vader's theme.

No way.

I slapped my ears, hoping that I was hearing things. Nope. The theme music got louder, which was followed by loud shouts of complaints coming from the lobby. I looked longingly at the elevator and my chance to escape. But I had a duty as the matchmaker in charge to look out for my matches. I couldn't leave them in the hands of the Empire. I decided Fionnula could wait while I saw what the commotion was about.

In the lobby, Mayor Robinson was going toe to toe with Darth Vader. The mayor was about a foot taller than his opposition, but Darth had his backup stormtroopers with him, who were pretty imposing.

The mayor's usual backup, Mary Trench, was sitting shell-shocked on a chair, her legs flopped open, giving an eyefull of her Spanx. George Trench wandered in, holding a bottle of booze in one hand and a blond forty-something in the other. He was still smoking a cigar, and he had lost his tie. His mouth was turned up in a huge smile.

He was a pig in shit.

"No more crazy morons to suck up my money!" he shouted, as he walked through the room. "You want to see my snowmobile, doll? I just bought it." His doll seemed more than happy to see his snowmobile. Mary moaned and dropped her head between her knees.

"These are not the droids you've been looking for," Darth Vader told the mayor.

The mayor snorted, choked, and fingered his cufflinks. "What on earth are you talking about? This is my event. You're bogarting my event. My people don't want a crazy, delusional mayor."

At the very least, it was an ironic thing to say.

The face-off was a great sideshow. It was getting a lot of attention from the ski resort's guests. The staff was not amused, however, and they were trying to break it up between the politicians. Young men and women wearing khakis and golf shirts with the resort's logo on their breast pockets were going after the mayor and his entourage and Darth Vader and his stormtroopers, trying to kick out anyone who was politically active.

It was all hands on deck.

All except for the guy at reception, checking in Fred and Julie. He was too busy screaming and trying to staunch the flow of blood from his hand.

I ran past the melee in the lobby and made a beeline for Fred and Julie at the reception desk. "What did you do? What did you do?" I demanded.

"Nothing," squeaked Julie. "Well, I might have stabbed him with the pen."

I turned on Fred. "You let her sign in?" I screeched.

"I got distracted," he said, wringing his hands.

"I'm dying!" the guy at reception was panicking pretty bad. He held his hand up, and blood dripped down, splattering the counter. The world spun around, and I gripped onto the counter to steady myself before I passed out. I couldn't stand the sight of blood, no matter how many dead people I had seen.

"I'll save you," Julie squeaked.

"No!" I shouted. "Fred, get her out of here before she kills another one."

"Kills another one?" the reception guy moaned. His cow eyes swirled around in their sockets.

"I have a Band Aid," Fred announced, happily.

"Get out of here!" I yelled.

With his good hand, the reception guy handed them

their key card, and they trotted away past the mayoral candidates, who were being ousted by the resort staff. "I'm going to sue you," he told me. "I'm going to have you arrested."

I rolled my eyes. "Amateur," I said.

His bleeding got the attention of another resort employee, and he was taken away to get bandaged up. Meanwhile, the lobby action had degenerated to dangerous levels. Pushing and shoving was involved. Half of my matches were caught in the fray.

"Perfect," I muttered. I tried to extricate a couple, but they didn't seem to want to leave the action. It was bedlam. It was Altamont.

If two dozen khaki-wearing athletic types couldn't stop the fracas, I couldn't do a thing. So, I threw in the towel. My event had turned to crap. A disaster. I was a failure again.

Outside, I pulled my singed shearling coat around me and breathed in the cold fresh air. Back inside the ski resort, the mayor and Darth Vader had staked out the lobby, both refusing to budge, trying to prove some kind of point about their territory and their claim to political power in Cannes.

Four of the Romance for the Holidays participants left Romance For the Holidays early because of the mayoral campaign ruckus, George Trench's smoking, and a general fear of Julie. Five others wanted to leave, but I convinced them to stay by starting the Hot Toddy class early and getting them blotto.

Now my group was either sleeping it off in their rooms, getting it on in their rooms, or in Bridget's case, sleeping off a second breakfast and in Fionnula's case, hiding from me. I was hiding, too. With all the commotion, my Grandmother's carefully crafted schedule was turned around, and I didn't know how to re-organize it.

And I needed to breathe without anyone approaching me with problems, concerns, or complaints. I was overwhelmed and didn't know how to get back on track. I didn't know how to fix it.

So, I was hiding outside where nobody could find me. Until…

"What are you doing? Are you hiding?"

"Oh my God," I said, startled. "What are *you* doing here?"

CHAPTER 14

Tell your matches this: never talk about the ex. You get me? Never. Why do they always want to talk about the ex? Ex is the past. Forget about it! Unless they're an archaeologist, they need to leave the past in the past. Move on! The future is where it's at. Or at least it's where it's going to be. So your heart was broken. So, he said this or she said that. So what? What does that have to do with the here and now? With the current? Just like fish, go with the current. Yep, tell them that, dolly.

Lesson 75, Matchmaking Advice from your
Grandma Zelda

"What are you doing here?" I demanded, again.

Spencer was dressed in an expensive ski suit, pants and a parka, black from head to toe with reflective sunglasses that shot my image back to me. I looked surprised and slightly pissed off. I was. These days, Spencer's presence meant that something was going to explode or I was going to find a dead person or get fired or all three. He was always around when I screwed up.

He pointed to the two tall skis that he held with his right hand. "What do you think I'm doing, Pinky?"

"Now? Here? Why?"

He gestured to the building behind me. "Ski resort. Snow. The perfect time and the perfect location to ski. Don't you think so?" He arched an eyebrow and smirked his annoying little smirk. "Why?" he continued. "Do I make you nervous?"

"No."

He stepped closer. "Do you feel your heart racing? Your body quivering? Your loins on fire?"

It was like he was a mind-reader. "No," I lied. "Just annoyed."

"From unresolved desire?"

"From annoyance."

He raised an eyebrow and leaned forward. He smelled of pine and vanilla icing. "From desire?" he purred low in his throat.

I unbuttoned my coat and fanned myself. "I thought you were going skiing."

"I was just being cordial."

I stomped my foot. "Listen, don't mess with me. I have Romance for the Holidays. I'm in charge."

"Oh, a promotion," he said.

"Exactly. I'm a professional, now. No more crap jobs. This is going off without a hitch."

The front doors of the resort burst open, and Darth Vader and his stormtroopers marched out. "No Mexican cartels in our town!" the mayoral candidate shouted through his helmet, which had some kind of microphone device that blared his message to the skiers.

"You were saying?" Spencer asked me.

"I can't help it if it's an election year. It has nothing to do with my event."

"Don't turn around," Spencer said.

"Why?"

"Don't turn around," he repeated.

I turned around.

Mary Trench had me in her sights. She pushed a couple of stormtroopers out of her way and double-timed toward me in her Chanel suit and sensible heels. "You!" she shouted.

"I think she's talking to you," Spencer pointed out.

She wagged her finger in my face. Mary was scary when she wasn't angry, but now she was madder than hell and terrifying. Her initial shock had turned to rage. Her husband had left her in the most humiliating way possible, and she wanted revenge. "What did you do to him?"

"Me? Nothing!"

"Tell the truth, Pinky," Spencer said, smirking. "What did you do to him?"

I wanted to stab him in the eye.

243

"I didn't do a thing!"

"You made him go crazy," Mary growled. "You and your meth lab and Mexican cartel, chopping up his baseball team. You did this!"

"It wasn't me!"

"Look at the time," Spencer said. "I have to mosey over to the slopes. I want to get in a couple of runs before the weather changes. You want to come with me, Pinky?"

"No. Why would I want to do that?"

"She's not going anywhere," Mary spat. "She's going to make this right. You're going to talk to George."

"You sure you don't want to go with me, Pinky?" Spencer asked.

I looked from Spencer to furious Mary and back again. I stepped behind him. "You have a point," I said from behind Spencer's back. "I have to do a run before the weather changes, Mary. How about we talk about this later?"

Mary Trench was a difficult woman to convince. There was no way she was going to let me get away, no matter how much I begged and slapped her hands as they grabbed for my coat's lapels.

But Mary reacted to Spencer's badge when he fished it out of his parka and flashed it at her. She reluctantly let me free with the warning that she would catch me later, and I would make restitution, whatever that meant.

"She's mean," I told Spencer, straightening my coat, after Mary left. "Do you think I need to worry about her?"

"How fast can you run?"

Spencer snapped on his skis, and we went toward the ski lift. I was wearing non-waterproof boots, and my feet were getting wet, but it was better than taking my chances with crazy Mary.

"Shall we start again?" Spencer asked. "Funny meeting you here."

"Yeah, it's a laugh riot."

"You can make a roundtrip on the lift. By the time you get back, she'll be long gone, and you can continue hiding."

"I wasn't hiding," I lied.

I watched the chairs hover on a thick wire, climbing up and down the mountain slowly. It didn't look safe, but I didn't want to be a chicken in front of Spencer, and besides, he was right. It was a good way to give Mary Trench the slip, and perhaps when I returned, everything would be back to normal.

Spencer was right about the weather changing, too. It had gotten darker and windier. Most of the skiers were returning inside the resort for the promise of hot cider and roasted marshmallows. The ski lift line had thinned out completely, and the chair lift was row after row of empty chairs.

"Get ready," Spencer said, and gave me a shove. The chair came around, and he hopped on. I was having more trouble, running to keep up as I tried to get the seat under me. Spencer's arm came around my middle and hoisted me up. A second later, we were ten feet off the ground and twenty feet a second after that. I held on for dear life.

"I'm not sure I'm seeing the logic of throwing yourself off a mountain in the freezing cold," I said.

"I don't throw myself off. I become one with nature, skillfully and masterfully conquering the slopes like an Olympic athlete."

I wanted to make fun of him, but he looked like an Olympic athlete just sitting on the chair next to me, so I could imagine what he looked like mastering the slopes.

Imagining it made my mouth turn dry and my insides heat up.

"I like seeing you like this," he said. I touched my face, self-conscious.

"I can't get the hang of it. I do the right one just fine, but the left is always wonky."

"I don't mean your eyebrows," he explained.

"Oh."

He put his hand on mine, and my heart raced. "I meant seeing you as the matchmaker. It suits you," he said.

I studied him, trying to figure out if he was lying or not. "What are you talking about? You didn't see me matching. You only saw me hiding."

"I might have seen you before that."

"You what?"

A gust of wind hit us, and the chair swung sharply on the wire. I scrambled against Spencer to catch my balance, but I was terrified that even if I didn't fall out of the chair, the chair was going to fall off the wire.

"I've got you," Spencer said, hugging me. "The chair will stop swinging in a second."

I settled into his arms, which wrapped around me easily. My head rested on his chest, and I could hear his heart beat even through his thick parka. He was warm and all kinds of comfortable. He was also right about the chair. It stopped swinging. In fact, we stopped moving altogether. We hung in the air, high above the ground, like birds sitting on a wire.

His hands moved on my back, and I leaned in, wrapping my arms around him. It felt good. Better than good. It felt like home. Ever so gently, his lips touched the top of my head. I sighed, exhaling a body full of emotions that I had denied for months.

My warning bells about Spencer were drowned out by our quiet, honest moment. There were no lies in his embrace, and for the first time since I met him, I trusted him.

We balanced precariously on a wire with a cold wind blowing. It was a metaphor for any sort of relationship that I could have with Spencer. Did I want a life lived in fear of falling? No, I didn't. I wanted a life on the safe ground, not balancing on a thin wire.

I didn't have to worry about relationship metaphors for very long because our quiet moment only lasted a minute. Another gust of wind hit us, and this one was twice as strong as the last. It came out of nowhere and whipped our chair from side to side. It wasn't a one-time shot. The gusts kept coming, and they brought snow with them. From one minute to the next, we were surrounded by what seemed like a tornado. It was complete white-out.

"I'm slipping!" I shouted. My body fell out from under me until I was hanging off the chair, held on only by Spencer's hold around my middle. "Do you have me? Do you have me?" I yelled, panicking.

"Nope!" he yelled back.

"Nope? What do you mean, nope?" His grip slipped from around my middle to my arms and then down to my wrists. "How about now? Do you have me now?"

"Nope! I said nope! Don't you understand nope?" he shouted. "I don't have you! I don't have you! Haven't you figured that out?"

"Don't get pissy with me!"

He grunted and tried to pull me up, but with the wind, snow, and his skis, he was getting nowhere. "I'm not getting pissy!" he bellowed, his voice strained.

The chair was being blown around like a ride at a carnival. I figured I was dead either way, but I preferred to take my chances with my butt in the chair. "Pull me up!"

Spencer grunted, as if he was going to pass a kidney stone and then miraculously, he yanked me up. He had saved me. I managed to right myself and sit on the chair, but while I did, I didn't notice that Spencer had lost his balance and was going over.

"Sonofabitch!" he yelled.

I watched him fall over face first, as if he was Greg Louganis, diving into a pool instead of a blizzard. My mouth opened to scream, but nothing came out. I had gone mute from the horror of watching Spencer fall to his death. The storm had gone from bad to Wizard of Oz in a matter of seconds. I held on to the chair as it whipped around. But I wasn't scared about my personal safety anymore. I was stuck on the fact that I had killed Spencer.

No matter how much of a womanizing jerk he was, he didn't deserve to plummet to his death. He had died saving me, and I didn't know how to live with that.

I started to weep. Big tears dropped from my eyes and froze on my cheeks.

"Help!" I heard a small desperate cry. It was my guilt talking to me. I would never get over Spencer's sacrifice. I would be forever altered. Traumatized.

"Help! Help! Sonofabitch! Help me!"

My guilt sounded a lot like Spencer. A dead-ringer. The memory of him was already haunting me. But in the off-chance that it wasn't my guilt talking, I leaned over and looked down.

Spencer's skis had been knocked off, and his legs were hooked on the metal bar under the chair. He was hanging there like a bat. A naked bat. His pants had gotten hooked on the chair as he fell and were pulled down to his ankles. I got an eyeful.

"You're naked," I said.

"No shit."

"Isn't this how we met?" I asked. I had first seen Spencer when I was hanging upside down on a telephone pole and he was part of my rescue team. Now the tables had turned, although there was no sign of first responders coming to his rescue.

"Help me up!"

"But I was wearing underpants. I didn't know you went commando, Spencer."

I could hear him growl over the sound of the raging blizzard. "Underwear chafes me," he said.

I gave him a good look. "You don't have much commando there, Spencer. I was expecting…I don't know…more."

His body shook, and he threw his arms around like he was slapping an invisible Gladie. "It's cold!"

"Uh huh," I said.

"My junk is out in a blizzard. What do you expect?"

I shrugged. "More. A lot more."

"If I live through this, I'll show you more. Help me up. I'm slipping."

With one hand, I held on to the chair railing, and with the other hand I managed to grab onto his ankle. I yanked on him, but he didn't budge.

"What are you doing?" he demanded. "Take my hand! Take my hand!"

He stretched his hand out. I let go of his ankle and I leaned down as far as I could go and tried to grab his hand.

But his hand was too far away.

The good news was that when I fell off the ski lift, I knocked Spencer free. More good news was that there was a large snowdrift underneath us that broke our fall. I mean, broke Spencer's fall because Spencer broke my fall when I fell on him.

"I'm alive!" I cried, surprised when I landed on him.

We didn't spend any time checking for broken bones. Spencer insisted that we get to shelter before we were killed by the blizzard. He pulled his pants up over his frozen privates and took my hand, which was also frozen. My beautiful shearling coat wasn't made for blizzards, and it occurred to me that Spencer was right: I wouldn't last long in this weather.

Even though it was the middle of the day, it was dark as night and treacherous. We were high up on the mountain, and there wasn't another person in sight. There were no sirens, and it didn't look like anyone was coming to our rescue.

I had no idea where we were or where we were going, but I held on tight to Spencer's hand and followed him, as he trudged through the snow. If he had a plan or not, I didn't know, but within a few minutes, we had crossed over the run into a stand of trees.

Walking in the snow in my boots was difficult but probably not as difficult as walking in Spencer's ski boots. Under the partial shelter of the trees, he stopped and looked around, getting his bearings. It was all trees to me, and I could see no discernible way out of our mess. I stomped my feet, trying to stay warm, but I was starting to freeze.

Spencer took his gloves off and gave them to me. "I can't take those. You need them," I said.

"Put them on. Don't argue."

As I put them on, there was a loud noise, and we ducked. "Was that a gun shot?" I asked, squatting low to the ground.

We heard the noise again, and I covered my head with my hands. "No," Spencer said. "It's not a gunshot."

He yanked me up, and we walked as fast as we could. Spencer seemed to have a destination in mind, and I hoped he was right. We trudged through the snow, past countless trees. I was exhausted, cold, and wet, but I didn't dare stop, and I didn't dare complain. The blizzard was worse now without any end in sight.

Just as I thought I couldn't go on any longer, we stumbled on to a large cabin. Its front door was open, and it slammed shut from the wind as we approached. It was the noise that I had mistook for a gun firing.

"Come on," Spencer said.

It was obvious that the cabin was empty, but it wasn't abandoned. The outside was painted and well cared for. Welcoming. We practically skipped toward it and quickly entered, closing the front door behind us.

Spencer tried the light switch, but the electricity was out, and the inside of the cabin was dark but maneuverable. A large fireplace was the centerpiece of the living room, and there was plenty of firewood next to it. Spencer stacked the wood and built a fire. I went into the kitchen, which was stocked with some staples. I turned on the gas stove and heated water for tea. When the water boiled, I filled two mugs with hot tea and brought them into the living room along with a box of saltines.

The living room had warmed up quickly under the power of the roaring fire. Through the living room's windows, I could see that the blizzard was getting even more serious. I was grateful for a place to wait it out.

Spencer sat on the sofa in front of the fireplace. He had taken off his boots and parka, and I did the same. I put my wet socks near the fire to dry. When I took my coat off, I discovered the jar of peanut butter that Bird had stuck in the pocket.

"Hallelujah!" I shouted in victory, holding up the jar of crunchy.

I sat on the couch next to Spencer and offered him a cup of tea. He took it gratefully, and we both sipped the hot liquid and watched the flames in the fireplace, enjoying our miracle.

I put my feet on the coffee table and let the fire warm them. I was feeling comfortable again after our harrowing ordeal. Finishing my tea, I opened the peanut butter and scooped some out with a saltine cracker, handing it to Spencer.

"Thanks. That hits the spot," he said, munching on the cracker. I scooped up some for me, too.

"This is cozy," I said. "Much better than naked in a

elise sax

blizzard, right Spencer?" I shot a look at his crotch.

"Hey, I'll show you Mr. Happy now that I'm not frozen, Pinky."

"You mean Mr. Tiny?"

"One word, and I'll strip down, but I'm not sure you can handle the awesome power of my hugeness."

"Hugeness, huh?"

He put his thumb in his waistband and gave it a tug. I shook my head. "Okay. Okay. I believe you. No need to free Mr. Tiny. I mean, Mr. Happy."

"Poor Mr. Happy," he muttered, scooping more peanut butter out of the jar with another cracker.

"Do you go skiing often?" I asked, changing the subject from his penis.

"Nah. I've only skied a few times. Mostly, I went on ski trips in high school. You know, for the girls."

"Duh."

"Duh," he agreed.

"So your womanizing jerk ways go back a long time," I said.

"I've chased a few skirts, but I'm working on only one woman these days."

My heart sank. I lost my appetite for peanut butter and crackers. "Svetlana," I said. Of course, the model. I sucked in my stomach.

"Svetlana? No. I don't like to sleep with a bag of bones."

I let my stomach relax. "*You* don't like to sleep with a

254

bag of bones. You?"

"What are you saying?"

"You've slept with every model in Southern California."

He raised an eyebrow. "Slight exaggeration. I'm sure I missed a few."

"Man whore."

He shifted his weight onto one hip and turned to look at me. "Since we're talking about whores, Gladys..."

"Don't call me Gladys. Or the other thing."

"Just sayin'." His face was inches away from mine. His lips were chapped red from the cold, and he had perfect dark stubble on his face. But his eyes said a lot of things I didn't want to hear.

"I haven't touched a model," I said.

He counted on his fingers. "An explorer. A UFC fighter. An explorer while you were with a UFC fighter."

"Not true," I said, desperate to defend my reputation to him. "I was never serious about the UFC fighter."

"You were pretty serious about him."

"No I wasn't," I insisted.

"Yes you were. You were over there all the time."

"Not true. Just once in a while and not for long. Hey, how do you know? Were you spying on me?"

Spencer got up and put another log on the fire. "I don't spy," he said with his back to me. "I'm a cop. I do twenty-four hour surveillance with the world's best technology."

He came back to the couch and plopped down. "Twenty-four hours?" I asked.

He shrugged. "In this case, random surveillance bursts. You were there a lot."

I smiled. "Oh."

"Oh?"

"You were jealous."

"Jealous is a stretch," he said, running his hand over his hair.

"Jealous," I repeated. "You have a thing for me."

"Yes I do, and I'll show it to you now that I've warmed up." His smile dropped, and he turned serious. "I have no idea what you saw in the guy."

"He has a very nice Mr. Happy."

Spencer squirmed in his seat. "Pinky, never tell a man about another man's Mr. Happy."

"What if he's a urologist?" I asked.

He ignored that comment. "But it's over?"

I nodded. I noticed he didn't ask about Holden. I also noticed he didn't say a thing about his intentions. He was jealous, but was he even interested in me? It was insulting that he would grill me about my sex life but he wasn't offering anything to replace it. He wasn't offering himself.

"I'm sick of the whole thing," I said.

"What whole thing?"

"The dating. The game. The first guy who asks me to marry him, I'm going to say yes." I didn't know what I was saying. The idea of marriage made the back of my neck break out in hives. Spencer didn't look any more comfortable than I was.

"How did we get on this topic?" I asked, changing the subject. "I thought we were talking about skiing. You love to ski."

"No. I didn't say that. I'm a baseball man."

"Baseball's the one with the hoop, right?"

"No. You can make fun of a lot of things, Pinky, but don't make fun of my baseball. That's sacrilege."

His breath smelled like peanut butter and something else. Something serious. But with the baseball talk, he relaxed. He put his feet up on the coffee table next to mine and grabbed the jar of peanut of butter. I handed him another cracker.

"Were you upset about the Prickly Pears? Were you a fan?" I asked.

"I'm a Padres fan, you know. But I like to support minor league teams, as well. The Prickly Pears are local, so sure, I was upset. It's a beautiful sport, and I don't like to see it mired in illegal activities."

It was shocking that a Mexican cartel was active in our little community and that it's representative was the trainer of the local baseball team. It had set off a chain of senseless murders and scarred our town.

I wondered if it had also scarred the owner of the team, George Trench, and that's why he went bonkers and decided to divorce his wife, suddenly.

Spencer's mind went to the Trenches, as well. "Mary

Trench sure was pissed at you."

"She blames me for her husband dumping her. How is that my fault?"

He arched an eyebrow. "No comment."

"He's really enjoying the whole divorce thing," I said. "He already bought a snowmobile and a blond. He's only seconds away from getting a yacht and a Corvette."

"Do you blame him?" Spencer asked. "He's free from that witch. If I were him, I would skip down Main Street, shouting *yahoo*."

"Once she realizes he's serious, she's going to take him for everything he has."

Spencer scooped more peanut butter with a cracker and handed it to me. "Well, he's worth a lot less now, you know."

"What do you mean?"

"The team. Its entire management got murdered. The team is worth next to nothing now. It has to be rebuilt. George Trench can buy his wife out for peanuts."

The atoms in the air rearranged themselves. Matter itself changed form. I heard a buzzing noise as the room filled with electricity. I replayed Spencer's startling words in my mind. *George Trench can buy his wife out for peanuts.*

Two plus two was finally equaling four.

I froze, raising my arms out at my sides, as if I had to catch my balance. A lightning bolt had hit my brain, and it was swirling with deductive reasoning, throwing me completely off balance. I was jittery, ready to explode.

Forget Miss Marple; I was Sherlock Holmes. We had been so wrong. Totally wrong. But now I had figured it out. I was sure I was right. I had solved a mystery that nobody thought existed. I was itching to blurt out what I had realized, how I had solved the murders of the Prickly Pears team, and that the truth was nothing like anyone thought. Not the police. Not the FBI. Not the DEA. I was the only one who knew the truth.

But I had to play it cool in front of Spencer. He didn't like it when I sleuthed, and he would be annoyingly bossy and condescending if I let on about my epiphany. He might not even believe me. He would tell me to mind my own business. I had to wait until I could prove I was right.

"You're getting a look in your eyes," Spencer said. "I know that look."

"No look," I said. "I have no look."

I bit my lip and tried not to have a look. But my body was vibrating. I didn't know how long I could hold back.

"Why are your arms out to the side?" he asked. I couldn't stand it any longer. I was going to blow.

"Holy shit!" I yelled and stood up.

"Did something bite you?"

"Oh my God! Oh my God!"

I had to tell him or tell someone. Now that I knew who the real murderer was, I couldn't hold it in. As much as I was freaking out, Spencer freaked out more. He jumped up and ran his hands over his head. "What is it? Are you okay? Are you having a stroke? I'll get you something to drink." He ran into the kitchen and came back with a warm can of root beer.

He opened the can and handed it to me. I swigged half of it and belched loudly. The desire to blurt out my revelation calmed, and I was in control, again. I could hold back telling Spencer anything until I could prove I was right.

"Better?" he asked.

I nodded and slumped down on the couch. He sat next to me and put his arm around my shoulders and pulled me close. "I know why you're acting this way," he said. His voice was soft and deep and made my insides turn to mush.

"You do?" I asked, breaking into a sweat.

"Yes. Of course. It's about what you told me the day your mother was arrested."

I had no idea what he was talking about. "Huh? What are you talking about?"

He caressed my arm and nuzzled my ear. It felt wonderful, and my body reacted to him. My mouth dropped open, and I sighed.

"You know. Don't deny it," he said, softly.

I scooted closer to him. "Don't deny what?"

"The thing you said."

"What thing?"

He stopped caressing my arm and pulled away from me. "The thing. The thing."

"I have no idea what you're talking about."

"The thing. You know. The thing."

"What thing?"

Spencer pursed his lips, as if he had eaten a lemon. He removed his arm from my shoulder and got up to stoke the fire. After a couple of seconds, he whipped around and sliced his hand through the air, as if he was karate chopping an invisible person.

"You told me you loved me!" he shouted.

I gasped. "What are you talking about? I did no such thing."

"Yes, you did." He was so head up that he spit when he talked.

"Are you kidding? No, I didn't."

He paced the floor in front of me, gesturing with his hands with each word. "I dropped you off at your Grandma's. You said goodbye, and then you said you loved me."

"I think I would remember if I said something like that," I insisted.

But then I stopped talking. A kernel of a memory popped in my brain. "Oh my God," I breathed. He was right. When he dropped me off at my house, I had told him I loved him and ran into the house.

"But I didn't mean it," I said.

Spencer stopped pacing and pointed at me. "You meant it."

"I was distracted. It was just reflex, a figure of speech."

"Not a figure of *your* speech, Gladys!"

"Don't call me Gladys!" I rubbed my temples, trying to clear my head.

Spencer sat back down. He took my hands in his. "I

didn't come to the resort to ski," he said. "I came for you."

The earth shook. My reality shook. My hands shook in his.

"For me? I don't understand."

"I came for you to be with you because…you know."

His eyes were dark with emotion and focused entirely on me.

"I know?"

"Because you know… that thing you said to me."

I cocked my head to the side. "It's like you have reverse Tourette's."

His forehead was covered in a layer of sweat, and it was dripping down his face. "You know. The thing you said to me."

I knew, but I wasn't going to say it again. Not unless he said it, and even then, I wasn't sure my mouth could say the words.

"You…the thing I said?" I asked.

His chest rose and fell with his deep breathing. His eyes were dark with passion. I gasped. It occurred to me that it might be possible that Spencer Bolton loved Gladys Burger. I started to sweat, too. Could it be true? After all these months, watching Spencer womanize, he really loved me? The player was done playing, and he wanted to get serious with me? It was like hearing that the sun was going to rise in the west from now on. I was disoriented.

"I…" he started.

I leaned forward to be sure to hear the words when he

uttered them, but he didn't say the words. Instead, Spencer was interrupted when the door burst open. A gust of wind and rain hit us, and I could have been knocked over with a feather when George Trench walked in.

"The world's coming to an end out there!" he announced, stomping his snow boots on the floor. "My damned snowmobile ran out of gas. I thought it was good for a few hundred miles. Who knew?"

He walked straight to the fireplace and warmed his hands, seemingly not at all surprised to find Spencer and me in a cabin in the middle of the woods on top of a mountain during a blizzard. Spencer introduced us to him, again, because he didn't seem to recognize us. He was too centered on himself and his newfound freedom from his wife.

"I should have bought a yacht," he said. "Yachts don't run out of gas, and they're warmer. I guess I'll buy one after this trip. It'll go great with the new house I'm buying in Key West. What's that? Peanut butter?"

He sat down and dug into the peanut butter. He regaled us a while longer about how his wife was a bitch and how he was going to buy every large luxury toy he could find. After a life of working hard, he explained, he was going to live the life he wanted. That meant living large with toys and women and not rotting in a small town and suffering fools like the mayor.

As he continued with his narcissistic monologue, I surreptitiously backed up toward the fireplace and grabbed the poker. I whipped it around and brandished it at him.

"Get back! Get back!" I shouted at him.

Spencer swiped the poker out of my hands. "What are you doing? That's dangerous."

It was now or never to announce my revelation. Without proof, I had to tell Spencer what was what and hope that he would believe me. It was a matter of life and death. I pointed at George Trench. "You're the murderer! You! I know the truth. Cartel smartel. You killed them to lower the value of the team so you could get a better deal in your divorce!"

"Gladie, have you lost your mind?" Spencer demanded.

"He did it. He did. With the team's value shot to hell, he could buy Mary out for peanuts and lead the life he wants. He probably has all kinds of money socked away, but the team would have cost him big."

George's mouth dropped open, giving me an eyeful of half-eaten peanut butter. After the initial shock, he seemed to enjoy my announcement. He leaned back, relaxed, and smiled.

"I wasn't going to kill them at first, you know," he started, like he was as happy to tell us about being a murderer as he was about his plans to buy a yacht. With his first words, relief and satisfaction washed over me. I was Sherlock Holmes. I had been right. I glanced at Spencer. Now his mouth was open.

"I started with the manager, just asked him to fire the pitcher and the first baseman to lower the value of the team,"

George continued. "He refused. He said we were going to have a winning year next year, and he wasn't going to let his best players go. Well, I couldn't let that happen. A winning season would ruin my plans. So, I got mad and hit him with a handy baseball bat. Easy."

A handy baseball bat. So, that's how he did it.

"So easy that you did it two more times," I said.

He nodded. "I didn't even ask the other two to fire the players. The players were gone for the winter so I got rid of the management. It turned out it was just as efficient. The value of the team plummeted. The problem was the bodies."

"You dropped off a body part wherever you went," I said. He had been at my grandmother's house for Thanksgiving and the restaurant where I found the head. It all made sense, now.

"I did my Christmas shopping and dropped off a toe here and a hand there," he supplied. "It was pretty easy, actually. Like the good old days when we were allowed to litter."

He smiled, pleased as punch with himself. "All righty then," he added and then in a blink of an eye threw the jar of peanut butter at Spencer's head with surprising force. He jumped up from the couch and ran outside.

I ran after him but Spencer stopped me. "You stay here! I'll get him."

I ignored him. When Spencer ran after him, I followed. Out into the blizzard in my bare feet, I ran around the outside of the cabin. It didn't take long to find George.

He was standing behind the house, next to his snowmobile. He pulled a snow shovel from behind his back and held it high.

"I'm great at beating people to death," he announced, proudly. He was nutty as a fruitcake. Bonkers.

"You're going to snow shovel us to death?" I asked.

He didn't answer. He went after Spencer first, but Spencer was a lot younger and a lot stronger. He wrestled the snow shovel out of George's hands and threatened him with it. I thought it was over, that Spencer had bested him quickly, but George wasn't finished. He fished a gun out of his pocket.

"I brought this, too," he said. "You know, just in case."

"Put it down," Spencer ordered while wielding the shovel, but he took a step backward.

"Don't bring a shovel to a gunfight, Chief Bolton," George growled.

He aimed his gun at Spencer, ready to fire. "No!" I shouted and lunged for him. It was my turn to be bonkers. After all, it was crazy to throw myself in front of a gun, but I couldn't bear to see Spencer shot full of bullet holes. After all, he almost said he loved me. At least I thought he had.

I lunged for the gun, but I wasn't fast enough, and thankfully, neither was George. Before he had a chance to shoot his weapon, little Irving Schwartz, otherwise known as Darth Vader, came out of nowhere and tackled George Trench to the ground. It was shocking to see Darth Vader there outside of the cabin. He normally went nowhere without his stormtroopers and his theme music. But here he was going after George Trench like he was Obi Wan, except that neither had a light saber.

Darth and George rolled around in the snow. Darth was small, but he had the element of surprise on his side. Darth's cape wrapped around George's head. George waved his gun, but he couldn't see to aim. It was a tossup who was going to win. George had a gun, but Darth had a helmet. Before it was over though, Spencer jumped into the fray and separated them, quickly disarming George.

Spencer forced George onto his belly and held him down with his foot. Darth Vader struggled to stand, adjusting his helmet and cape.

"I saw the whole thing. Heard every word," he said, excitedly, his breathing louder than usual. "I had gotten lost in the blizzard and found you guys. This is going to play great at the polls. 'Darth Vader Subdues Murderer.'"

With the murderer on the ground on his belly and Darth Vader assured of winning the mayoral election, the skies cleared, and the snow and wind stopped. The ski patrol found us within minutes, and they escorted us down the mountain, where Darth's stormtroopers waited for him, and my matches waited for me, as if we were conquering heroes.

I didn't see Mary Trench, but I figured she owed me

one. With her husband in prison, she would have total control over the checking account.

Irving Schwartz aka Darth Vader told the crowd a harrowing story of being separated from his stormtroopers, of wandering through the blizzard with only his cape and his plastic chest plate to keep him warm. When he stumbled on our cabin, he thought he was saved, but then he heard George Trench's confession, and Darth Vader decided to throw away his evildoer persona to save the day.

I tried to interject about how I actually figured out who the killer was, but it was hard to compete with a Star Wars figure's charisma. So, I took a back seat to Darth Vader. But my friends knew better. They were used to me solving murders.

Lucy gave me a hug. "Damn. Did I miss another one, darlin'? One more murderer captured by Gladie Burger. You get all the fun."

"We almost died," I told her.

"I heard he tried to kill you with peanut butter. I can't wait to tell Bird that her diet food is deadly."

"You kind of had to be there to understand about the peanut butter. And he had a gun," I said. Peanut butter didn't sound very life-threatening.

Lucy nodded, but she didn't seem impressed by the gun. "Who'd have thought Darth Vader had it in him? And you and Spencer alone in a cabin during a blizzard? When am I going to hear the juicy details about that? Should I block off a few days? Should I order in for that talk? Maybe Indian food?" Then, she froze. "Uh oh," she said, looking behind me.

I turned around to see what had her immobilized.

Standing in the snow, breathtaking in his jeans, boots, and parka, was Holden. Lucy stepped aside, and he embraced me in a big bear hug. Out of the corner of my eye, I saw Spencer grimace, and I could practically hear him grind his teeth.

"You want me to shoot him?" Uncle Harry asked Spencer.

"Nobody's going to shoot anyone," I said. "Right?" I asked Holden.

"Right," he said. Then, he got down on one knee and presented me with a ring box. "Gladie, you're the most special woman I've ever known. I love you, and I want to spend the rest of my life with you. Would you do me the honor of becoming my wife?"

CHAPTER 15

In love and life, in beginnings and in the end, the most important thing is to listen. If you listen, you'll probably hear the truth. Don't let the truth fly past you, dolly. Be there when it's given to you. And believe it.

Lesson 33, Matchmaking Advice from your Grandma Zelda

I stood in Grandma's driveway, spying on the house next door.

"Merry Christmas!" Mayor Robinson called from the street. He walked up the driveway, carrying a large, wrapped gift. "Isn't it a glorious day?"

It was. Our colder than usual winter was taking a break, and it had been sunny and seventy degrees since the blizzard ended. But even if the weather had been miserable, I suspected that the mayor would still be happy.

"Congratulations on the election," I said.

"Victory is sweet, Gladie. Very, very sweet."

The mayor's path to victory had some twists and turns. He had actually lost the election to Darth Vader with the largest election margins in Cannes' history. The mayor gave a tear-soaked concession speech to a half-empty room at the high school. But he didn't have to cry for long. Within thirty minutes of the election results, Darth Vader was disqualified when it was discovered that he was actually Canadian and in the country illegally. So, instead of creating a galactic empire, Irving Schwartz went back to Vancouver, and Dwayne Robinson continued for a fourth term as our mayor.

Grandma opened the front door and welcomed the mayor for her The End of the Year Isn't the End of the World lunch. It was one of her most popular annual happenings.

"Don't be too long," Grandma called to me. "Bridget's on her way, and she wants you to talk to her stomach."

"I'll be in soon," I called back.

Grandma shut the door, and I went back to spying. I peeked through the hedges that separated Grandma's property from the house next door. Holden's truck was in his driveway, packed high and tied down with a tarp.

Holden had been a class act when I rejected him in front of hundreds of people at the ski resort. I tried to let him down gently, but when he got down on one knee and proposed, the only thing I could think to answer was: "Uh…"

That was enough. He got the picture. It wasn't the normal reaction of a woman, who's presented with a three-carat diamond ring by the man she loves. He closed the ring box and gave me a sweet smile. I took his hand, and we walked inside to talk with a little more privacy.

"I'm dumb. I'm an idiot. You're perfect. You're every woman's dream man," I said, as we stood face to face in a small alcove.

"But not *your* dream man," he said, lightly caressing my cheek. "Your dream man is standing outside, debating with himself whether or not to give me another black eye."

"He's not my dream man," I said. "He's a womanizing jerk."

But I had a feeling I was lying about Spencer not being my dream man. I chewed on the inside of my cheek. Why was Spencer my dream man? He didn't give me a three-carat diamond. He didn't concern himself with my every desire. He wasn't an internationally-known explorer and author of several coffee table books.

Holden was all of those things, and I was kissing him goodbye. He was the second man in a week that I had kissed goodbye. I was good at goodbye. I had years of practice.

It didn't take Holden long to pack up the rest of his house and fill the back of his truck with his belongings. Now, while Grandma was preparing for her End of the Year Isn't the End of the World lunch, I was watching the end of

Holden in my life, as he prepared to drive away.

A hand touched my back, and I jumped three feet in the air. It was Spencer, dressed in his usual metrosexual perfection with slight razor stubble, which made me go weak in the knees.

"Take it easy, Pinky. Guilty conscience?"

"Shh. Get down," I hissed. I yanked Spencer's arm, pulling him down to squat next to me.

"What are we looking at? Oh…"

We watched in silence as Holden left his house and opened his truck's driver side door. He got in and started it up. Slowly, he backed out of the driveway into the street. I ran down the driveway and watched the back of his truck as it receded into the distance.

Spencer took my hand. "Are you okay, Pinky?"

I was okay. I felt like slime, rejecting the perfect man who loved me and wanted to take me around the world and pamper me like I was a princess. But I was okay.

Holden had been gracious about my rejection. He wasn't bitter, and he never said an unkind word against me. But he was sad, and I was sad that I made him sad.

Spencer faced me and cupped my face with his hands. We had been shy with each other since our discussion in the cabin. There was a lot of unfinished business between us, but I felt we had moved forward in our relationship.

If we had a relationship.

He kissed me gently, ever so softly grazing his lips against mine. "It's just you and me, Pinky," he said. It was a scary thought, and I pushed down my fight or flight response. Were we committed now? Was he done with models?

"What happens now?" I asked.

"Well, we could eat lunch or watch an Adam Sandler movie or…"

He smirked his annoying little smirk and arched an eyebrow.

"Or finish telling me that thing you started to tell me?" I asked.

"What thing?"

"The thing."

"You want to see my thing?" he asked, grabbing my ass and avoiding the subject.

"I've seen your thing, remember?"

Spencer's face dropped. "Not when it's seventy degrees out."

"Grandma has a house full of people."

"Well, I'm not into that, but I could be, if that's your thing. Is that your thing? You want to get your freak on? You want to see my red room? How about ginger root? You like that?"

"You are five years old."

"But in a good way, right?"

We walked up the driveway, passing the oil slick where I used to park my car.

"How will I ever afford a new car?" I asked.

He opened the door to Grandma's house. "I know of a moped you could buy for cheap."

FIELD OF SCREAMS

THE END

Don't miss *From Fear to Eternity*, the next installment of the *Matchmaker Mysteries* Series. Keep reading for a preview!

And don't forget to sign up for the newsletter for new releases and special deals: http://www.elisesax.com/mailing-list.php

FROM FEAR TO ETERNITY EXCERPT

CHAPTER 1

    I get a lot of matches. People come to me from all over the world. Did you know that, bubeleh? One time I even got a lovely gentleman from the North Pole. Business is good. I can't complain. But did you know that a lot of people want to come to me, but they're afraid? Fear is a strong enemy of love. What are they afraid of, you might ask. That they're not beautiful enough. That they're not smart enough. That they're not rich enough. That they're not lovable enough. But the number one biggest fear is that they're too old. Too old for love…have you ever heard of such mishegas? Yes, I bet you have. Something happens to our thinking as we get closer to our final days. Instead of visualizing ourselves as vessels full of a lifetime's worth of wisdom, kindness, beauty, and love, we see ourselves as reaching our "use by" date. We picture the last of our wisdom, kindness, beauty, and love draining out of ourselves, just like our supply of estrogen and skin elasticity until there's gornisht. Bupkes. These matches see themselves as worthless bags of skin never to feel again the euphoria of the first sparks of passion with a new love. I don't blame them too much. After all, a sixty-year old tuchus isn't usually a thing of beauty. But that doesn't mean that that tuchus doesn't deserve as much love as a twenty-year old tuchus. How to alleviate your potential matches' fears, you might ask? The proof is in the pudding, dolly. Don't wait for them to ask. Push them off the cliff and match them, even if they're too scared to ask. Go to them. Match their tuchus.

Lesson 76, Matchmaking Advice from Your Grandma Zelda

My grandmother thought I shared her gift for knowing things that couldn't be known, but that Tuesday, I had no idea that old man Dwight Foyle was about to be murdered and that I was going to find his body...as usual. Maybe Grandma was right, and I did have a third eye waiting to make its appearance, but for now, it was being distracted by Spencer.

Oh, Spencer.

He smelled like really expensive sex. Like a young Hugh Jackman-- but much better looking-- mixed with kajillion-dollar men's cologne, mixed with a testosterone supplement that the EPA would have listed as one of the most dangerous substances on earth, mixed with a whole bunch of holy moly.

Gobs of holy moly.

Massive quantities of holy moly.

"Holy moly." I moaned, as his hands roamed my naked body searching for my erogenous zones. He found them all. "This is so good." I moaned again. It was good, and I knew it was going to get better. After all, we had only just started. We were naked, slick with sweat, our limbs intertwined, rolling around on the floor of the National Museum of Natural History as tour groups of tourists walked by, enjoying the dinosaur display.

Spencer looked deeply into my eyes. "Bubeleh, you want Danish or bagels for breakfast?" he asked. "I got prune Danish and pumpernickel bagels. I hear that pumpernickel is very good to keep you regular. But prune is gangbusters for a speedy bowel. How's your pooping these days?"

"Huh?" I asked the naked, muscly Spencer.

His blue eyes were dark with passion. "Your poop. How's your poop?"

"Excuse me?"

"Dolly, did you hear me?" Spencer asked.

His gorgeous face shimmered and then faded away. I grabbed for him, but he was gone. Disappeared. So was I. I was no longer naked in the Natural History Museum, no longer getting it on with the man who was supposedly in my life.

Instead, I was waking up in my bed in my grandmother's house. Speaking of Grandma, her ancient, slack face was hanging over me, and she tugged at my pajama sleeve. Her hair was covered in rollers, and she was wearing her favorite blue housedress. "Well, bubeleh?" she demanded. "Danish or pumpernickel bagel? Hey, I got a good idea. Why don't we do both? I think we're going to need our strength today. We could carbo load like marathon runners."

I rubbed my eyes. "I was dreaming," I said.

She nodded. "Boy, were you dreaming. Porno dreaming. If you don't seal the deal with Spencer, you're going to blow up."

She was right. It had been two weeks since Spencer and I sort of committed ourselves to a relationship with each other. I had inadvertently said the "L" word, but when it was his turn, he sort of choked on his tongue. I hadn't seen much of him since. I didn't know if he was hiding from me or if I was hiding from him. In any case, it had been a quiet two weeks. My body was getting impatient. My grandmother was right; I was going to blow up any minute.

"I'm not going to blow up," I said, pulling the covers up under my chin. "We're just taking it slow." I could see my breath as it hit the cold air. "Grandma, it's freezing in here."

"Cold makes you sleep better. But you can get up now. I turned on the furnace. It'll be toasty in no time. We got the *New Year, New Love* meeting in an hour."

That meant I didn't have a lot of time to get my prunes and pumpernickels in me before Grandma's house was invaded by the desperate and lonely. My grandmother insisted that the cold might make you sleep better, but it was terrible for finding love. There were a whole lot of miserable people wearing long underwear in our town of Cannes, California, during this frigid January. Hopefully, the *New Year, New Love* meeting would help match up a few of them. I had moved in with my grandmother eight months before to help her with her matchmaking business. It was a steep learning curve. Grandma had a way of matching people with an almost magical gift. She assured me that I had the gift, too, but there was little evidence of it so far.

I wrapped my blanket around me and padded my way

to the bathroom. I scratched a place on my arm, which was raised in an angry welt. Despite the cold January, we were getting an influx of mosquitoes. Every morning for the past week, I had been getting up with new bites on my body. It was like the mosquitoes were confused about what season it was, or they had decided to spend the winter in Grandmother's large Victorian house.

After my shower, I put calamine lotion on my bites and decided to make an effort to look the part for the day. Just as Spencer and I had sort of decided to be a couple, I had sort of decided to finally be a real matchmaker, once and for all. A professional. So, this morning I made a point to put on professional makeup and professional clothes and put my hair back in a professional ponytail. "Not bad," I told my reflection in the mirror. I looked respectable in my black turtleneck, dark green skirt, and black boots.

Downstairs, I smelled the coffee brewing. I found Grandma in the kitchen. She had stuffed her ample body into a Stella McCartney-knockoff beige power suit. Her hair was teased into submission, and she was still wearing her plastic slippers, which clacked on the linoleum when she walked around the kitchen.

"Grab the milk out of the refrigerator, Gladie," she told me.

I took out the milk and the cream cheese. The table was already set, and I picked up one of the plates as the toaster oven dinged with our pumpernickel bagels. I sat down across from Grandma, and tossed one of the bagels onto her plate. She poured coffee into a "Don't Mess With Texas" mug that she must have gotten as a gift because my grandmother never left her property line.

"Good coffee," I commented, taking a sip.

"What a day it's going to be!" she exclaimed, scratching at a mosquito bite on her neck.

"It is?" I asked, concerned. The past two weeks had been quiet, and I didn't want to ramp up any excitement in my life. Not after my December, which had been packed with dead people and things exploding.

"You should probably eat double. Get your strength up."

I scratched at a mosquito bite on my leg. "I'm not sure I have any more strength." But I did as she told me and ate double. It was always a mistake not to listen to my grandmother. She had a way of knowing things that couldn't be known.

Just as she took the first bite of her second Danish, she froze in place. Her eyes fixed at the air above my head, and I looked to see what she was staring at. There was nothing there.

"What is it? Are you okay?" I asked.

Her face was a picture of fear. "Someone's here who shouldn't be here."

That could have meant a good hundred people. Grandma's house was the Grand Central of the town. People came and went every day. But this was different, according to my grandmother. In defense against the unknown intruder, I grabbed my butter knife with a smear of cream cheese on it. "Should I call 911?"

She blinked. "Our home has been invaded, Gladie. Something's definitely not right."

My instinct was to run like crazy, but Grandma insisted that we search the house for the unseen invader. She stood behind me and my cream-cheese smeared butter knife as we walked from one room to the next, investigating every closet and under every bed. But we found no one.

"Maybe your radar's off," I said when we reached the downstairs, again.

She thought about that a moment. "No, I'm seeing pretty clearly today. I wish I could get a handle on the invader, though. That's a bit fuzzy."

The front door opened, and a parade of women of all shapes and ages paraded in. They were repeat offenders, women who had more problems in the love arena than the average person. But my grandmother was eternally optimistic that their matches were out there somewhere. She had created the *New Year, New Love* meeting specifically for them to give them a boost for the year. Without being instructed, the group set up folding chairs in the parlor. They laid out cookies and a big pot of coffee and sat down, chatting among themselves.

"Okay, bubeleh, let's get cracking," Grandma told me.

I took a seat next to Grandma, and she nodded toward me to begin. Being responsible for other people's lives got me really nervous and I wondered if I would ever get used to it. Despite sweat breaking out on my upper lip and under my arms, I knew I'd have to soldier on. Having my grandmother with me helped. She was the backup that I needed because I knew she wouldn't let me fail while she was around. I smiled back at her, giving her a sign that I was fully on board as a professional matchmaker. She smiled back and crossed her legs. I noticed then that her heels had formed a thick crust. Normally, my grandmother was very concerned about her upkeep. Every Monday, Bird Gonzalez, the local hairdresser, would visit and give my grandmother a head-to-toe tune-up. Come to think of it, Bird hadn't come this week, which was odd. Usually, nothing came between Bird and her clients. Crusty heels or gray roots in town was bad advertising for Bird. I wondered what was wrong, and if Bird was okay.

"I'm fifty-two years old," Darlene Scholz complained. "I've already given up on my ovaries, but soon I'm going to have to give up on my vagina. You know what I mean?"

I had no idea what she meant. I shot a panicked glance at my grandmother. "Your hoo-ha has got years before it gives up the ghost," Grandma told Darlene, reassuringly.

Darlene didn't look totally convinced. I got the impression that she gave her vagina a lot of thought and knew something that we didn't know. I didn't give my vagina any thought at all, and now I was wondering if I should have. How much thought should women give to their vaginas? The fact that I didn't know made me doubt myself as a matchmaker, again.

Grandma patted my knee. "You're doing fine, Gladie," she said.

"Even with the bad weather, we need to get out and show ourselves," I began. "January is a bummer with the weather and short days. So, get out there and participate in the town's events."

"I'm allergic to the cold," Christine Lansberg interrupted. "And I can't do anything involving hot cider or hot chocolate. It throws off my numbers."

I didn't know what she meant by numbers. Did hot chocolate have a number? I shot Grandma another desperate look, and she signaled to the binder on the coffee table. I picked it up and quickly searched for Christine in it. Grandma's notes said that Christine needed a man who liked quilting and who knew how to use an EpiPen. My forehead broke out into layer of sweat.

Then it hit me. "You're right, Christine. That's why I think you should visit Henrietta's Notions." Henrietta's son had just come back from Afghanistan, where he served as a medic. He had potential as a great match. Grandma gave me an approving nod.

I was pumped up with self-confidence. This matchmaking business wasn't as hard as I thought. Maybe I really did have the gift.

The meeting went on for about another twenty minutes before we stopped for a cookie break. I hadn't had any more brainstorms, but Grandma seemed to know where three of the women should go to find their forever loves. It was all going smoothly until the front door opened and the sound of men's boots echoed through the house, stampeding like Clydesdales at the start of a Budweiser commercial.

"Oh, dear," Grandma breathed.

"What the hell?" Darlene shrieked.

I don't know why, but I shut my eyes tight. Maybe it was some sort of survival instinct.

"Save our town's good name!" a man yelled from the entranceway. I kept my eyes closed, but I could hear the *New Year, New Love* participants get up and move around. Fools. They wanted to see what the action was, but I had experience with action, and it never turned out well. I wanted nothing to do with it. Fool me once, okay. Fool me a dozen times, and…well, I had no intention of getting involved, no matter what it was. I had moved into a crazy town full of crazy characters. Normally, I got sucked into the craziness, which made me crazy, and occasionally put me in the hospital, but now I needed a moment to just be normal. Was that so much to ask?

Yes. Yes, it was.

"We're going to have truth this year, no matter what!" another man yelled. I recognized his voice. It was Jose, my grandmother's gardener. Usually he was very mild-mannered, but now he was spitting mad. He had worked with Grandma to create her prize-winning roses and crossed himself a lot around her, probably because he believed that she was a witch.

"Get that pickaxe away from my face!" another man

yelled. "You want some of my axe?"

"I dare you!"

"I'll pound you one, head-in-the-sand moron!"

"Communist!"

I opened my eyes. The women of the meeting had shuffled out of the room, and Grandma was still sitting next to me, shaking her head, like she was disappointed that girls were wearing their skirts too short this year.

"You interrupted our meeting!" I heard Darlene yell at the men in the entranceway. "Now what am I going to do about my vagina?"

That seemed to quiet down whatever argument they were having. "Grandma, do you ever think of retirement?" I asked.

"Sometimes I think about becoming a welder, but I don't like heights."

She got up and walked into the other room. Reluctantly, I followed her out. The entranceway was crammed with the single women and five men armed with pickaxes and other tools that they were wielding like weapons. It would have been a great matchmaking opportunity normally, but the single women didn't look interested in the men. That was probably because the men were dressed as 19th century, filthy gold miners, and they were giving off an authentic old-timey smell, not to mention that they were wild-eyed, fighting mad, and ready for hand-to-hand combat.

"Zelda, we came here because you got to help us work this out," one of the men implored my grandmother.

"Certainly, Ralph. How can I help?"

"Jose here is rebelling against tradition. We're in a crisis that could bring down this town."

The women gasped. I sniggered and put my hand over my mouth. It would take a lot to bring down the town. We had already had a cult invasion, a flying donkey, and body parts in the freezer section of Walley's. And the town was still intact.

"Our tradition has been wrong all these years, Zelda," Jose said. Ralph threw his pickaxe on his shoulder like one of Snow White's dwarfs and huffed. Another man nodded in agreement with Jose. It was like the civil war all over again.

"I thought the gold mine was closed," I said. It had just dawned on me that the mine had closed down over one hundred years ago. Cannes was a small mountain town east of San Diego. It had been founded with the discovery of gold in the middle of the 1800's, but the gold ran out pretty quickly, and now it was just a tourist town, filled with pie shops and antique stores.

"Of course it's closed," Ralph said, annoyed.

"Every January, the town puts on a historical play. It's been the same play since as far back as I can remember." Grandma explained. As far back as she could remember was a long time. "I'm guessing you're having creative disagreements this year?" she asked Jose.

It was my first January in Cannes since I was a little girl. I didn't remember the play at all.

"Jose and his cabal want to change the soul of this

town!" one of the men shouted and shook his pickaxe.

"Fascist!"

"Lenin-loving Stalin!"

"These are not creative disagreements, Zelda," Jose said. "It's about the truth. The real, dark history of our town."

Time seemed to stand still, and there wasn't a sound in the room. We seemed to stop breathing, while we waited to hear what the "real, dark history of our town" was.

Jose opened his mouth, ready to reveal all, when another woman and man stepped through the front doorway, interrupting him.

It was like Grandma's entranceway had become the vortex for the town, the whirlpool where everyone came to drown, or at least to voice their discontent. The woman looked slightly familiar. She was mousy, in a long skirt, stretched out cardigan, and a long wool coat. The man was Andy Griffith.

"Uh," I said.

"Liar!" the mousy woman shouted and pointed at me. I looked behind me to see who she was shouting at. Nope, nobody there. She and Andy Griffith pushed their way past everyone to get into my face. "Liar! Fraud! Phony!"

"Is this part of the meeting?" one of the matches asked. "Like a show?"

"How did you get Andy Griffith for an appearance?" Darlene asked.

"I thought he was dead," Ralph said.

"It's not Andy Griffith," Grandma explained. "That's Gordon Zorro."

"Andy Griffith is Zorro?" I asked.

"He sure looks like Andy Griffith," Darlene said.

"Whistle your theme song," a man with a pickaxe demanded.

Andy Griffith or Zorro or whoever he was waved a paper in the air. "Gladie Burger, you're being served."

For a few seconds, I thought he was delivering pizza or Chinese food. Grandma caught on more quickly and retrieved the paper from his hand.

"You told me that I was going to fall in love, and I didn't," the woman screeched, her finger hanging in the air, pointing at me. All heads turned toward me...the matches and the costumed townspeople.

"I'm sorry?" I said like a question. "Do I know you?"

It was the wrong thing to say. Her eyes got huge, and she began to pant like a Chihuahua, trying—I assume--to find the right words to express her outrage.

"Maybe I know you," I said to pacify her, actually she did look familiar to me. Grandma remembered every name and face of every person that she met or saw a picture of, but I was terrible with names and faces, which was just one more sign that I probably didn't have my grandmother's gift for this business.

"Fionnula Jericho," Grandma said, gently taking her hand in hers. "What can we do for you?"

Fionnula Jericho. Fionnula Jericho. The name was

familiar, too. Oh! "Fionnula Jericho!" I cried. "Of course. You were at Romance for the Holidays. I remember you." She had been dressed pretty much the same as she was now at the meeting a couple weeks before, and instead of angry, she had been depressed. The rest was fuzzy. I remembered telling her something about falling in love, but that was it.

"You told me that I would fall in love! You're a fraud! I'm not going to rest until everyone knows it and I take every penny you have."

"I have like three pennies," I said.

"Fraud! Phony! Come on, lawyer," she said, tugging on the arm of the Andy Griffith-lookalike.

"Bye y'all," he called, and they walked out.

"Was that part of the show?" one of the matches asked.

"Are you sure that wasn't Andy? He even sounded like him," Ralph said.

My grandmother handed me the paper. I blinked twice and read through it three times because I couldn't believe my eyes. According to the paper, Fionnula Jericho was suing me for eight-hundred-thousand dollars, and Gordon Zorro was her lawyer.

"Eight hundred…eight hundred…" I hyperventilated.

"Put your hands up, bubeleh."

I put my hands up, letting the subpoena float to the floor. "Eight hundred…"

One of the men whistled. "That's a lot of clams."

"What did she do to get sued for eight-hundred-thousand, Zelda?" Darlene asked.

"She must have poisoned her dog or burned her with hot coffee. Those are big lawsuits," a man commented.

A match nodded. "Yep. Saw that on Judge Judy. I'm no expert, but it doesn't look good for you."

"It doesn't look good," I repeated, my voice hitching up like I had sucked helium. "It doesn't look good!"

"If Fionnula has Gordon Zorro, you can't mess around," Grandma said seriously.

"I can't mess around," I repeated. "Eight hundred…Eight hundred…"

"You're going to have to hire Cannes's second-biggest shark," she told me.

"Second-biggest shark? Why not the first biggest shark?"

Grandma shook her head. "Cannes's biggest shark is Gordon Zorro. So, you'll have to hire number two. John Wayne."

"John Wayne? Andy Griffith against John Wayne?"

"Don't be ridiculous. It's Zorro against John Wayne. Go now. John Wayne has a slot available until twelve o'clock. And don't stare at his face."

I nodded. "Twelve o'clock. No face."

The eight hundred thousand number had me in a state of shock. I knew that my grandmother was speaking to me, but I couldn't understand a lot of the words. I started to push my way through the crowd to visit the second biggest shark.

"Cannes police department," a gruff, authoritarian voice bellowed at the front door, stopping me in my tracks. I knew that voice. Usually it was chastising me for something or trying to get into my Spanx, but it was still the same voice.

Spencer Bolton, the police chief and my maybe, sort of, oh-who-knows boyfriend was pushing his way into the bursting-out-of-the-seams entranceway. He pushed past the single women and pickaxe-bearing men until he spotted me.

"Are you kidding me?" he demanded.

Don't forget to grab your copy of *From Fear to Eternity* today!

ABOUT THE AUTHOR

Elise Sax writes hilarious happy endings. She worked as a journalist, mostly in Paris, France for many years but always wanted to write fiction. Finally, she decided to go for her dream and write a novel. She was thrilled when *An Affair to Dismember*, the first in the *Matchmaker Mysteries* series, was sold at auction.

Elise is an overwhelmed single mother of two boys in Southern California. She's an avid traveler, a swing dancer, an occasional piano player, and an online shopping junkie.

Friend her on Facebook: facebook.com/ei.sax.9
Send her an email: elisesax@gmail.com
You can also visit her website: elisesax.com
And sign up for her newsletter to know about new releases and sales: elisesax.com/mailing-list.php

Made in the USA
Las Vegas, NV
26 July 2021